The Prosecco Pact

KILTIE JACKSON

ISBN-13: 978 – 1999866679

DEDICATION

To Mark Fearn.
My Beta-Reader Extraordinaire.
xxx

Also by Kiltie Jackson

The Lovestyle Series

A Rock 'n' Roll Lovestyle
An Artisan Lovestyle
An Incidental Lovestyle
A Timeless Lovestyle

The Since Forever Series

Waiting Since Forever

Standalones

A Snowflake in December

The Bay Series

The Bay of Lost Souls

**Available on Amazon in ebook, Paperback
And Kindle Unlimited.**

ACKNOWLEDGEMENTS

Once again, it's time to open a few bottles of fizzy stuff and raise a glass to all the wonderful people who helped to make this book happen and who give their never-ending support along the way.

The first glasses go to John Hudspith, my amazing editor who continues to fix my terrible punctuation with great patience, Berni Stevens who creates the most stunning covers and always 'gets' exactly what I want and Zoe-Lee O'Farrell for her fabulous book tours which she works so hard on to make a success.

The next bottle of bubbles is for my little band of cheerleaders who stand and shout about my offerings at every opportunity – Miriam O'Brien, Sue Baker, Kathleen Becker, Meghan Gibbons, Joanne Byrne & Karen Harrison. Thank you for being so wonderful.

For my next thank you, I need to open a few bottles to get round all the great book bloggers who take time to read my work, write up reviews and then share them across social media and the internet. You are all very special and I am deeply grateful for all that you do.

Time now for a big crate of fizz because that's how much is needed to ensure all the members of the following great Facebook groups get a glass – Kiltie Jackson's Book, Bits & Bobs; The Fiction Café; Chick Lit & Prosecco; Heidi Swain and Friends, Jenny Colgan and More Great Books, and the TBC Reviewer's Group, especially the lovely Helen Boyce who puts so much effort into ensuring all reviews are shared.

The posh crystal glasses have been polished off and are being raised to the following extra-special people who make me happy just by being their wonderful selves – Mark Fearn, my much-loved Beta Reader for always being honest with me, Stuart James Dunne, my BFF who always makes me smile and helps me to understand all the marketing stuff, my mum for reading my books so often she knows the stories better than I do and my dad for doing the same.

The bottle of Cristal Champagne is for Kym, my best friend in the whole wide world because not only is she just amazing but she's also a posh bird and Cristal is her favourite!

The Moggy Posse aren't allowed wine but will be more than happy with their cat treats as spending time with these fluffballs takes me down off the shelf when the words won't come.

The shot glasses of O'Donnell's Wild Berry Moonshine are for my Mr Mogs who has now learnt to just go with the flow. As always, I will love you till the end of eternity… and a day!

And finally, the most important people of all – my incredible readers who keep on reading the books, keep leaving the all-important reviews and keep sending the much-appreciated messages telling me how much you have loved my scribbles. You keep me going and the biggest toast of the night is for you.

Till the next time,

Slàinte Mhath!

Kiltie

xxx

ONE

Lydia Beaumont glanced in the mirror at the clock on the wall behind her as she snapped the last curler closed on her client's head. Four thirty. After more than twenty-five years of transposing the numbers in her head, she now did it as automatically as breathing.

'There you go, Edna. Fifteen minutes under the dryer and you'll be setting hearts racing at the community centre tea dance this evening.'

Edna gave a hearty chuckle and Lydia discretely flexed her fingers a couple of times while reaching for the floaty, chiffon scarf to place over the top of the rollers. She scrunched her toes at the same time, trying to ease the ache which had set in from being on her feet for most of the day.

She wheeled across the free-standing dryer, placed it over the top of Edna's weekly shampoo and set and fiddled with the timer to give the allotted fifteen minutes of low heat required to gently dry her client's baby-fine hair before walking over to give the sinks a final clean before closing time. Heather, her assistant, had already swept up before she left at four o'clock to be home for her kids so all that was required, once Edna's curls had been brushed, teased and hair-sprayed, was to give the floor a quick wash and then she was out of here. It was Tuesday night and she didn't hang about on those; they were the nights she lived for. Hell, they were the only sniff of a life that she had!

It was ten minutes after five when she pulled down the shutters on the front of the shop and locked them. After giving a sharp tug to check they were properly secured, Lydia glanced up, as she did every night, and smiled when she saw the name on the board across the top – "Gracie's" with the word "Hairdressers" in smaller font underneath. Her grandmother had been so proud when she'd stepped into the arena of self-employment and some of Lydia's happiest memories were of being in the shop with her gran and mum, sweeping the floor with a broom three times taller than herself while they chatted and laughed with their clients. There always seemed to be a happy atmosphere and Lydia strived to ensure she still created the same ambiance today. It had been a natural choice for her to follow in the footsteps of her grandmother and mother but she was now beginning to understand why they'd both retired when they'd turned fifty-five; standing for eight or nine hours a day, six days a week really did take its toll and her back had started aching just that little bit longer over the last eighteen months or so.

She walked the handful of steps to the bus stop and her stomach gave a little rumble as she looked across the road at the bright neon sign advertising the local Marks & Spencer Food Hall. It was so tempting but tonight was "Pie & Prosecco" night with the girls and being good now meant she could be far more decadent later. Besides, she could see the bus just turning in at the bottom of the road and she didn't want to miss it as she was planning a nice soak in the tub to ease her aching bones before she headed out.

A few minutes later she was on the bus and smiled again as it slowly trundled past her shop. "Gracie's" shone out in the light of the street lamp and it was her grandmother's name that had helped to bring about her being friends with the girls she was meeting tonight. They'd known each other for barely two years but they'd become friends after meeting on a first-aid course. Given their differences, they would never have met under any other circumstances and despite being the eldest of the group at forty-two, she never felt that way when in their company.

Lydia tried not to think of the years that had gone by but with her tired reflection staring back at her in the bus window, it was hard to ignore it. She let out a sigh while reaching up to press the "Stop Bus" button and felt her good mood plummet as she stepped down onto the pavement knowing she now had to run the gauntlet that was her husband and son before she could make her escape. It was a thought that had the butterflies scurrying for cover in her stomach before the heavy feeling of dread settled in.

The sensation within her grew heavier as she trudged up the stairs to their flat and put her key in the front door. She could already hear Davie's music before the door was opened and it was an assault on her ears as she turned to close it behind her. Dropping her handbag on the floor and undoing her coat as she stormed up the stairs, she reached her son's bedroom in a fury and threw his door open without bothering to knock. What was the point? He wouldn't have heard it anyway.

'FOR THE LOVE OF ALL THAT'S HOLY, WILL YOU TURN THAT BLOODY RACKET DOWN!'

She walked over to the player and yanked the plug out of the wall.

'MUM! I was listening to that!'

'Yeah, and so was half the neighbourhood, except they

3

were getting no choice in the matter. You got those bloody expensive earphones for Christmas, try bloody using them!'

With that, she spun around and walked out, slamming the door behind her.

'Hey, what's all the noise?'

She walked down the stairs to find her husband standing in the doorway of the lounge. Well, he was standing there, his beer belly was halfway to the kitchen.

'Are you for real? He's sending the neighbours deaf and you're moaning over a door slamming?'

She threw her coat over the bannister, barged past him into the kitchen then stopped in her tracks when she saw the mess in front of her.

'What the hell?'

The casserole dish that had held the cottage pie she'd planned for their dinner and should have been warming up in the oven, was now on the kitchen table, devoid of any mince and potato contents. The fryer was gaping open on the worktop with a flattened frozen chips bag next to it and two empty baked beans tins sat beside the saucepan which had cooked the contents but now only contained the sticky, congealed remnants of tomato sauce that was a bugger to remove without soaking first.

She turned to look at her husband and it took every ounce of effort not to shudder with disgust at the sight of him. Fat, bloated and slovenly, he looked nothing like the man she'd married twenty-four years before.

'Well, since you both made the mess, you can both clean it up. I'm going out.'

'Er, what about me dinner?'

'Excuse me?'

Was she hearing him right?

'Me dinner? When you cooking that?'

'You've just eaten it.'

She swept her hand around the kitchen, pointing at the empty plates lying discarded there.

'That were just a snack to keep us going coz we were famished when we got in.'

Dave was a mechanic and part-owner of a garage over in Balham and she'd often thought of late that it was a good thing they no longer had the pits there for working underneath cars because they would require a crane to get him out, such was his bulk these days. Unfortunately, Davie Junior thought everything about his father was the gospel of how life should be and had followed in his every footstep, right down to the ever-expanding girth and misogynistic attitude to women. Hard as she'd tried to instil a modicum of modern decency in her one and only child, his father had always managed to overrule her and when he'd turned fourteen, she'd given it up as a bad job. He'd followed his father into the garage and the two of them were peas in a pod. She despised them both.

'Well, if you're still hungry, you can order in a takeaway. You know where the menus are.'

She tried to step past him to go upstairs but he slammed his hand against the wall at the side of her head, his arm blocking her path.

'You, woman, are not going anywhere until you cook us a dinner. It's time you learnt your place around here. You'll go out when I say you can go out.'

She glared at him for a moment before ducking down and under the offending limb.

'And you need to drag yourself into the twenty-first century. It doesn't work like that anymore, Dave. When are you gonna learn that you don't frighten me? Now fuck off out of my sight!'

Lydia ran up the stairs and into the bathroom, quickly locking the door behind her. She perched on the side of the bath for a few minutes, waiting for her heartbeat to slow down. She didn't expect Dave to come up the stairs after her, that would be too much of an effort, but she couldn't help but feel that one day, given how much their relationship had deteriorated over the years, the abuse would not stop with an exchange of words.

TWO

The gentle tap on the office door had Grace Mitchell ready to fire off an expletive until she looked up and saw her secretary, Emma, standing there.

'Yes, what is it, Emma?'

'Err, you asked me to let you know when it was five o'clock.'

Grace noticed the buttoned-up coat and scarf in hand, ready to be wrapped around Emma's neck. She looked out of the office window and saw the darkness of the evening on the other side.

'You're right, Emma, I did. Thank you. I take it that's you going now?'

'Yes, I am. Unless you need me for anything?'

Grace registered the look on the younger girl's face and knew the offer had been made from a sense of duty rather than a desire to work extra hours.

'No, I don't. You get yourself off. Are you doing anything nice?'

'I'm meeting some friends in Leicester Square. We're having dinner in Chinatown and then going to see the latest

Tom Cruise movie.'

'That sounds like a lot of fun. Have a great time and you can tell me about it tomorrow.'

'Will do. Goodnight.'

Just then, the sound of raucous laughter floated in the door, over Emma's head.

'What's going on out there?'

Emma gave a small grimace. 'Seb Andrews relaying some story about an argument he had with his client's financial department while trying to sort out a contract. You know what he's like, all full of bluster.'

'Yes, more likely he was rude and someone shut him down on it but we'll never hear that one being told.'

'I think you're right there, Grace. I reckon his untold stories are the ones which are more interesting. See you in the morning.'

With a little smile, Emma pulled the door closed behind her, cutting off the noise in the outer office and allowing silence to return to the room once more.

Grace glanced down at the contract in front of her but it was no use, her concentration had been broken and she wasn't going to get back into it tonight. Besides, it was Tuesday, and she had her "Pie & Prosecco" with the girls to look forward to. This was the first time they'd met for about four weeks, thanks to Christmas and New Year getting in the way and the year was already into its second week. She hadn't realised how much she'd missed them until now but hearing Emma say she was meeting up with friends had brought home how much she was looking forward to this night out.

She closed the file, making a note first on where she'd read up to, and locked it away securely in the filing cabinet. The keys for the cabinet were then dropped inside the tampon box in the bottom drawer of her desk, covered up with said tampons and, after also placing her laptop in another drawer, the desk was locked too. The key for that resided on her Snoopy keyring along with the key to her front door. It wasn't that she was paranoid or anything but industrial espionage was a real thing and she wanted to ensure nothing untoward occurred on her watch. She also didn't trust Sebastian Andrews as far as she could throw him and given that he was the size of a rugby second row forward, that wouldn't be very far. The man took ambitious to a whole new level and while he wouldn't do anything to harm the company, he could easily do something to harm her position within it. They were both gunning for a partnership and it was a case of may the best person win. She fully intended for it to be her.

She took her coat off the stand, put it on and cast an eye around the room while she fastened it up. Nothing was out of place which was just how Grace liked it. She was a neat-freak, she openly admitted to it, but her thought process worked better when everything was in order around her.

She locked her office door, said goodnight to the few stragglers still staring at their PCs and braced herself for the cold outside. A dark, gloomy and icy January night was waiting for her on the other side of the front doors and she wasn't looking forward to her walk to the tube station.

'Goodnight, Ms Mitchell.'

'Goodnight, Bill.'

She smiled warmly at the doorman as he held the door open for her. She'd observed some of her fellow solicitors being rude to the older gentleman who was only doing his job, just like everyone else. It annoyed her to see this so she always made a point of being polite to him and those around her. Her father had an "us and them" attitude which she deplored and, these days, she found being in his company outside of the house, more often than not, embarrassing.

It took less than ten minutes to reach the tube but she

felt every one of them as the wind off the river whipped up through the lanes and alleys between the City and the waterway. The warmth of the underground station was a relief although she often felt differently in the height of the summer when the tube system turned into a sweltering, sweaty cesspit and most passengers became grumpy little gremlins. A train was just pulling in as she reached the platform and checking it was one that would take her home – more than once she'd found herself either halfway to Ealing or unexpectedly late-night shopping at High Street Kensington – she jumped aboard while taking it as a good omen for the night ahead that she was even able to get a seat.

It was a mere five-minute walk from the tube to her house when she reached her destination but Grace was sure the temperature had dropped several degrees by the time she was stepping through the black, cast-iron gate, along her short black and white tiled path and in the pretty red front door which looked so bare without the gorgeous Christmas wreath that had adorned it for the last four weeks. Once inside, however, the décor was considerably starker even though Grace had lived here for two years. The small terraced house had been an old rental that her father had decided to release from his portfolio of properties. It had taken much begging on her part to get him to sell it to her as he hadn't thought Parson's Green was a suitable area for her to be living in. The snobbery behind him feeling this way simply made her want it all the more. Finally, he'd relented and agreed she could buy it and while he'd reduced the price by a reasonable amount, the mortgage payment still made a sizable dent in her monthly income.

Once her name was on the deeds and she was safely moved in, the first thing Grace did was have it gutted out and restyled. Being an ex-rental, the property had become tired over the years but with the assistance of a good architect and an even better builder – she'd struck it lucky with both of them – her little piece of heaven was now fully renovated and modernised with its cosy lounge, open plan kitchen-diner, two bedrooms upstairs and a converted loft which currently served as a study but could be a third bedroom if needed.

She loved her house and she was sure she would love it even more if she could find the time to get it properly furnished. The only room that came close to being decorated was the study and that was mainly because she spent most weekends in there, working her way up the ladder to that partnership.

Her handbag was placed on the small dining table and she walked over to the patio doors, giving a cursory look out into her small courtyard garden before closing the curtains to keep the heat in.

She was walking through to close the shutters on the windows at the front of the house in the lounge when she heard a light tinkling sound coming from her bag. She turned around, walked back, stuck her hand in to retrieve the ringing mobile phone and with a quick look at the display to check it wasn't a work-related call, answered it with a smile on her face.

'Hi, Debbie.'

'Hey, Grace, you alright?'

'I'm very well, thanks. Yourself?'

'All good here. I'm just calling to make sure you're definitely coming along tonight.'

'I'm already home and about to treat myself to a nice warm shower before calling a taxi.'

'Not walking tonight?'

'Nope! It's too damn cold out there.'

Debbie's light happy laugh danced into her ear.

'I have to agree with you on that one. So, I'll see you in

just over an hour then?'

'You sure will. And, Debbie…'

'Yeah?'

'I'm really looking forward to it. Wanted you to know that.'

'Ah, you daft softie. I'm really looking forward to it too. Although my waistline may not be!'

'Well, you can worry about that another day. I'll see you in a bit.'

Grace continued to smile as the phone was returned to her bag. Debbie was one of those people who had the knack of making you feel completely at ease within a few minutes of being in her company. She had a gorgeous, sunny and happy soul – something which Grace truly envied and hoped a little would rub off on her one day so she might manage to be less uptight in her own life. She was still smiling as she walked up the stairs to her bedroom to get changed.

THREE

Debbie Stanford put the phone back down on the counter and glanced at her watch. Almost six… oh, to hang with it, she could get away with closing the shop a few minutes early. It wasn't like anyone was beating a path to the door in order to buy themselves a nice vintage dress with a handbag and matching shoes thrown in. In fact, even someone casually strolling down to purchase anything would have been nice. She gave a sigh as she stepped out the front door of the shop and pulled across the old-fashioned diamond-shaped shutters. The kind that still allowed people to see the goods in the window without letting them have the opportunity to run off with them. She then closed over the grill for the door, secured it and stepped back into the shop, throwing the bolts home top and bottom and turning the big key in the lock. Another day was over.

She turned to walk back to the counter and caught her reflection in one of the full-length mirrors. Stopping, her last words to Grace came back to her. Her waistline really wasn't going to be happy at the sight of "Pie & Prosecco" tonight. The over-indulgence of the festive season had added to her already generous curves and she was in serious danger of no longer having a waistline at all. It didn't help that she loved food and that her fiancé, Dale, was such a whizz in the kitchen. More than once, she'd wished she looked like Grace. That woman was elegance personified with her Nordic good looks and sleek blonde hair which was either swept up in a smart-but-casual bun or sitting in perfect place on her shoulders, not a single strand daring to be out of place. Debbie's own curly, dark-brown locks did their own thing and were quick to rebel whenever she tried to drag them down into some form of submission. Where Grace had cheek bones you could cut glass with, Debbie had little chunky rosy apples that had been pinched far too often by over-zealous aunties over the years. Finally, and the thing Debbie was most envious of, was Grace's slender, almost fey-like, frame. No matter what she wore, she just had the knack of looking totally put-together. Debbie, on the other hand, just had the knack of looking like she'd been pulled apart and then put back together in the dark! No matter how hard she tried, elegance didn't so much as pass her by but run past faster than a bullet train. She'd long since figured out that if she stuck to wearing period-style clothing, which had been designed with real women in mind, she stood a better chance of looking as though some thought and effort had been put into her attire. And thus, her passion for vintage clothes had been born.

When all was said and done, the only thing she had in common with Grace in the looks department, was their blue eyes although where Grace's were a pale, ice blue, hers were a startling electric blue, flashing out through her dark lashes and they were the only part of her appearance she liked. People always commented on them which she didn't mind as they detracted the attention away from the ample chunkiness lower down.

She let out a small humph, ran her hands down the A-line skirt she was wearing and stepped behind the counter to switch off the shop lights. In the darkness, she walked over to look out one of the bay windows into the little mews outside. The street lights cast their orange glow and the damp cobbles glistened beneath them. She loved this quaint little lane. Located just off Putney High Street, if you happened to sneeze while walking by, you would miss it. It ran behind the main road shops and many people, the locals included, often mistook it for the trade entrance to the High Street retailers. It was only if you raised your head a little that you saw the board on the wall advertising the secrets which lay down the lane if you were brave enough to explore.

The first shop the modern-day David Livingstone would encounter was Bet's Bakery although the other retailers in the mews referred to it as Bait's Bakery for it was often the warm tantalising smell of freshly baking bread that drew in the unsuspecting passer-by.

After they'd sampled some of her wares, they were then enticed further by the old-fashioned sweet shop which sat just on the bend of the old cobbled stones – jars upon jars of bygone school-day goodies adorned the walls within. Next, and hidden entirely from view of the main road, came a dying breed – a proper, traditional cobbler who would also make you a nice pair of shoes by hand if you were prepared to spend the money. Debbie had been surprised to find that not only was this still a thing in this day and age but that he did a roaring trade in this department.

The cobble stones inclined downwards and her vintage clothes shop rubbed shoulders with the shoe-maker on one side and a gentleman's tailor on the other although there was a small alleyway between her and the cobbler, allowing rear access to the shops and the flats above them. Debbie had tried to get Cedric, the always-smiling proprietor and tailor, on board with offering alterations for her ladies' attire but he was having none of it. He said women changed their minds too often and he "didn't have time for all that palaver!". Directly opposite Debbie's windows was Bobby who owned the jeweller's shop which specialised in antique jewellery and watches. The dead-end of the mews was home to a small Italian restaurant with its own wine bar beside it. In the summer months, with the light, sunny nights, Debbie changed her opening hours to try and capture some of the wine-bar's clientele when tables and chairs were placed outside and it usually paid off rather nicely. She would be making sure she did that again this year although, right now, summer seemed an awful long way off.

Luigi, the owner of the restaurant whose real name was Derek although no one ever called him that, came out to place the "Specials" board on the pavement. He looked over and seeing her through the window, gave her a wave before going back inside. He and his wife, Sonya, lived "above the shop" as did she and Cedric next door but everyone else resided elsewhere and mostly used the flats above as store-rooms although Bet had occasionally rented hers out only to complain afterwards that doing so was more bother than it was worth.

Debbie stood looking out the window for a little while and would have most likely stayed longer had she not glanced down at the 1920s Cartier watch on her wrist, picked up for a song at Camden Market due to it being covered in grime and filth and lacking in motion. She'd spent several hours painstakingly cleaning between the links to make it shine again and Bobby had brought it back to life with his magic touch. It now told her just how much time she'd spent day-dreaming and that she needed to get moving or she'd be late. Again!

Grace and Lydia were always teasing her over the fact that she had the least distance to travel to get to their favourite meeting place, The Black Swan Pub, but she was always the last to arrive. She'd vowed to herself that she'd be the first one there this time but that wasn't going to happen if she didn't hurry up and get a wriggle on.

She ran up the back stairs to the flat, dived into the bathroom and turned on the shower to warm up while she got some clean underwear from the bedroom. She threw her clothes on the bed and was glad that Dale was working a late shift tonight as she'd have time to tidy up her mess when she got home later. As much as she loved her fiancé, his obsessive tidiness could sometimes be a touch overbearing.

'But,' she sang out as she made her way back to the bathroom, 'what he doesn't know won't harm him.'

And with a wide grin on her face, she climbed into the shower.

FOUR

Lydia stood on the train platform, turning her collar up on her coat and her back to the icy wind that was blowing through the station. An older lady, standing two or three feet away, was staring at her. For a minute she was a bit nonplussed at the scrutiny and then remembered her shocking pink hair with gold highlights and purple tips.

She smiled at the woman. 'I'm a hairdresser and my trainee's got a thing for pink.'

'I like it,' came the reply, accompanied by a grin. 'It suits you. I wish I was that brave.'

'Feel free to pop down to my shop – I'm sure Coral would be more than happy to sort you out. Pink seems to be her forte.'

'Tempting but I think my husband would have a heart attack if I came home looking so bright. Although,' a small wicked smile crossed the woman's face, 'it would be a good way of getting shot of the miserable bugger! I'll keep it in mind.'

They were both laughing as the train pulled in and before Lydia alighted one stop later, she slipped a business card into the woman's hand and said, with a little wink, 'For the day when your patience has been stretched to the limit.'

'Cheers, duck. Like I said, I'll keep it in mind.'

Lydia gave a small wave through the window as she walked off along the platform and was pleased to see the card being slipped inside a purse. With a bit of luck, she may have found herself another customer.

When she exited the train station, she turned right, glad that the pub was less than five minutes away. She'd barely had a chance to warm up on the train and her feet were beginning to feel more like blocks of ice than plates of meat. Thermal socks be damned, she thought, as she tried to wriggle some feeling back into her toes.

She glanced at her watch and saw she was going to arrive early but she didn't care. Dave had continued to be an arse while she was getting ready and where she'd normally have a cup of tea and a breather before she left for the train, tonight she'd left as soon as she was dressed. She was, therefore, surprised to see Debbie sitting in their preferred booth when she walked through the doors.

'Hey, Debs, great to see you. I thought I was going to be sitting here on my Jack Jones for at least ten minutes.'

'I was determined to prove to you both that I *can* be on time, once in a while! Make the most of it, I'm not promising to make it a habit.'

The two women hugged before Lydia shrugged her coat off and put it in the corner of the seat on top of Debbie's.

'Have you checked Gracie is on her way?'

Debbie gave her a small smile. Lydia was the only person who got away with calling Grace, "Gracie". 'Yes, I have. She was about to take a shower when I called her so she should be here soon.'

'That girl works far too hard. I swear, if it wasn't for our nights out, she wouldn't have any kind of social life worth talking about.'

'You know that and I know that but don't try and tell her that…'

'I know! She would just tell me to stop being an old mother hen again.'

Lydia loved these two women like they were sisters but she did have to work at not mothering them. Being older than Grace by four years and Debbie by nine, her natural instinct was to look out and care for them but as they'd told her more times than she could count, being out with them was her time off from being a wife and mother and she should just be letting her hair down and relaxing.

She picked up the menu and ran her eyes down the pies on offer that evening.

'Oh, the chicken and mushroom sounds tasty. *Tender breast of chicken slow cooked in a chestnut mushroom sauce with a shortcrust case and buttery puff pastry lid.* My mouth is watering just thinking about it.'

'They all sound good to me,' Debbie smiled as she too perused the menu.

'Hey, you two, I hope you're not planning on starting without me.'

'Gracie, darling, you know we'd never do that.'

Lydia stood to gather her friend up in a bear-hug, delighted to see her. Grace returned the embrace with equal fervour before turning and giving Debbie a hug of the same magnitude.

She'd only just taken her place in the booth when the waitress arrived with three glasses and a bottle of Prosecco in an ice bucket.

'Oh, Alyson, are we that predictable?' Lydia laughed as the waitress worked on opening the bottle.

'I prefer to think that I know what my favourite clients like to drink and do my best to look after them. I don't give this level of attention to anyone else you know.'

She grinned at them and they all grinned back. After eighteen months, it would have been more of a surprise had the waitress not known what they liked. They'd tried a few other pubs on the high street for their first few meet-ups but it had been Alyson's friendly professionalism which had made them decide this would become their regular haunt.

Once the wine had been poured and the fizz had settled, they raised their glasses to each other.

'Happy New Year. May we all have a good one.'

They chinked the glasses together and took a drink.

'I'm famished. Shall we order first and then exchange news. I can't believe we haven't been together for so long. It's been ages!'

'That, Gracie, sounds like a good idea. I've already decided on the chicken pie. Debs, do you know what you're having?'

After giving their orders to Alyson, Lydia leant forward, placed her elbows on the table and asked, 'So, how was everyone's Christmas? Did you have good ones?'

She was not at all surprised by the rather muted responses she received. None of them had been looking forward to the "Big Day" and it sounded like their low expectations had been more than met.

'Gracie?'

Her friend pushed her blonde hair behind her ear, took a drink of wine and grimaced as she replied, 'Well, Father decided to turn up with some piece of candy-floss on his arm, didn't warn me beforehand so I hadn't cooked enough veg and the two of them sat being nauseating with each other the whole day. She behaved like a ten-year-old schoolgirl out with her first crush and he lapped it up like the sad old, middle-aged fool that he is!'

'Ouch!'

'Yes, Debbie, "ouch" indeed. Talk about feeling like a

spare part in your own home. The only upside was that her being with him meant he didn't stay the night as originally planned and they left just after six. After that, I enjoyed my day!'

'Gracie, I know you. "Enjoying your day" means you ended up in your study working, didn't you?'

'Oh, Lydia, you have got me so sussed. Yes, I did, but I felt better for doing so. It meant I was ahead of the game when I returned to work, which is more than can be said for some of my colleagues.'

'I'm guessing you mean Seb Andrews?'

Lydia and Debbie were totally up to speed on the love-hate relationship Grace had with her office rival.

'Yes, I do. Anyway, stop giving me grief, Lydia Beaumont, did you finally tell your mother-in-law to sling her hook or did you let her boss you around in your own home like you've done for the last eighteen Christmases?'

Lydia let out a sigh.

'Okay, you've got me. Yes, the Out-Law from hell arrived on Christmas Eve, left the day after Boxing Day and made my life miserable the whole time she was there. Sat on her fat arse and never once offered to help.'

'At least you know where Dave gets it from.'

'Debbie, I swear, the three of them treated me like their skivvy the whole time. Other folks look forward to Christmas but I can't see it gone quick enough. Anyway, less of my woes, how was yours?'

'Oh, pretty fabulous... not! Dale, at the very last minute, took on a double-shift for the day – cover for someone who was ill – which meant I was off to my parents on my own. Cue the perfect scenario for my mother to nag me senseless about setting a date for our wedding. Of course, without Dale beside me, I was totally defenceless.'

'But, don't you want to get your date set? You've been

22

engaged for a year now. If you leave it any longer, you'll be getting married in your fifties as the waiting lists for the best venues seem to grow longer every year.'

'And how would you know that, little Miss Bachelorette? Something you haven't told us?'

Grace laughed as she answered.

'Get away! You know my thoughts on marriage. I just happen to hear the girls at work talk about these things and the lads at work moan about them.'

Just then, Alyson arrived with their food and their chatter ground to a halt while they ate.

FIVE

'Oh, that was tasty. Although I just know I'm going to regret it in the morning when I'm getting dressed and trying to find something to fit.'

Debbie pushed the plate away from her, the last bit of custard having been wiped up on her finger and consumed. As much as she liked a main course, puddings were totally her downfall and she simply didn't have the will power to refuse them.

'Don't be so daft, Debs. Did you enjoy it?'

'Ohhhh, yeah! I've yet to meet an apple crumble and custard that I didn't like. And therein lies the problem! I'm going to look like a white, hot air balloon by the time I get married.'

'Well, you'll just need to get Dale to do some bedroom workouts with you. That'll burn off a few calories.'

'LYDIA!'

Debbie and Grace burst out laughing as Lydia pulled a leery face and gave her a few winks.

'What? I'm just suggesting a more enjoyable form of exercise.'

'Well, for that kind of exercise to happen, we'd need to spend time together and these days, it feels like we're ships in the night. As I finish work, he goes off to it. I honestly can't remember when we last spent some quality time together.'

Debbie felt tears well up in her eyes and looked down at the table as she tried to blink them away.

'Hey, hon, it's okay.'

She felt Lydia's hand covering hers while Grace gently rubbed her back.

'I'm sorry, I didn't mean to let it get to me like this. It must be the wine.'

'No, it's not, Debbie, don't do that. This is something that matters to you so come on, out with it.'

She gave Lydia a watery smile as she tried to think of the best way to express her feelings.

'I'm just... I don't know... tired of waiting for the next step in my life to happen. As you said, Grace, we've been together three years, engaged for one so, surely, we should by now be planning our wedding but I just can't seem to get Dale to give me a straight answer when I bring it up. And the last few months have felt like he's being even more elusive.'

'In what way?'

She looked at Grace as she answered, 'The hours he's been working. Don't get me wrong, I know how busy they are at the hospital and there's never enough staff to cover but it's as if Dale has become a one-man nursing machine. If there's a spare shift going, he's taking it. I spent nearly all of Christmas alone and I was in bed at ten o'clock on New Year because he was working again. I don't know how much longer I can take this.'

Debbie felt the tears coming again and quickly rummaged in her bag for a hankie.

'You poor thing. He's not being fair on you, Debbie.

You really need to make a stand. It's time to get him to face up to the next step in your relationship. No doubt he's being a typical bloke – happy to dip his toe in the water by being engaged but too scared to dive right in on the marriage part. You need to sort him out.'

'What, like you've sorted out your Dave and his lazy-arse ways? How long have you been saying you've had enough; you're going to leave yet you're still there? These things are easier said than done, Lydia. You of all people should know that.'

Lydia's face fell at her harsh words and Debbie immediately felt bad for what she'd said.

'Lydia, I'm sorry. I shouldn't have said that. I lashed out. I'm so sorry.'

This time, it was her turn to reach across the table and take her friend's hand, giving it a squeeze as she apologised.

'No, don't apologise, Debs, you're right. Totally right. Who am I to sit here and tell you how to resolve your relationship when my own marriage resembles a nuclear fallout? It is too easy to just let yourself be carried along with the flow. So many times I've thought I was ready to make the break but then bottled it. I also know that if I don't make some changes soon, it's going to be too late and I'll be stuck with the life I have now for good. And the thought of that scares me more than you know. Unfortunately, being on my own scares me just as much. It feels like a no-win situation.'

'Hey, being alone isn't such a bad thing. You never need to queue for the bathroom, never have to fight for the duvet, you can be as quiet or as noisy as you like, eat what you want when you want and NEVER have to relinquish the remote control for the television. So far, I'm seeing a lot of wins there.'

Grace's dry commentary caused Debbie to begin

giggling. It grew into a laugh and within seconds, Lydia had joined in and soon all three of them were laughing fit to burst.

'Well, Gracie,' Lydia gulped down some air as she tried to bring herself under control, 'when you put it like that, I'm moving out tomorrow. I can't think why on earth I've waited this long!'

'The way I see it, ladies, this is the perfect time to look at making those changes in your lives. New Year is when life-changing resolutions are made, so why not make yours tonight. You have to start somewhere. And if we all pledge to make a stand or a change in our lives, we've got each other for support to ensure we don't fall by the wayside on the journey.'

Debbie looked across at Lydia and they both turned to look at Grace as she finished her little speech.

For a moment there was silence and then Lydia said, 'Okay. I'm in. Let's do it.'

Debbie blinked at the strong tone of her friend's voice. It was a tone that stated she was all for this and Debbie knew she had to step up, if not for herself but for Lydia who had to find the strength to free herself.

'Okay, I'm in too.'

'Hang on a minute…'

Lydia got up, went to the bar and spoke with Alyson. When she returned five minutes later, the waitress was behind her with three glasses of Prosecco on a tray. She placed them on the table, cleared away their pudding plates and took their empty wine glasses. After she'd gone, Lydia said, 'I feel like we should seal our deal with a drink and as our bottle was empty, I got us some more.'

Debbie looked at the glass in front of her for a brief second before picking it up and holding it in front of her, said solemnly, 'I swear that by next January, I will have set my wedding date.'

27

'January?'

'You can't rush these things, Grace.'

Lydia picked up her glass and holding it aloft as Debbie had done, said, 'I swear that by next January, I will be my own woman and a woman living on her own.'

They both looked at Grace.

'Oh... erm... I swear to be a partner in the firm by the time I'm forty.'

'Grace! Seriously? That's already a given.'

'Well, there's nothing else I can think of...'

'Yes, there is, Gracie. You know what I mean.'

Debbie watched as Lydia gave Grace a hard stare and was surprised to see Grace almost wilt beneath it.

'Okay. I, Grace Mitchell, swear to spend a bit less time working and a bit more time on myself. I swear to have my house fully decorated by next January.'

Lydia nodded her approval and they chinked their glasses together before each taking a big gulp of the fizzy liquid.

'You know,' Debbie said with a smile, 'people used to make blood pacts to seal their agreements but I have to say, a Prosecco Pact works far better for me.'

SIX

Grace walked down the stairs and wandered through into the kitchen. It was Saturday morning and she was still at home. Normally, she would have gone into the office for a few hours but she'd overheard Sebastian Andrews saying he'd be going in this morning and she really didn't fancy being stuck in the building alone with him. She'd brought some files home with her instead and she planned to bury her head in them as soon as she'd made herself a hot drink.

She put the coffee on to brew before going to open the shutters in the lounge. Picking up the remote control, she flicked it in the direction of the television as she dropped down onto the sofa.

A brief second later, she was catapulted onto the floor as, with a sharp crack, the front right leg snapped in two. She had just narrowly missed clouting her head on the coffee table.

'Oh bugger!'

Still sitting on the floor, she twisted round to inspect the damage and felt a surge of sadness when she saw the errant piece of furniture tilting at a drunken angle. She'd picked the sofa up for a few quid at a flea market when she'd moved into her first student bedsit and it had dutifully followed her around London as she'd rented flat after flat, working her way up to owning her first home.

'I'm not giving up on you just yet, baby. Let's see what we can do here.'

Grace carefully turned the sofa onto its back and proceeded to remove the other three legs along with the broken half that remained. After doing so, she pulled the sofa back into an upright position and looked down at it.

'Okay, you're not perfect but you'll do for now.'

After collecting a mug of coffee, she carefully lowered herself down onto her new, semi-futon style, piece of furniture and took a long drag of caffeine. From this less elevated position, she looked around the room, seeing it from a new perspective.

If I had to describe the décor in here in one word, she thought, it would have to be "sparse". With a capital S!

The sofa, what was left of it, was positioned a few feet in front of the window. Behind her, and to her left, in the alcove between the window wall and the chimney breast, was a bookcase rammed full of law-related missives. Not a single book for pleasurable reading sat among them. A small television unit sat at an angle in the other alcove with the television on top and a satellite box and DVD player on the shelf underneath. In the corner, on the other side of the window, resided a bean bag, also from her student days, which Grace sat on when she had guests. However, as the only guests she'd had to date had been her father and his candy-floss at Christmas, her bottom very rarely made an indent in it. In fact, it was more often used as a footstool on the occasions where she decided to chill out with a pizza and a movie. Such occasions were rare though and it had spent most of its life in this house stuck in the corner.

A sigh squeezed out of her lips. It was time to face up

to how impersonal and cold her home was. There were no photographs on any of the windowsills. No pictures upon the walls. No plants for her to water and no other life-form for her to tend to. If she died tomorrow, anyone coming into the house would have no idea about her as a person.

This realisation dropped on her like a lead weight and she suddenly felt very alone. She no longer had any close friends – her intense ambition to climb the career ladder had alienated those who'd once mattered to her. Weddings and babies had also pushed a wedge between the few people who'd tried to maintain some kind of relationship. All they could talk about was the impossibility of finding a decent plumber and the abhorrent cost of organic disposable nappies. The latter she definitely couldn't comment on but now that she was in a position to give an opinion on the former, there was no one around to listen. Lydia and Debbie were the only people she could now think of as friends but despite all they shared on their Tuesday nights, their lives never crossed paths at any other time. She had a vague idea of where Debbie's shop was but had never been in it. She knew roughly where Lydia lived but had never visited. It was as if their Tuesday nights were just little pockets of time when they came together before dispersing again.

This thought only added to the feeling of desolation growing inside her. Sure, she loved her job, she tried to reason with herself, but was it really the b-all and end-all of her existence? Was that really all she had to offer to the world?

Grace drained her mug while trying to remember the last time she'd even had the merest sniff of a relationship. Certainly not since she'd bought the house, that was for sure. The only blokes she met were through work and she was far too professional to date the clients. This left work colleagues which was a total no-go area – the thought of getting it on with Sebastian Andrews made her teeth clench and her body shudder – or the other faceless, suited wonders who milled around the pubs in the City after work on a Friday night. They were even less appealing than Seb Andrews and that was going some.

Hauling herself up from almost-the-floor, she walked back to the kitchen with the intention of refilling her mug when the Prosecco Pact conversation came to mind. Her part of the deal had been to get her home properly decorated, by which she really meant furnished. The decorating part was complete and had been for about ten months. No, it was turning her house into a home that was her stumbling block. Buying the right furniture took time, patience and effort – three things that were in short supply when you were grasping onto the rungs of the career ladder. It also seemed that most people decorated their homes these days with big Swedish flat-pack pieces which was all well and good but too many of the items required two pairs of hands to assemble. She was already down at the first hurdle.

'Oh, to hell with this!'

Her exclamation was followed by a couple of colourful expletives and the coffee mug was all but thrown into the dishwasher.

'Girlfriend,' she muttered aloud, 'it's time you had a day off and got this place sorted out.'

She ran back up the stairs to her bedroom and forty-five minutes later, she walked out her front door determined that, by the time she returned, she would be the proud owner of at least one item of "proper" furniture.

SEVEN

Grace pushed open the door to what felt like the hundredth furniture shop she'd been in so far. In truth, it was only the seventh but she was getting bored now because despite all the sofas she'd seen, nothing was hitting the spot.

The problem she had was that she didn't know what style of furniture she liked best. There were some modern designs which she sort-of liked but then she also had a leaning towards the heavier, traditional items. Finding something which was a fusion of the two was proving to be impossible.

'Can I assist you with anything?'

The sales assistant walked towards her and with his greasy, parted hair, glasses and supercilious approach, she was immediately put in mind of James Spader's character in the film "Mannequin". Obsequious… that was the word she would use to describe him.

'No, thank you. I'm just looking at the moment.'

'No problem, madam. If anything catches your eye, I'll just be over here.'

'Thank you.'

She gave him a polite smile and strolled away through the showroom. The fact of the matter was that she no longer had any expectations of finding something she liked today, and had only walked through the door as it was the last shop in the row and it would have been daft to pass by without looking.

The stylishly displayed items in front of her were, unsurprisingly, leaving her cold and, as she walked towards the back of the shop, the furniture ceased being "displayed" for the simple reason that it was all crammed together. To say it was crowded was an understatement and she found herself having to squeeze between chairs, tables and sofas as she pushed her way towards the far corner. After all, since she'd made the effort to come into this final shop, she may as well have a good look around before crossing it off the list.

Finally, when she reached the spot she'd been aiming for, she was surprised to find a small alcove and when she stepped across to the entrance, she stopped and stared in pure delight, for sitting in pride of place in the centre of the space, was the most glorious sofa she had seen all day. She instantly fell in love and walked towards it in an almost reverent fashion.

The first thing to tug on her heartstrings was the colour. It was a deep, rich crimson which she knew would look stunning alongside the grey panelling in her lounge. It had a high back and equally high arms shaped in a soft wing-like style with a gentle roll-top. They created the perfect corner for snuggling into. The legs were dark wood – the label on the arm said walnut – and were carved in a manner not dissimilar to the legs on a Queen Anne chair but decidedly more ornate and not as high as the chair legs would be.

She slowly sat down, expecting it to be quite firm, for that was how it looked, and was surprised to find herself sinking into the soft seat. It almost felt as though she was being embraced. As she sat, Grace felt herself begin to relax and the tension that had been with her since she'd left the house, seeped away.

She didn't know how long she'd been sitting there but the sales assistant had a rather concerned look on his face when he came round the corner to find her.

'Is madam okay?'

'Oh, yes, thank you, I am. I'm just enjoying this gorgeous sofa. It's wonderful.'

'Ah, yes, you have good taste. That's a JVF piece. They're excellent quality.'

'JVF? It's not a name I'm familiar with.'

With great reluctance, she pushed herself off the sofa and back onto her feet.

'Jake Valentine Furniture. He's a local designer and furniture maker who is fast becoming quite something within the interior design circuit. His pieces are now much sought after. This sofa only came in last night and is due to be moved to the front window on Monday. We don't expect it to be there for long.'

'I can fully understand why. It really is something. I love it.'

'Maybe it won't make it into the window...'

She heard the hopeful tone in the assistant's voice and knew she was going to have to burst his bubble.

'I'm very sorry, but as much as I love it, and I really do, I can't buy it.'

'It's a very reasonable price and we do offer instalment payments if that helps.'

'It's not the price that's the issue... it's the size! It's blooming massive!'

And it was! The sofa could easily seat four people. Five if they were on the skinny side! Had it been smaller, like a standard three-seater sofa, her credit card would already be slipping through the electronic device on the shop counter.

'Ah! I see.'

She turned to look at the assistant and saw his name badge on his tie.

'Barry, trust me, it's the only thing that's stopping me buying it. There is just no way on the planet that this would fit in my lounge, no matter how much I might wish it could. If there is any way of getting a smaller one, then I would be thrilled to take it off your hands.'

'Sadly, Jake Valentine only does one-off pieces. Every item is unique.'

'Damn!'

Strangely, Grace felt like bursting into tears. It was only a sofa but somehow, it had come to be more than that. She liked the way it made her feel safe and protected when she sat on it. The high back and arms felt as though they were wrapping themselves around her and soothing away her troubles. It was almost as if the sofa was returning the love she felt for it. Her logical, lawyerly mind was telling her she was thinking nonsense but her heart whispered, *'I hear ya…'* and gave a little clench of sympathy.

'I'm sorry you're unable to give this item a home, madam, but Jake is still doing bespoke commissions. I can give you his card, if you like? I wouldn't hang around too long though, regarding getting in touch with him, because the way his star is rising, he may not be offering that service for too much longer.'

'Oh, I would love to have his contact details. Thank you.'

She followed Barry back to the front of the shop but not before taking several photographs of the sofa on her phone first. She was most definitely going to be contacting this Jake fellow and she hoped she might be able to persuade him to put aside his "one-piece-only" rule on this occasion.

EIGHT

Lydia swept into the pub and headed straight for their booth. She was the first to arrive this time but wasn't surprised as Gracie had sent her a text to say she was running late and Debbie hadn't managed to be on time since their first meet up in January.

She tugged off her coat and undid the buttons on her cardigan. They may have just crawled into February but it was still perishing outside and even the extra layer hadn't kept the chill out as she'd waited for the train.

Alyson, the waitress, smiled as she walked over and deposited three menus on the table.

'You nearly didn't get your booth tonight, Lydia. I had to do a quick manoeuvre and redirect a couple of lads who were heading right for it.'

'Oh, thank you, Alyson, that's much appreciated. How did you sway them?'

'I just told them, if they were intending to watch the football on the big screen, the view from here was rubbish. That soon shifted them!'

Lydia laughed along with Alyson and they were still

chuckling as Debbie and Grace walked in the door.

Alyson gave them all a smile and said she'd be back for their order in a few minutes once they'd settled themselves in.

After hugs and greetings had been exchanged and they were all seated with their glasses of Prosecco in front of them, Grace piped up with a big smile on her face, 'You'll never guess what I did on Saturday?'

'Do you actually want us to guess or would you rather just come straight out with it?'

'I'm going to come right out with it! I went furniture shopping! I have begun to work on my pact offering.'

Lydia looked at the happy expression on Gracie's face and couldn't help but return her wide smile.

'You go, girl,' she said, 'tell us all about it.'

For the next few minutes, Grace filled them in on the events of Saturday and they all had a good laugh as she verbally painted the picture of being thrust headlong off her old sofa when it collapsed on her. She then told them about traipsing around the shops and becoming more demoralised in each one as she couldn't find anything she liked but then she showed them the photographs of "the" sofa and Lydia could see why she'd fallen for it. It really was a gorgeous piece of furniture but she could also see where Gracie was coming from when she said the size was a problem.

'Can the shop order in a smaller one?' Debbie asked as she expanded the photos on the screen to get a closer look at the detail.

'Sadly, no, as the bloke who makes them only does one-off pieces but...' she paused for effect, 'he does do commissions and I not only have his phone number but I also have an appointment to meet him on Saturday morning. His workshop is in Wimbledon so not far to go, which is a result.'

'Oh, that *is* a result! Nice one. Do you plan to ask him to recreate this one in miniature for you?'

'Well, Lydia,' she smiled, 'I'm certainly going to try. If he won't, then I'll see if he can make something quite close to it. I'm sure if I explain to him what I liked about it, he'll be able to come up with some ideas.'

Lydia felt a little buzz of pleasure at her friend's obvious happiness. Grace often carried a look that suggested there was something missing although it only appeared when she wasn't aware she was being watched. While Lydia didn't think a solitary sofa was going to fill the space, it was doing its job in making Grace step outside her usual rigorous routine – after all, not working two Saturdays on the bounce was a big deal for her friend.

'So, has anyone else made moves on their Prosecco promises?' asked Grace, taking a sip of her bubbles.

Handing the phone back to Grace, Debbie followed suit on the fizzy front and as she replaced the glass on the table, she grinned, 'I have!'

Lydia sat up straighter at this news,

'What? You have a date for us? Am I buying a summer hat or a winter one?'

'Noooooooo, silly lady, I'm not that far down the path but…' she inserted a dramatic pause of her own, 'we ARE having dinner together on Friday night.'

'And, do you think Dale will turn up?'

'Oh, yes, Lydia, I do because he's been told – in no uncertain terms I would add – that his life won't be worth living if he bails on me. I pointed out how long it's been since we had a proper meal together so he promised me he would be home.'

'Do you think he'll go for setting the date?'

'Grace, I'm taking a leaf out of your book – presenting him with a number of options, none of which is the word "no". I've listened to you talk about how you approach some of your most awkward clients and I'm using your methods. I've made a short-list of the venues I like and which I think he will also like. And, I've spoken with them to find out which dates are available, those have been collated into a spreadsheet and I now have three dates which are contenders. He doesn't get to leave the table until one has been confirmed. I'm putting my foot down with a firm hand, as my old granddad used to say!'

'Good for you, girl! He'd better step up after all your efforts.'

Debbie turned at Lydia's words and said in a tone which suggested she wasn't messing about, 'Lydia, if he doesn't, then I won't be wearing this ring when we meet next Tuesday. I'm thirty-four later this year and while that is not old by any means, I would like to have children while I'm still young enough to actually enjoy them.'

'Fair enough. Just be absolutely sure though, Debbie.'

'Oh, I am! It's almost fourteen months since he popped the question, it's time he came good on his proposal.'

'Here we are, ladies, "grubs up", as they say!'

Alyson put their plates on the table and took away the empty Prosecco bottle. She returned a few minutes later with a new one.

Over dinner, they discussed the various venues Debbie had considered, which ones had been discarded and those who'd made it onto the short-list. She adamantly refused, however, to share the potential dates stating that she wasn't prepared to risk jinxing anything until she had one set.

After Alyson had returned to clear the table, Lydia found herself being scrutinised by two pairs of blue eyes.

'Right then, Lydia, you were the one who instigated all of this, so, where are you at?'

'Erm…' She gave a small cough and began again. 'Erm, I've got an appointment on Thursday with one of the estate agents in Tooting to go through my options. I need to find somewhere to live before I can do anything else.'

'If I'm being too personal, Lydia, just say so but... how are you fixed financially?' Grace put her hand up to stop Lydia replying immediately. 'Let me finish. I don't want to know the minute details but I'm just aware that Dave could be entitled to half of anything you possess, which could leave you in a pretty bad place. After all, you mentioned once, if I remember rightly, that the flat you're in at the moment is a council flat?'

'And that's where the problem lies, Grace. It's all very well and good wanting to leave, but if I can't afford somewhere to live... London has become so bloody expensive now. I wandered down to have a look in the estate agent's window the other day and just about passed out when I saw the prices. How on earth do people manage?'

'With difficulty! If it wasn't for Dale's share of the monthly expenses, I'd be struggling. It was okay a few years ago but the management company has increased the ground fees three times in two years and it's becoming harder to keep the shop going as I'm barely making a profit these days. Do you have rooms over the shop, Lydia, that you could move into?'

'Sadly, no! I've rented them out to a beautician and she's done them all out to accommodate her business which means that, even if I was to give her notice, the space wouldn't be practical for living in without further work being done.'

'Is the shop in your name?'

Lydia looked at Grace. 'Yes, Mum took her share when she retired and transferred it over to me.'

'Hmm, that's a bummer because Dave could come after you for half of it.'

'If he does that, I'll go after half of his share in the garage! After all, I gave him half the money.'

'I'm sorry, what? Run that one by me again?'

'Dave bought into the garage about five years ago. The boss at the time had gambling debts so offered Dave a buy-in option and fifty percent of the business. Up till then, he'd been making a reasonable wage and had some savings but it wasn't quite enough to meet what his boss was asking for. Because we knew the reason behind the offer, we played hard-ball, got the price knocked down by £10K, and I gave Dave the difference.'

'Do you have the arrangement in writing?'

'Grace, are you getting all lawyerly on me here?'

'Damn right I am! I want to make sure no one tries to screw you over.'

'Well, I don't have my share of the actual payment in writing but the money can be traced from my business bank into our joint account – the good thing about internet banking! – and then the payment value can be viewed going out. The timing will match up with his name going onto the business deeds which I made sure he got sorted just in case Roger, the boss, tried to pull a fast one. But he didn't, it was all legit and Dave became co-owner.'

'Has he ever paid back the money?'

'Nah, don't be so daft! The very notion of that wouldn't even cross Dave's mind.'

'Well, that's a relief. I have to be honest, Lydia, it has been niggling at the back of my mind.'

'Do you think I'll have any problems there, Gracie?'

A twisting sensation began growing in her gut as she asked the question. The thought that Dave might try to take a portion of her business was one that hadn't occurred to her but now that Grace had brought it up...

'To be honest, Lydia, I wouldn't like to say. It really comes down to how good a solicitor you get and the same with Dave. Of course, if you can keep it amicable – he doesn't touch the shop and you don't go after his share in the garage – it will make it considerably easier on both of you. Do you think it could be an amicable split?'

'I... I don't know. Dave can be quite possessive with his belongings and I'm kind of lumped into that bracket. As you know, a lot of Dave's thinking is still in the twentieth century, especially when it comes to women and our rights.'

'Lydia, we're here for you and don't feel we're pushing you into something you don't want to do. We're not going to tar and feather you and walk you down Putney High Street if you don't come through on your part of the deal.'

'Speak for yourself there, Debs, I fully intend to do all of that and more!'

Lydia couldn't help but laugh at Gracie's expression of mock indignation and she felt the tremors inside seep away.

'Thank you, Debbie. I know I have to do something though – I can't carry on like this, but now I'm on the verge of beginning the process... I can't help but feel scared. I do worry if I'm doing the right thing or will it end up being worse than it is now.'

'Or... it could be so much better! You could meet someone who really cares about you, values you and respects you.'

'Oh, puhlease! Who's going to want to hook up with a worn-out, old-forties-plus divorcee? Huh? Get real!'

'Now you just look here, lady...'

Lydia sat back a little in surprise at the vehemence in Debbie's voice.

'You are not old and you most definitely are not "worn-out"! You're lovely! You're slim and well fit – no doubt from standing all day at work – you have a great personality and you're so outgoing, you make friends with ease. Hell, it's because of you that we're sitting here now. You cut straight through Grace's ice-queen act when we were on our course and you saw how shy I felt and made a point of talking to me and including me in the tasks. You will have no problem meeting someone nice, although you might fare better with the gorgeous blonde locks you're currently sporting than the bright pink of last month!'

'She does have a point on that one, Lydia. The blonde suits you far more than the pink.'

The two women sniggered as Lydia rolled her eyes.

'Very well, I shall break poor Coral's creative heart by insisting on no more pink hair. You do know she'll be devastated.'

'Time for her to learn the valuable lesson of "the customer is always right" then!' Grace said in a dry tone.

'I will put the blame firmly at your door, Grace Mitchell.'

'Yeah, you do that!'

They laughed again and Lydia sat back, her drink in her hand, and listened to the easy banter going on between her friends. While she was still dreading the visit to the estate agent on Thursday, it was only a reconnaissance trip to get a feel for what she could or couldn't afford. She didn't have to make any moves yet; she wasn't being forced into a decision. All she was doing was gathering information.

The tension eased out of her shoulders and she leant forward to re-join the conversation which had gone off on some strange tangent about Debbie's wedding dress looking like something from a Disney movie. Seriously?

NINE

Debbie leant forward and straightened the candle slightly in its holder. She was so excited for tonight and had made a point of putting every effort into making it special.

The dark green tablecloth had been brought out and the few pieces of lead crystal received when they'd become engaged, had been washed, polished and carefully placed on top of it. The gold platters she'd bought for their Christmas dinner but ended up not being used were laid out and the bowls for the chilli sat on top of them. She did regret that chilli con carne wasn't the most romantic of dishes but it was the one she could cook well and she'd felt compelled to produce some kind of home-cooking. She had to make sure that Dale couldn't come up with any excuses for not setting their wedding date and while she was under no illusion that her actual cooking was going to sway the odds in her favour, the fact that she'd made the effort just might.

She smoothed down her skirt and went out to the mirror in the hallway to check her hair and makeup hadn't wilted under her efforts in the kitchen. While making the chilli had been quite straightforward – thanks be to the creators of slow-cookers – the rice had been more of a challenge as she'd side-stepped the easy option of the microwave packets and had chosen instead to make it from scratch herself. No mean feat as they'd sat down in the past to rice that had such a "bite" it was still crunchy, or the other extreme of a disgusting mushy mulch that bore more of a resemblance to wallpaper paste! Debbie was determined that tonight, it would be perfect.

Her phone pinged through in the lounge so after popping back to give the rice another gentle stir, she replaced the lid on the pan and went through to find a text from Dale saying he'd been a bit late finishing his shift but he was leaving now and should be home in about twenty minutes, which prompted a quick return to the kitchen where she turned off the heat under the pan, leaving the rice to slow-cook in the hot water.

To kill time, she walked into the spare room, which was more of a large box-room than a spare bedroom. Sure, she'd managed to fit a single bed in it, and it was perfectly functional as long as you didn't mind getting in and out via the bottom of it as walking up the side wasn't an option. At the opposite end of the long, narrow space, however, was the reason Debbie was smiling because this was her "stock" room. All the beautiful clothes she didn't have space for downstairs were kept in here and it was also where new stock came to be cleaned, assessed and priced before going onto the shop floor. And she'd received a wonderful surprise, which had unfortunately come with some sadness, earlier that morning.

A young woman had come into the shop dragging a large suitcase behind her and it transpired that her grandmother, Martha, had recently passed away. Martha had visited the shop every few months to sell one or two of her old designer outfits in order to supplement her pension, often staying for a couple of hours while they discussed the merits of high-end couture over "off-the-rail" pieces that many of the fashion houses now offered. She had always enjoyed the company of the older lady and while deeply sorry that their discussions were now a thing of the past, she'd been secretly thrilled to learn that she'd left her entire wardrobe of clothes to Debbie in her will. The granddaughter had made a point of saying how relieved the family were that they didn't have to bag and drag the contents of Martha's dressing room to a charity shop and had gone off to return with two more suitcases.

Debbie was betting her last pound coin on the family being completely unaware of the value of some of the items of clothing and was hoping that many of the dresses and suits Martha had talked about were lurking inside the as-yet-unopened gifts. She hadn't wanted to delve into the unexpected cache of goodies in front of Martha's granddaughter because she'd known that she wouldn't have been able to contain her excitement if she had come across something immensely collectable and therefore, valuable. Thankfully, the offer to empty and return the suitcases there and then had been declined and she'd lugged them up the stairs as soon as she'd seen the car drive up the hill and out of the mews.

She'd just clicked open the first catch when she heard the footsteps coming up the metal stairs outside and with a sigh, she closed it again. As much as she wanted to lose herself in the frothy contents, tonight, she had bigger fish to fry.

The forkful of rice and chilli that Debbie had been holding clattered down into her bowl as she looked across the table at Dale who was now saying words her brain was struggling to comprehend.

'I'm… I'm sorry…' she stuttered, 'but can you just repeat that, please.'

'There isn't going to be a wedding, Debbie. I can't marry you.'

Her head filled with dizziness and she was sure she felt herself sway. She grabbed the edge of the table, closed her eyes and held her breath, trying to quell the listing sensation inside her. She then exhaled very slowly through her mouth before taking another deep intake of air through her nose. She repeated this three times before opening her eyes and looking at the man sitting across from her. His hazel eyes looked back, full of concern and sadness.

'Why?' she whispered, 'What did I do wrong?'

She turned her gaze down to the table as tears blurred her vision and felt the vibration of Dale's chair moving on the wooden floorboards. A second later, he was kneeling on the floor beside her, holding her hands and softly rubbing her back.

'Oh, Debbie, you have done nothing wrong, I promise you. This all rests entirely on me. You are absolutely perfect, just… not for me.'

She turned her head marginally to her right to look at him.

'What do you mean, not perfect for you?'

Dale stood up and held out his hand. 'Come, let's talk on the sofa.'

She allowed him to pull her to her feet before he bent over to blow out the candle and pick up their wine glasses. He glanced at the bottle on the sideboard and she grabbed it. He grinned at her and she again silently questioned why he would be breaking off their engagement when they were so in sync with each other.

She followed him across the front room, where the open

curtains allowed a view of the dark, unlit buildings opposite, and sat down beside him when he patted the sofa for her to do so. She put the wine bottle on the small table and from force of habit, placed a drinks coaster underneath. For goodness' sake, she thought, my life is in the process of falling apart and I'm worrying about rings on the bloody table?

'Debbie,' Dale took her hand and held it gently in his. 'There's no easy way for me to say what I need to tell you but I hope it will help you to realise that my breaking off our engagement has nothing to do with you or anything you've done.'

'Dale, of course it has something to do with me. You loved me enough last year to propose but now you don't. I must have done something to make you change your mind.'

'No, you haven't, Debs. Trust me on that. You are the same lovely, sweet and gorgeous girl you were last year, and the year before that and, I hope, will be for many years to come. But I can't give you what you want from life. I can't marry you or give you children.'

'Why not? I thought that was what you wanted too?'

'I do, I still want all of that but we can't have them together.'

'Why can't we?'

She turned to face him, wanting him to look her in the eye when he came up with some pathetic reason to let her down gently with.

The expression on his face changed several times, quicker than she was able to decipher what they meant. Eventually it settled on one which she recognised as being resignation.

'Debbie, the reason I can't marry you is because...' he paused, swallowed hard and then copied her previous breathing technique, exhaling twice before saying, 'I can't marry you because I'm gay.'

Debbie stared at him for a second or two before she burst out laughing. Did he honestly think she was going to fall for that? He'd never been a big joker but this sure made up for the lack of practical funnies throughout their relationship except… when she looked back at Dale, he wasn't laughing with her. He was now the one with the tears in his eyes.

Abruptly, her laughter stopped, the last chortle quickly dying in her throat.

'You're serious, aren't you?'

He nodded and she became aware of how tightly he was now gripping her hands.

'But… how? Why? When?' She shook her head. 'I'm sorry, Dale, I don't know what I should be asking or saying here.' She pulled her hands away from his as she spoke.

'It's okay, I get why you're confused. If it helps, I have been too, for a very long time.'

'But now you're not?'

He shook his head ever so slightly. 'No, I'm not. Not anymore.'

'What changed?'

He hung his head and she had to lean closer to hear him.

'A new doctor at work. He started nine months ago and the attraction, for both of us, was instant. I've never felt that before. I'd… I'd looked at men in the past and felt a twinge of something inside – sometimes it would be stronger than others – but I was always able to ignore it. With John, however, it wasn't a twinge, it was like being hit by a wrecking ball and ignoring the feelings wasn't an option, although I tried, Debs, I really tried.'

The earnest expression on his face left her in no doubt that he had.

'I believe you,' she said quietly. 'Carry on.'

'For the first few months, I did everything I could to

avoid him – changed my shifts so we wouldn't be working together, swapping my days off to when he'd be working so there would be fewer occasions for our paths to cross, and socialising less with my colleagues; only going out when I knew for sure he wouldn't be around.'

Debs nodded as she remembered when she suddenly didn't have a clue what his shifts were and the rota pinned on the fridge with a fridge magnet was the opposite of what he was working.

'What changed?'

'I was asked to do a double shift and it threw us back together. Unfortunately, we lost one of our patients that night and it left us both vulnerable. You know how it is when that happens.'

'I do.'

And she did. Twice Dale had come home and cried in her arms over the pain of being unable to save the life of a patient. All the doctors and nurses took it personally when it happened and it sometimes took several days for them to move on.

'Things got a little physical in the immediate aftermath, at the end of the shift, and then very physical a couple of days after that. Since then, I've been living a double life and it's been hell.'

'So, all those extra shifts you were doing?'

'Weren't all extra shifts. Some were but others were me avoiding coming home.'

'Why?'

'Because I hated deceiving you and I was sure you would see the guilt on my face. Staying away was the easier option.'

'The cowardly option.'

'Yes.'

Debbie sat back on the sofa but left her hand in his. She looked up at the orange glow in the dark sky outside the window – the streetlight trying to throw some warmth into the chill seeping through her bones.

'Why did you ask me to marry you, Dale, if you'd been having these twinges? Surely you must have been aware of the uncertainty of the feelings within you?'

'Yes, I was aware but I was also trying to ignore them. I know it will break my mother's heart and I dread to think what my father will say. Mum kept going on about me getting married, having children, how much she adored you and what a great wife and mother you'd make and I caved. You saw her face when I asked you after Christmas dinner. I honestly thought that you and I could make it work. I was convinced we had what I needed to see me through.'

'Did you love me?'

He turned and placed his hands on either side of her face.

'Debbie, I loved you then and I love you now. I will always love you in the deepest part of my being and if I was straight, there is no other person in this world that I would want to spend my life with.'

'So, if this John hadn't arrived on the scene...'

'We'd have already set a date and be on our merry way towards becoming mister and missus.'

'Instead, here we are, breaking up and you sharing the biggest secret of your life. I just don't know what to say, what to think or how to feel. I'm numb, I really am. I mean, you say you love me but how can I believe you? How do I know that it wasn't just easier to be with me because I didn't question you too closely?'

She racked her mind, trying to find the clues which, if she'd just looked a little closer, would have alerted her to what she'd so clearly missed. On the face of it, there were many things that she could have questioned – how well he dressed and always looked so good regardless of what he was wearing. The more-than-good skills in the kitchen. His set-in-stone facial routine and, now that she came to think about it some more, his unexpected pleasure in the manicure they'd shared when they'd gone on holiday for the first time. She could also add his near-obsessive cleaning of the flat to the list but then, her own mother sat on the cusp of being OCD when it came to housework and she definitely wasn't going to be leading the line on a LGBT parade anytime soon, so even that wasn't a giveaway.

The truth be told, she thought, we're now living in an age where we're told not to judge, not to jump to conclusions, don't make assumptions and be more accepting of people's differences and while all of this is as it should be, it did mean the red flags which would have once had the old "gaydar" sounding, were now redundant... and look where it had landed her.

The emotions inside her were bouncing back and forth between the upset of them breaking up and the relief of knowing the reason behind it was out of her control. Neither one had the upper hand at the moment.

She stole a look at Dale and the sad, desperate anguish within him was seeping out from every pore. In that moment, she knew that whatever she was feeling was irrelevant. Sure, she might be upset and broken-hearted but she'd be able to pick up the pieces and move on. Dale's life, on the other hand, was about to implode and no one knew where the pieces might fall. How would his parents take the news? How was he even going to break it to them? How scared must he be right now?

She leant forward and this time, she wrapped her arms around him.

'I'm here for you, Dale. I love you and always will. This won't be easy for me but it's going to be a hell of a lot harder for you and I'm not going to let you go through it on your own. If you want me with you when you tell your folks, I'll be there. It's time to embrace who you really are and I'll do whatever it takes to make that easier for you.'

For the next few hours, they sat talking on the sofa until they eventually dropped off to sleep, wrapped up together in each other's arms but no longer together in the way that really mattered.

TEN

Grace walked slowly down the street, looking at the numbers on the doors and back at the street map she'd printed off the computer, trying to follow the bright yellow highlighter path she'd marked out. She'd come out of the train station and was now following Queen's Road which was turning out to be considerably longer than she'd given it credit for. She was looking for a small lane that was apparently slotted between two houses near the park and, at the end of it, she would find Jake Valentine.

As she walked along, she wondered what the man in question would be like. She'd tried to look him up on the internet but although there had been plenty about his growing popularity and his products fast becoming the must-have pieces for the name-dropping elite, there was little about the man himself. Even photographs were scarce and the few she'd been able to dig up had either been blurred or at an angle that gave little away. All she'd managed to ascertain was that he had dark hair.

She looked back at the map and checked the house number to her right. Damn! She'd been so busy day-dreaming, she'd walked right past the lane. Retracing her steps, Grace soon found what she'd missed. And how she'd missed it! The lane, while not massive, was certainly big enough for a Transit van to drive down. There was also a small enamel sign screwed to the wall which indicated that JVF was that way if you followed the arrow.

As she walked along the uneven surface, Grace made sure the GPS facility on her phone was activated and she'd sent Lydia a text that morning with Jake's address. For all that she'd spoken to the man on the phone and he'd sounded very pleasant, she was savvy enough to know that you don't take chances like these without some kind of backup. And her backup was that she'd contact Lydia within twenty minutes of her arrival to let her know she was okay. She had her arrival text ready to go and she hit the send button when she came to a large set of dark-blue double gates with an intercom. Duly pushing the button, she waited for a disembodied voice to float out to her and was slightly taken aback when the side-gate pinged open.

She gingerly pushed it to the side and stepped through into a large yard area filled with wood and timber of varying degrees. Some were as raw as the day the trees had been cut down, the bark and branches still evident. Some had been roughly sawn down where the beautiful wood inside could be seen but the edges were still lined with bark. An open shed revealed timber which had been fully cut down to equal sizes and was piled up waiting to be put to good use.

While the yard itself was open to the elements, she was standing in a small, covered walkway which led her to a door at the far end. It was ajar and with a small polite knock, she pushed it open. The first thing to hit her was the smell of wood. The lovely warm scent of freshly-sawn timber and sawdust assailed her nostrils and she found herself taking deep breaths, relishing the delicious odour.

She looked around but the workshop appeared to be empty of human life although a partially assembled chair was sitting on a nearby workbench. She walked over to have a closer look and almost jumped out of her skin when a disembodied voice suddenly said, 'Watch out for the soldering iron, it's switched on and blooming hot. It likes to give nasty burns.'

'Oh!'

Grace found herself stepping back from the bench and swivelling round to find the man the voice belonged to walking towards her with a warm smile on his face and his hand stretched out to shake hers.

As she placed her hand in his, he said, 'I was just putting the dog away in the house as he can sometimes get a little too excited with my visitors. It doesn't always go down so well.'

'Oh, I wouldn't have minded, I like dogs.'

'Do you have one of your own?'

'Sadly not. Until they can be taught to walk themselves and feed themselves, it's better for all that I don't. My working hours are barely human-friendly, never mind animal-friendly.'

'That's a pity. There's a lot to be said for the comfort an animal can give.'

She had no reply to that, so Grace said nothing and waited for him to continue.

'Anyway, I'm rambling. Let me introduce myself properly and then we can discuss your requirements. Hi, I'm Jake Valentine, thank you for taking the time to come to my workshop and for considering commissioning a JVF piece for your home. What did you have in mind?'

'Well, I visited a shop just off the King's Road last weekend and they'd taken a delivery of one of your sofas. I have pictures…'

Grace scrolled through her phone before holding it out

for Jake to look at.

'Ah yes, I was very pleased with, and especially fond of, that one. I had a piece of timber with these glorious curves on one side and it felt like a sacrilege to trim them off. So, I let it stand against the wall until inspiration struck and I had the idea to use it as the back of a sofa. To ensure I didn't lose any of the beauty, I had to make a large sofa as cutting the timber to size wasn't an option in this case.'

'It is a stunning piece of furniture and I fell in love with it the instant I set eyes upon it.'

'But?'

'Sorry?'

'Why didn't you buy it if you loved it so much? Was it the price? Because I have to advise you now that commission pieces are usually ten to fifteen percent more than the retail price of non-commissioned items.'

'No! No, it wasn't the price that was the issue, it was the size! It was too big so I'm here to ask if you would consider making a second one but smaller.'

Jake gave her a gentle smile and something in her stomach made a "twanging" sensation. There was no denying the man was good looking but in a totally un-obvious way. She guessed he was in his early forties judging by the small amount of salt and pepper in his short side-burns and tidy, goatee beard. His hair was predominantly dark, cut fairly short but with a small sticky-up quiff effect at the front. His facial structure leant towards being oval with his brown eyes, a little paler than milk chocolate with some hazel streaks, being the stand-out feature. Stature wise, he was about five inches taller than her, making him about six feet and fairly solid in the way of a middle-aged man who maybe liked one or two more beers at the weekend than he worked off during the week. Nothing about him would ever feature on the list of attributes she'd like to see in her ideal man but he certainly had something going on. Combined with his low, but softly-spoken, voice – think Professor Brian Cox but dropped a few octaves – he exuded a warm, charming charisma and Grace found herself being inexplicably drawn to him.

'Hmm, I'm afraid I can't make the exact same sofa because **A**, I created it around that particular piece of timber and **B**, I like every item to be unique so that the owners of them know that what they have is completely individual.'

Grace felt her mood drop and she tried not to let her disappointment show.

'That is not to say, however, that I can't create something which you could love just as much, if not more. Come, let's have a seat, a cup of something hot, and you can tell me what it was that appealed to you.'

He led her over to a door and when she stepped through, she had to work on not gasping out loud. She'd been expecting an office with blokey-stuff in it, instead she'd walked into a tastefully decorated room featuring wall-to-wall patio doors with an expanse of decking on the other side and a green lawn beyond that. The room itself was bright with pale-yellow walls, white woodwork and a selection of individually designed, comfortable-looking chairs placed around a slightly-taller than usual coffee table which held a selection of large drawing pads and a tub of different coloured pencils.

'Please, take a seat.'

Jake gestured towards the chairs while walking over to a coffee machine sitting on a shelf.

'Any particular chair I should sit in?'

'No, any one is fine with me. Would you like tea, coffee or hot chocolate? I have these pod things which seem to offer a wide spectrum of options.'

'A black coffee would be perfect, thank you.'

Grace turned back to the chairs and chose the one facing out towards the garden. A couple of minutes later, Jake placed two mugs of coffee on the table and sat in the seat by her side. She hadn't expected this, thinking he'd sit opposite her, and was taken slightly off guard. Something in her face must have shown this because he picked up a pad and explained, 'It's easier for me to sketch as you watch because then you can point to where you want changes made as I draw rather than trying to amend a finished sketch, which can look messy.'

'Oh, right, yes, that makes sense.'

'So, please, tell me why you loved the sofa. What did you notice first?'

Grace tried to think back to the previous week. So much of the sofa had shouted at her at once that it was difficult to try and put the varying emotions and aspects into any kind of order.

'Well, I think…' she paused, 'I think it was the colour. I love dark red. The panelling in my lounge is mid-grey, so my first thought was how good the colour would look against it.'

'Okay. What next?'

She closed her eyes to help her focus.

'The high back and arms. Something about them gave me a sense of… peace? Safety? I'm not sure but it was a nice feeling. When I sat down, it felt like I was being—'

She suddenly stopped and her eyes flew open.

'Felt like what?'

'Erm…'

She could feel the colour racing up her cheeks but the gentle look on Jake's face and his quiet question gave her the confidence to speak out.

'It felt like I was being embraced. As if warm arms had wrapped around me and were saying everything was going to be alright.'

'Good. Good. Thank you. I would be happy to make something for you.'

'Oh, I thought that was already a given...'

'Not always. Like any artist, it's nice to know that the love we pour into our creations is felt by the recipients. Some people don't get that. I prefer to work for those who do.'

He smiled at her and Grace gave a gentle smile back. Just then, her phone suddenly burst into life and Ed Sheeran was blaring out his Bad Habits, breaking the peaceful tranquillity of the room.

'Oh, I am so sorry. It's my friend checking that I'm okay.'

'Ah, a safety call. Very wise. Please take it. And if she wants to check up again in twenty minutes or so, I'm good with that.'

Bloody hell, thought Grace, as she swiped to accept the call, she hadn't expected that level of understanding.

'Hi, Lydia, thanks for calling. Everything is really good here. No, no concerns at all.'

The colour that had recently just receded from her cheeks came rushing back. Jake was focusing solely on the pad that was propped up on his bent knee but unless he'd suddenly been struck deaf, there was no way he was missing out on hearing the one-sided conversation.

'Thank you but no, there's no need to call me back again. I will drop you a text, however, once I leave, if that's okay?'

After Lydia had agreed, Grace ended the call and turned the phone to silent to ensure no further interruptions.

'Sorry again, about that.'

'Don't worry about it, no problem. Now, did you take photographs of the room you want the sofa to go in as I requested.'

'Yes, here...'

The phone that had just gone into her handbag came out again and she passed it over once she'd brought the photographs up.

'Hmm... right... yes... oh good... interesting.'

He swiped back and forth between the six photographs and enlarged them for a closer look.

Eventually, he sat back and returned the phone to her.

'I like how you've decorated it, not too fussy.'

'I prefer the idea of the furniture being the showpiece in the room rather than the décor, if that makes sense.'

'Yes, I get it completely. Interesting sofa you have at the moment – did you buy it from the seven dwarves?'

With a laugh, she explained what had happened the previous week and Jake was laughing with her by the time she'd finished.

'I applaud your ingenuity, but I can see how it's not a long-term fix. And the bean bag, where does it fit into your proposed scheme?'

'It doesn't really. It's just there as backup if I have any visitors.'

'I see. Would I be right in guessing there haven't been too many of those?'

Out of nowhere, Grace felt as though she'd just had a punch in the stomach. A sharp pain hit her as she thought of how few people had actually been inside her home in the time she'd lived there. The builders didn't count which left the solitary visit from her father and his candy-floss at Christmas.

'Erm, no, there haven't,' she replied in a quiet voice.

'Probably a good thing. You don't want to be facing a lawsuit brought on by injuries caused from a collapsing sofa now, do you.'

The warmth of Jake's words and the laughter in his voice instantly made her feel better.

'No, I suppose not,' she smiled.

'Right. So, I know you have a thing about high backs and arms – have you noticed those elements of the chair you chose to sit in, by the way?'

Grace looked at her chair and it dawned on her that it held similarities to the sofa.

'Oh, no I hadn't…'

'I use the chair method to help me see what people prefer. Their unconscious choice goes a long way to ensuring I deliver something they will love.'

'Very clever.'

'Thank you, I like to think so. Now, back to your sofa… I can see your room doesn't have a lot of footage to spare which means your sofa will be the main seating area. What will you do when visitors do come round? After all, you'll be the proud owner of a JVF piece, I expect you to show it off to all and sundry.'

'Bean-bag?'

'Not really a good option. For a start, you will be sitting at a lower height than your guests which puts you at a psychological disadvantage within your own home. You should always be the same height or higher. There's a reason why kings and queens sit in seats which are raised above everyone else.'

'I hadn't thought of it like that.'

'Well, what I'm thinking – and do say no if it's really not what you like – is a corner sofa.'

'Oh!' Grace sat back in her chair. 'That's a left-field suggestion. I hadn't thought about that.'

'Well, the way I see it is, it will give you the extra seating you'll need for all your visitors but is neat enough to maintain the minimal look you appear to favour.'

He threw her a little wink, accompanied by a cheeky grin, and Grace's innards twanged once again, although more strongly this time and she could feel herself being pulled deeper under his spell. She crossed her legs and squeezed the muscles around her middle as tightly as she could in the hope of preventing any more untoward twinges while hoping she could reach the end of her appointment without saying or doing anything that would make her look like the infatuated fool she was rapidly becoming.

ELEVEN

Lydia stood looking around in dismay. The bedsit she'd come to view was really not much more than a hovel. No wonder it was one-hundred and fifty pounds cheaper per month than everything else on the market – it was disgusting. The "kitchen" – she used the term loosely – was a two-ringed hotplate sitting on the draining board of a scratched, filthy, stainless-steel sink. She only knew it was stainless-steel from the design of it as the actual steel colour couldn't be seen beneath the grime.

A wardrobe leant drunkenly up against the wall in the corner and the bare mattress on the bed, which was being held up in one corner by a couple of bricks – a possible long-lost relation of Gracie's sofa perhaps? – was not only stained but she was sure the foul odour in the room was emanating from it. The dirt-smeared windows appeared to be painted closed which meant getting rid of the smell could only be achieved by disposing of the mattress, but going by the black mould lurking in a few of the corners and underneath the sill of the windows, she'd be just be swapping one form of something nasty for another.

The light from the bare bulb above her head was struggling to illuminate the room to any great degree and Lydia found herself being grateful for this as she didn't think she could cope with seeing deep into the eyes of the cockroaches she was convinced she'd be sharing this hellhole with.

She turned to the man standing by the door, eyeing him as he inspected his dirty fingernails before giving the hairy beer-belly poking through the buttons of his shirt a good scratch and she felt her stomach actually heave. He fitted every caricature of a slum landlord you could ever hope to meet and she couldn't wait to get away from him and this dump that he had the absolute cheek to ask over seven-hundred pounds a month in rent for.

'Erm, thank you,' she said with a tight smile as she squeezed past him and out the door. 'I've got a couple more to see before I can make a decision.'

'Right you are, love. Don't wait too long though – a bargain like this'll be snapped up in no time.'

'I'm err… sure it will,' she replied.

But not by me, was her silent response as she scurried out the front door of the old Victorian building.

She traipsed back to the shop and tried to plaster a smile on her face as she walked through the door, the little bell tinkling above her head. She hadn't told Heather where she was going and her assistant threw a brilliant smile her way, none the wiser to her dilemma, as she walked to the store room where they hung their coats and made the beverages for the clients and themselves. She stuck a teabag in a mug and flicked the switch on the kettle. What on earth was she going to do? While the business made a more than reasonable income, the actual salary she drew from it wouldn't cover two weeks rent on a studio flat, never mind a month. Yes, she could give herself a wage rise but she'd still struggle to pay all her bills along with feeding and clothing herself. How on earth did people like nurses and teachers manage it?

Her next option was to look at places that were not on a tube line. The estate agent had explained that the closer the property was to the transport system, the more expensive it was inclined to be. Lydia had approached it from a different angle – the closer she was to the shop, the less she'd have to pay each month for travelling. Well, that was an angle which had just slammed its door in her face so it looked like she would be casting her net further afield.

The double-whammy she had to face there, however, was that the shop was in a central location and she had to be within a reasonable proximity to it. Her parents had upped sticks and moved to the Lake District when they'd retired so there was no chance of bunking up with them for a time and unfortunately, the "reasonable proximities to the shop" were Wandsworth, Clapham, Balham, Putney and all the other places in between that had become uber-trendy and over-priced in the last few decades. There was nowhere "cheap" in London anymore and for a forty-two-year-old woman, trying to leave her husband and start a new life, it was the worst possible place to live.

TWELVE

Lydia looked across the table and saw her own disbelief mirrored on Gracie's face. She turned to Debbie and her heart clenched at the misery the girl was clearly suffering.

'And you had absolutely no idea?' she asked gently.

'No. Well... I don't think I did. I've been questioning myself all weekend. Were the signs there but I subconsciously chose to ignore them? Or was Dale just really good at keeping that side of himself hidden and I didn't stand a chance of picking up on it? I mean, some men live a whole life where they manage to hide who they really are from their wives and children for years.'

'You must be so pissed off.'

'Oh, Grace, I wish that I was – it would make it all so much easier but how can I be angry or pissed at the bloke for having the courage to open up to his true feelings. He shouldn't be living a lie to make me, or anyone else, feel better. That would be all wrong and I wouldn't want him to do that. No, it's right that he's taken this step but knowing he's gay doesn't stop me loving him and wanting to be with him.'

Lydia placed her hand on top of Debbie's and gave it a squeeze.

'Your feelings can't be turned on and off like a tap, love. Of course, it's going to be painful for you and confusing too. But your understanding will help Dale to move forward into this new part of his life. I've got no doubt that he's dealing with his own pain and confusion and I expect there's a big chunk of guilt in the mix too. Hurting you is the last thing he would have wanted to do.'

'I know, Lydia. He said exactly that. I have told him not to feel guilty; it's not fair on him to have to deal with that too. When all is said and done, this is a small blip in the path of my life but it's a massive big turn in the road for him.'

'So, what happens now? Is he moving out or what?'

Grace refilled the wine glasses and Lydia saw her give Alyson a discrete nod to bring over another bottle as she asked the question.

'No, he's going to continue living in the flat for now but he's moving into the spare room. I don't want him to rush into anything and, if I'm being a bit selfish, his share of the rent is a godsend at the moment so I'm glad he's sticking around.'

'Is this the spare room that's so small it has a wall-to-wall carpet tile?'

'That would be the one.'

Lydia was pleased to see the little smile on Debbie's face at her pithy comment. She was such a happy girl and it really hurt to see her like this.

'That's going to be cramped.'

'All the stock has been moved into my larger bedroom and it was fun and games on Sunday, trying to rearrange the furniture in there so that I didn't fall over the rails in the middle of the night when going to the loo. Although, weirdly, changing the room about has kind of helped me to deal with Dale no longer being in there. It's not "our" space anymore, it's "my" space now and getting used to looking at a different perspective when I'm in bed helps my head at night.'

'Would that be the perspective of a Chanel dress or a Dior one?'

'Actually both!'

Debbie began telling them about the suitcases she'd received on Friday and Lydia felt herself relax a bit as she listened. Yes, Debs was hurting now but it would pass and no doubt something far better was coming her way. At least, Lydia hoped it was.

'You know, Grace, you should pop into the shop and take a look at a couple of the dresses Martha has given to me; with your slim figure, I think they'd be perfect for you. There's a stunning black Gucci one which I just know would look amazing on you.'

'Oh, I might do that. My LBD is beginning to look a bit worn out and has seen more work do's than one dress should.'

'Talking about work, Gracie, or rather, you doing less work... how did it go on Saturday? I am fully aware of how long it took you to text me that you were on the train back home.'

'Oh, yes, you had an appointment with that furniture bloke...' Debbie smiled as she took a swallow of her wine before looking at Lydia and giving her a wee cheeky wink. 'Was he hot to trot and totally fanciable or did you end up meeting the eighth dwarf complete with huge big feet, a long beard and bad breath?'

'Did you drown your sorrows by watching "The Hobbit" trilogy over the weekend?'

'Hey, you know they're my favourite films – what else was I going to do!'

'Well, no, he isn't a dwarf and I was there for ages

because he's making me a corner sofa and we were discussing what I like and what I don't like because it needs to be perfect.'

'A corner sofa, eh? That'll be nice. Lots of space to stretch out on.'

'Actually, Lydia, it's a case of more space for visitors to sit on.'

'Except, you don't do visitors.'

'I had to promise to invite people over to admire my new masterpiece otherwise he wasn't going to make it for me.'

Debbie burst out laughing and Lydia found herself joining in.

'But you don't do visitors...'

'Tell me about it! Somehow, though, this man seemed to sense that and made it a proviso if I wanted him to go ahead with the commission.'

'So, what was he like?'

Debbie took another drink of her wine and Lydia hoped she didn't overdo it. She'd barely eaten any of her meal and while the lass had every right to drink herself into oblivion, it never solved any problems and the resulting hangover only added head pain to the heart pain.

'He was very nice. Not at all what I was expecting.'

'What did you expect?'

'Well, Lydia, given how popular he's becoming, I thought he might be rather arrogant or overbearing but he was quite the opposite. He's a quiet man. I got the feeling he prefers to watch and listen rather than talk. He was soft-spoken. In fact, I'd go as far as to say his voice was almost hypnotic. I could listen to him talk for ages.'

'A bit of a charmer, then?'

'No, Debs, not at all. Charismatic would be a better description.'

'How long will it take him to make the sofa?'

Lydia took a small sip of her wine after asking the question and hoped Debbie might follow suit although given that she'd just drained her glass, it wasn't looking likely.

'He thinks maybe six weeks or so. The next step is for him to come to the house tomorrow night and take measurements of the space from which he'll design three options for me to choose from. Once I decide which design I prefer the most and pay my deposit, he'll begin. It should take about a month although as it is quite a large commission, he said there is a good chance it may take an extra week or so.'

Lydia placed her glass back on the table more firmly than she'd intended.

'Did you just say he's coming to your house to measure up tomorrow night?'

'Yes, why?'

'Oh, nothing. It's just that you haven't worked the last two Saturdays, you're actually buying furniture for your house which you intend to invite people to sit on, and now you're planning another early finish tomorrow to allow this man in your home. Who are you and what have you done with the real Gracie Mitchell?'

'Oh, sod off!'

'She's right though, Grace, you're leaping way ahead with your part of the pact.'

'Give over the pair of you, he'll be at my place for all of ten minutes – or however long it takes to measure a room – and after he's gone, I'll be upstairs in my little attic, working away until midnight. So there! Now, I'm changing the subject – Lydia, how's the flat-hunting going?'

'Oh, it's still early doors there.'

'Have you seen any yet? Don't go moving into the first thing you come to. It's a big step and you don't want to end

72

up wasting money by snapping up the first flat you see and then it turns out to be awful.'

'Let me assure you, Grace, that I will definitely not be doing that.' Her mind raced back to the hovel she'd looked at and she mentally shuddered at how abysmal it had been. 'At the moment, I'm still trying to decide where I want to live and when I decide that, I'll be looking at the cost.'

'Don't you want to stay in Wandsworth?'

'I don't know, Debbie. It would certainly be the most convenient option but I don't think I fancy running the risk of bumping into either my husband or my son. I know I would always be looking out for them whenever I'm doing my shopping or waiting at the bus stop. I certainly wouldn't be able to relax.'

'Or, God forbid, you were walking down the street or in the pub with another man.'

'Trust me, Debs, being with another man couldn't be further from my mind right now. The way I feel at the moment, being single for the rest of my days sounds absolutely perfect.'

Debbie grabbed her glass, held it up in the air and after hollering, 'I'll drink to that,' downed the contents in one gulp.

Lydia waited outside the train station until she saw Grace sit down inside the bus. They waved to each other and she turned to walk inside as the bus pulled away. She checked the time on the station clock, relief coursing through her when she saw it was only five minutes until her train arrived. Debbie had ended up being a little more sozzled than Lydia was comfortable with for her to walk home alone so Grace and herself had escorted her back to the shop and waited outside until they saw the light go on in the front room above it.

On their way back towards the train station, they'd both agreed to put in some extra calls to her, just to make sure she was okay. Grace had even mentioned that she had some work events coming up which she could ask Debbie to attend with her. It was better for her to be out and about than sitting at home moping.

'Blimey, duck, that was a big 'un!'

'Sorry?'

Lydia looked at the woman just along from her on the platform.

'The sigh you just let out; near on blew me hat orf!'

'Oh! I didn't realise...'

'No worries. We've all been there at one time or another.'

The woman gave her small nod and a look of understanding just as the train arrived at the platform. It made Lydia feel a little better as she stepped into the carriage and found a seat near the door.

Now that she was heading home, the butterflies had once again begun to churn in her stomach and the sensation intensified as the train grew closer to her stop.

She had chosen not to say anything to the girls as Debbie was already in a fragile state – she still couldn't get her head around that bombshell! – and even though she hadn't realised it, Gracie had clearly enjoyed the company of her furniture man, judging by the way her face had lit up when she'd spoken about him. Lydia hadn't wanted to say anything about how her home life was deteriorating by the day.

She and Dave barely spoke at all now and they'd taken to leaving the room when the other walked in. The atmosphere in the flat was so heavy, she could feel it pressing down on her the minute she stepped through the door. More recently, Dave had taken to spending his nights down the pub and rolled in just after ten o'clock whereupon he had a shower and went straight to bed. This meant she had to put up with Davie's nonsense on her own. He persisted in playing his music at ear-drum-splitting levels, leaving a trail of destruction from the kitchen to his bedroom, sometimes via the bathroom, and thinking it was alright to shout in her face when the hoodie he wanted to wear hadn't been washed because he hadn't bothered to put it in the laundry basket. How she'd managed to hold it together when he'd told her that she was a crap mother and that they'd all be better off without her, was still a mystery.

They would both be out tomorrow night at the local darts league which meant she'd have peace and quiet to do some more internet searching and hopefully, this time, she'd find the elusive little piece of paradise which she could call her own.

THIRTEEN

'Hi, come on in. Did you find it okay?'

Grace opened the door wider and stepped back for Jake to walk in. As he moved past her, he left a subtle waft of citrus and sawdust in his wake. It wasn't an unpleasant combination and she found herself inhaling deeply as she guided him through to the lounge.

'Your directions were easy, and it was pretty straightforward to get here. I came on the tube as it's only a handful of stops and much easier than driving.'

'Yes, I know what you mean. I have to make a point of taking my car out for a drive once a month otherwise it would never move. Sometimes I think I should get rid of it but there's something comforting about knowing it's there – you know, like for emergencies and stuff.'

Grace felt herself blushing as she realised she was waffling but Jake flashed his easy smile at her and agreed.

'I do know. My van is a business requirement but I also have a little MGB Roadster which I restored and I often feel I don't get to drive her as much as I would like. Do you like driving?'

'What do you mean?'

'Some people see driving as a means of just getting from A to B and will avoid it if they can, whereas other people get a thrill from driving. They love being behind the wheel and roaring along an open road.'

'Ah, I get you. Once I get out of London, I enjoy driving immensely but it's a pain in the butt to drive around the city.'

'Exactly! An open road, roof down, wind in your hair—

'You mean hair in your eyes, nose and ears frozen to bits, flies in your mouth...'

Jake burst out laughing and Grace felt a little surge of pleasure that she had caused him to do so.

'There speaks the voice of experience. How do you know of these open-air wonders?'

'My dad had a Cobra when I was younger and I was occasionally dragged out in it. I hated everyone looking at us when we were sitting at traffic lights and roundabouts. My dad, on the other hand, loved the attention and I'm sure he used to find the longest route with the most stops whenever we went anywhere in it. Those experiences kind of put me off.'

'Ah, I can see that. The mortifying moments of our youth stay with us long into adulthood.'

He gave her that smile again and Grace was sure she felt her knees give a small shudder. Bloody hell! What was it with this man? In the grand scheme of things, he wasn't all *"that"* at all but the effect he had on her was not something she'd ever experienced before and she wasn't at all sure that she liked this sensation of not being fully in control of herself.

'Can I get you a tea or a coffee while you're measuring up?'

'A black coffee would be nice, thank you.'

She walked through to the kitchen and stood on the small deck in her courtyard as she waited for the kettle to boil, willing the heat in her cheeks to reside. When the kettle clicked off, she poured the hot water into the cafetiere and by the time the coffee had brewed, she felt she'd managed to get her rebellious hormones under control.

Mind you, the rebellious hormones nearly had a field day when she stepped back into the lounge to find Jake bending over, taking the measurements, and his jeans-clad derriere was the first thing to hit her eye as she walked through the door.

Oh, for the love of all that's holy!

'Erm,' she gave a small cough, 'one black coffee, as requested.'

'Great! Thank you.'

He straightened up, took the mug from her outstretched hand and after enjoying a hefty sip, placed it on the table, ensuring a coaster was underneath it. This action gained him more points than he'd ever know in Grace's estimation as drinks straight onto tables was one of her pet hates.

'Your room is even nicer than your photographs led me to believe. The grey panelling isn't as dark as I thought it was.'

'No, the camera did darken it. I meant to say that to you on Saturday.'

'It's fine. This is one of the reasons why I like to visit the space I'm creating for. I now know what shade of red will work and what won't – that's if you still want red, of course.'

'Oh, I do, most definitely.'

'Now, is the fireplace your only heat source in here? There aren't any radiators…'

'Underfloor heating.'

'Ah! Very clever. That frees up your wall space and

opens up so many options.'

'Yes, that's what I thought.'

You lying cow, her brain screamed. She'd put in the underfloor heating because she hated wearing shoes or slippers indoors and didn't want cold feet all the time.

She stood in the doorway, watching him taking his measurements, logging them in a small notebook and taking photographs of the space. He certainly seemed to know what he was about.

'Right, that should do it.'

'Why do you need so much information?'

'When it comes to a bespoke item, you need to ensure it's a perfect fit. So, for example, your windowsill is slightly higher than some others which means I can give you the high back on your sofa that you like so much.'

'And if the sill had been lower?'

'We would be discussing alternative options at this point.'

'I see.'

He drained his coffee mug and handed it back, checking his watch as he did so.

'Have you eaten yet?'

'Excuse me?' Grace wasn't quite sure she'd heard him correctly.

'Have you eaten? I passed a rather quaint little Mediterranean restaurant on my way here and I now have a fancy for some Meze. Is the food good there?'

'Erm, I wouldn't know, I haven't tried it.'

'Oh, don't you like Med food?'

'I do. I've just not been to that particular restaurant.'

'Wow! If I had a place like that just around the corner from me, I'd have a bigger belly than I do already.'

'There's nothing wrong with your belly!'

Shit! Had she just said that aloud? Judging by the twinkle in Jake's eye, she had. Oh, bugger!

'That's very kind of you to say so but you still haven't said if you'll join me for dinner.'

'Maybe that's because you haven't actually asked me.'

'Oops! My bad! I got so carried away with the prospect of a Turkish cheese fondue, I forgot that bit. Please, would you join me for dinner?'

'Turkish cheese fondue? How could I refuse? Although, didn't fondue go out with the seventies?'

'It came back in again. Everything does eventually. Now, grab your coat before my stomach begins to rumble and I really embarrass myself.'

Grace looked discreetly around the small but cosy restaurant. It had fairy lights artfully wound around the hanging ceiling blossoms and the soft blue walls enhanced the Mediterranean atmosphere. She sipped her glass of wine slowly as she relaxed into the soothing ambiance. Also, she hadn't eaten since breakfast and didn't think getting tiddly would go down too well.

'So, Grace, tell me about yourself. How do you like being a solicitor?'

'Oh, I love it. Call me sad, but there's something about fine print and details that I— hang on, how do you know I'm a solicitor? I don't recall sharing that with you?'

'You didn't but my brother called me and asked me to take this commission as a special favour for him.'

'Your brother? I'm sorry? What?'

'You do work for McArthur Forbes, don't you?'

'Yes…'

'As does my brother. Apparently, he overheard you talking about the sofa you'd seen and saying to your secretary that you'd left a message on my voicemail asking me to call you back to discuss further. He knows I've stopped doing commissions because of the time involved so asked me to do this one as a special favour. He said it was for the very nice lady he works with.'

'Oh, I see. I wasn't aware of that. "*The very nice lady*" eh?' She grinned. 'I reckon I can live with that description although I don't know anyone in our office called Valentine.'

'Ah, you won't! He's technically my step-brother. His father married my mother. I was almost eighteen at the time so chose to keep my original surname.'

'Right. So, your brother is…'

'Sebastian Andrews. Or Seb, as he prefers.'

Grace swallowed and felt a touch light-headed. For a brief second, the blood thundered behind eyes that saw stars before clearing and seeing Jake looking at her with concern on his face.

'Are you okay, Grace? You've gone really pale.'

'Um, yes, yes, I am. Sorry. I'm just shocked that Seb would do that for me; we're not exactly the best of buddies.'

'Oh, I'm aware of that. You're his nemesis and I suspect he's yours. You both want the same prize so are constantly competing against each other. Yes?'

'That's a good way of putting it. We rarely speak to each other in anything resembling a civil manner which is why this is such a shock.'

'He speaks highly of you and respects you as a colleague. He says you challenge him to be better. That's quite a compliment. And he really does think you're a very nice lady.'

She blinked at this news and wondered how Seb would feel if he knew his brother was sharing this information with her.

'You do realise you've put me in a position where I have to be nice to him now! Tomorrow at work is really going to suck!'

Jake let out one of his laughs that was so contagious, she just had to join in.

'I don't think you need to go that far. I reckon it would be his undoing if you suddenly moved towards pleasantries. He may stop feeling the need to be so competitive and that would piss off his mother more than you can imagine.'

'His mother?'

'Yeah, Virginia Carruthers. The poor lad was going to be a solicitor whether he wanted to or not. She pushed him into law and she expects him to be on a par with her.'

Grace suddenly felt a little sorry for Seb – Virginia Carruthers was well-known in law circles and she took no prisoners. Her reputation for playing hardball was legendary and even after she'd married, she'd insisted on retaining the maiden name her reputation was attached to. If Grace was being truly honest, she was a little envious of Virginia and had, on occasion, tried to emulate her when facing down an adversary. If Seb had been told by his mother that he was going into law, then no amount of arguing would have gotten him out of it. Although, he did seem to enjoy it so maybe his mother's genes had come to the fore.

She was about to say as much when the waitress arrived with their starters and when she took her first bite of toasted sourdough bread fingers dipped in molten Turkish cheese with added bacon bits, she was so blown away with the flavour and her stomach suddenly telling her just how hungry she was, that all thoughts of Seb and the office went out of her head and she spent the rest of the evening discussing food and travel with Jake.

FOURTEEN

Lydia slowly trudged up the path towards the flats. She was shattered. Today had been a busy one and she'd stayed late to give one of her regulars a special "up-do" as she was going out for her wedding anniversary.

Wedding anniversary… she couldn't recall the last time she'd considered hers an occasion worth celebrating. Each passing year felt more like a prison sentence although she took a little bit of comfort from knowing that she was now trying to find a way out – *"trying"* being the operative word. Hopefully, tonight she might find a new home that was not only a step-up from something out of the sewers but also within her price range. It was darts night so she would have the flat to herself and some much longed for peace and quiet. She'd treated herself to a cottage pie and a half bottle of wine from the Marks & Spencer's food hall across from the shop and she would consume both while scrolling through the unlimited offers of accommodation that South London had to offer.

That, she mused, was probably the only good thing about renting a place in this city – if you couldn't find what you wanted one day, come back the next because there was sure to be another two-hundred and fifty new options to trawl through.

As she turned the corner and the flat came into view, the deep base sound of the hard rock that Davie liked to listen to, came flowing towards her, growing louder with each step she took towards home. In confusion, she checked the time on her watch. Davie should almost certainly be down the pub by now so why on earth was he still home?

She quickened her pace and gave a small grimace of apology to her neighbour who was standing glaring at her through the window. She hurried in the door, dropped her bags on the floor and ran up the stairs. When she threw Davie's bedroom door open, all set to release six shades of hell upon him, she was stunned to find the room empty. Stepping back out into the hallway, she went to the bathroom and was surprised to find it empty too.

She scurried back into her son's bedroom and turned off the noise, the immediate silence of the flat filling her ears. It was as she was walking out that Lydia stopped. There was a scent in the air which did not correlate with the body spray her son liked to douse himself in. Nor was it the odour of a man's bedroom. It was… something else. Familiar but not too familiar… What was it?

Her brain worked on trying to recognise it and it didn't take too long for it to spit out an answer. Cannabis!

The sweet but musty smell was very distinctive once you knew what it was.

And Lydia knew what it was!

Dave had gone through a phase of smoking it after Davie was born. He'd been a difficult baby – go figure! – and his incessant crying had stretched Dave to the limit of his patience resulting in him smoking weed to help cope with the stress. Unfortunately, he'd continued smoking it for quite some time after Davie had grown out of his awkward stage and it was only the threat of losing his job due to an accident when he was high that had brought him to his senses.

And now Davie was on it. Great, just what she needed.

She walked back into the centre of the room and stood looking around, ignoring the mess while trying to figure out where her son was hiding his stash. The chest of drawers was too obvious but wasn't hiding stuff in plain sight the new way of doing things? A quick rummage through soon proved that this obvious hiding place was just that – too obvious. She pushed the drawers back in but as she stepped away, her ankle clattered against the bottom one which was still sticking out.

'Damn thing,' she muttered, bending down to close it.

Except, it wouldn't close. Something was jamming it at the back. Lydia got down on her knees, pulled the drawer out of the casing and leant forward, sweeping her hand along the back of the cabinet. Her fingers touched something plasticky feeling and, wrapping her hand around it, she gently pulled out a sealed package the size and shape of a standard envelope and about an inch in depth. It was soft under her touch so she took it into the bathroom with its bright, overhead light, for a closer look.

Her suspicions were confirmed when she got a clear view of the white powder contained within. She was no expert but she had a good idea that this was cocaine although, with all these new-fangled drugs coming out, she wouldn't put a bet on that. Whatever it was, it told her one thing.

Her son was dealing drugs.

When Dave and Davie got home that night, Lydia was waiting for them in the lounge. Davie went straight up to his bed but Dave walked in, shocked to find her sitting there. Normally, she'd have been in bed long before now. It had been many a year since she'd sat up until he got in.

'Alright?' he grunted at her, walking over to the drinks cabinet in the corner.

'No, I'm not. In fact, I'm as far from being alright as it is possible to be.'

'Why, what's up? Someone run away with your favourite hair-dye?' he sneered while pouring out a hefty shot of whisky. He put the bottle away without bothering to ask if she wanted one. Even now, the selfishness of his actions registered.

'Actually, I've just discovered that our son is a drug dealer.'

Dave dropped down onto the chair next to where she was sitting on the sofa.

'Oh, give over! I've never heard the like. He might like the odd puff of the wacky baccy but dealing it? Don't be so daft.'

'I'm telling you, Dave, he's dealing drugs and it's NOT wacky baccy!'

'Yeah, right! And my great auntie is Vera Lynn.'

She'd known Dave wouldn't believe her so she picked up her phone, swiped it open and turned it around for him to look at.

'So, what do you reckon that is, then?'

Dave looked at the screen for a few seconds before looking back at her.

'Where'd you get that pic from? Somewhere off the internet?'

'Excuse me? That photograph was taken in your son's bedroom. Look, there's more, so you can see for yourself.'

She passed the phone back but Dave refused to look at it or the other damning pictures on it.

'So, when did you *find* these drugs and where are they now, eh?'

'I found them this evening – I don't know why you're having such a hard time believing this – and they're back in their hiding place because I wanted to discuss this with you first before speaking to Davie about it.'

'So, what if he is dealing, it's only a small batch. It's not like you're talking about some big, gangster style dude here.'

'Dave, are you even on this planet? How on earth can you sit there and say something like that? Surely you must realise that if he gets away with peddling this small amount, he'll soon move up to selling more. That's the way these things go and with respect, our son is not the shiniest spoon in the drawer, he's the one who'll get caught and be locked up. Is that what you want?'

'Oh, the police won't bother with small fry like him – they only ever want the guys at the top of the tree. Something our Davie is never going to be.'

'Dave, I really can't believe you're prepared to ignore this and behave like nothing is going on. We need to speak to him. I won't have drugs in the house. Not now, not ever.'

Dave stood up, leant over her and snarled, 'My son is not a drug dealer. What kind of a mother would think such a thing of her son? So, he might be selling the odd bit here and there but that don't make him a threat to society. It's just like you to always think the worst of him. You make me sick.'

He spat out the last sentence before straightening up and walking out the room, leaving Lydia sitting on the sofa in disbelief.

FIFTEEN

'We need to talk.'

Debbie looked up as Dale handed her a glass of wine. She took it from him and drank a more than hefty sip as he sat down on the sofa next to her. She knew what was coming and she was dreading hearing it.

'Debs... I'm moving out.'

Yup! There it was. The words she'd been waiting for since he'd broken off their engagement six weeks ago. It was inevitable really. They were no longer together and he had someone new. The irony was that they'd spent more time together in the last six weeks than they had in the last six months. Now that the truth was out, Dale no longer felt he had to avoid her. She'd even met John and she couldn't deny he was a very nice man. He doted on Dale and she could see his feelings were reciprocated. She couldn't recall Dale ever looking at her the way he looked at John.

'When?'

'I'll be out by the weekend. I'm sorry.'

'Hey, don't be so daft. There's no need to apologise. You need to do what you need to do; I get that.'

'But I hate that I've hurt you. I never planned this, it's not what I wanted for us.'

She could feel the sting of tears in her eyes and she blinked several times, willing them to recede. She had to be brave now.

'I know it's not, Dale. But you can't change the path you're on. It's just… it's just one of those things.'

He took her hand and squeezed it tightly.

'Please always be my friend, Debbie, I couldn't stand not having you as a part of my life. I'm sorry if that's selfish but I do love you. I just can't love you that way.'

'I know. And I will always love you too. I will always be your friend, Dale, but maybe an absent one for the next few months. You know… I still need some time to adjust. To get used to the change. I'm not quite there yet, but I will be. In time.'

'I know, I know.'

After that, they said very little. Just sat side by side on the sofa, drinking wine and wondering how long it would be until they did so again.

Debbie walked down the alley that ran along the side of the shop and turned towards the stairs that led up to the flat, her feet landing heavily on each metal tread. She'd been out walking along the river for several hours, not looking forward to when she had to return home but she hadn't been able to put it off any longer. She took a deep breath, put her key in the lock and opened the door. Even before she walked in, she saw the envelope lying on the mat and knew that Dale's key was contained within. She bent down to pick it up, the sob catching in her throat as she did so. This small act was the final curtain on their life together.

He was really gone.

She closed the door gently behind her and locked it. She was halfway across the kitchen before she turned and went back to throw over the bolts along the top and bottom. She hadn't done that for such a long time but tonight she felt vulnerable on her own. Even though Dale had spent many nights working at the hospital, she hadn't felt as alone as she did right now. Knowing that no one would be walking through that door tonight, or any other night for that matter, changed everything.

She wandered into the lounge after changing out of her jeans and jumper and tried to work out what made it feel different. She knew there would be items of Dale's that he'd taken but he'd also left much that he didn't need. The television for example as John already had that covered so he'd left it for her. It took a few minutes for her to really notice what was missing and she only sussed out why when she realised his graduation photograph with his parents was no longer on the shelf. He'd only gone and moved the other nick-nacks around to hide the space; to make it less obvious that he was no longer there.

This small, caring gesture was too much for her. The tears came again and this time, as she let them fall, the pain in her heart escaped through her lips as a high-pitched keening which she didn't bother to try and smother because there was no longer anyone around to hear her cry.

SIXTEEN

Lydia took a deep breath as she pushed open the door of the pub and forced a smile on her face. Somehow, she had to find it in her to be bright and breezy for the next few hours. No way could she let on how her life was unravelling. She most certainly couldn't tell the girls about Davie and the drugs she'd found. Especially Grace, given what she did for a living. Lydia wasn't exactly sure how it all worked but she had an inkling that if Grace knew her son was involved in something illegal, it could compromise her job and career. So, it was better to keep schtum. Unfortunately, hiding her emotions was something Lydia had never been good at.

'Well, girl,' she muttered under her breath as she made her way to their booth, 'time to put on your best Audrey Hepburn and deliver an award-winning act.'

'Hey, ladies, how are we all hanging tonight? Ready to hoover-up some calorie-filled pastries and glug down some alcoholic bubbles.'

'Hi, Lydia, you're looking good. Nice skirt.'

'Oh, this is an old thing that I forgot I had in the

wardrobe. I was doing a clear out and found it. I made it years ago.'

Debbie raised her head and looked closer, her interest piqued. Lydia didn't miss the red-rimmed eyes.

'You made this?'

'Yes. I used to do quite a bit of dress-making when I was younger. I really enjoyed it.'

'Why did you stop? This is really good.'

Lydia stood a bit longer, allowing Debbie to inspect the seam work and the stitching. After all, clothes were her business and those puffy eyes said she needed all the distraction she could get right now.

'Thank you, I take that as quite the compliment. I stopped, since you asked, because a sewing machine and a boisterous toddler are not a good combination. As time went on, I just never got back to it. Maybe I will again, one day.'

'You're obviously good with your hands – what with being a hairstylist and being able to sew. You must have very dexterous fingers.'

Lydia grinned at Grace as she slipped onto the bench seat.

'I suppose I have. I've never thought of it like that. And, while we're on the subject of "dexterous fingers" – how did it go last week with your Valentine?'

She gave a saucy grin which made both Grace and Debbie laugh.

'Oi, you behave yourself.'

'Well, did he measure up? And I don't mean just in your lounge?'

'As it happens, he measured up very well. On both counts!'

'Is that so? Tell us more. No, wait a second... Alyson's on her way over with the bubbles.'

Once they'd poured out the fizzy into the glasses, Grace

proceeded to fill them in on her unexpected night out with Jake.

'What? You're telling us that he's the brother of that Seb one from your office? No way!'

'Yes, way! In every blooming way! Well, they're step-brothers but from what I can gather, they're as close as if they were blood brothers. He definitely spoke fondly of Seb when he was the topic of the conversation.'

'And you say that Seb phoned and asked him to take on your commission? That was pretty damn decent of him and certainly not what I would have expected from the odious, jumped-up little oik that you have described to us over the last couple of years.'

Lydia took another sip of her wine as she waited for Gracie to answer because she had spoken the truth – Grace hadn't said a single nice thing about her office colleague in all the time they'd been friends.

'Okay, you've got me there. I confess – it would seem that I've perhaps been a bit over-zealous in maligning the bloke. There's something about him though, that just winds me right up and I probably vent more to you ladies than perhaps I should. I appear to have done him a degree of injustice and I apologise for that.'

'Are you going to apologise to him though, that's the big question?'

Debbie chuckled as she worded her question and Lydia joined in with her wickedness.

'Yeah, you can't be apologising to us, you need to say sorry to him.'

'Well, it'll be a cold day in hell before that happens so I suggest you both just drink up your wine and behave yourselves!'

Lydia and Debbie sniggered while Grace made a show of looking affronted which lasted all of five seconds because Alyson arrived with their meals and soon there was appreciative silence while they ate.

'Oh, I do enjoy these nights out – having a nice meal, that I didn't have to cook, and intelligent conversation. I tell you, it's the highlight of my week.'

Lydia sat back and gave her stomach a little pat, to emphasise how much she'd relished her dinner.

'How are things at home?'

She looked at Grace and took a sip of wine as she tried to think of how best to answer. She needed to keep as close to the truth as possible; she didn't want to lie to her friends but at the same time, she had to watch what she did divulge.

'Well... not good. Definitely not good. I am fairly certain that Davie is doing drugs.'

'Oh, Lydia, no. You're right, that's not good. How has this come about?'

She filled them both in on the smell she'd encountered in her son's bedroom the previous week and that there had been the odd occasion since, where she'd been talking to him, and he had been vague in his responses.

'You know that way, not so high as to be unable to communicate but high enough for something to not feel quite right.'

'What are you going to do? What can you do?'

'I talked to Dave about it but I might as well have been talking to a brick wall for all the use he was. Didn't want to know and thinks it's harmless. Nothing for us to be bothering about.'

'But you feel differently?'

'Yes, Debs, I do. I worry about where it could lead. A bit of weed today could be snorting cocaine tomorrow or shooting up heroin by the end of the month. Young folks today always seem to be looking for more extreme ways to find their thrills and cannabis could just be the start of something more serious.'

'Has this changed your mind about leaving? With Davie doing this?'

'I… I don't know. I'm his mum and I feel I should be there but if his father can't be arsed to show any concern, I wonder why I am. After all, they've both made it perfectly clear over the years that Davie is Dave's son, not mine. I honestly don't think either of them would miss me if I was out of the picture.'

She felt a lump grow in her throat as she spoke and had to take a deep breath to shift it, this wasn't the time to be indulging in self-pity. She'd known how the cards were going to fall around her family life a long time ago so why was she letting it get to her now?

'Lydia, far be it from me to be giving you any kind of advice but maybe being without you is what they need to realise how much they need you?'

'Oh, I have no doubt they *need* me – after all, who's going to clean their shit up after them, do all their laundry and ensure they have a home cooked meal at least four times a week? No other mug is going to do that. However, there's a big difference between "needing" someone and "wanting" someone and they certainly don't *want* me around.'

'Are you still looking for a place?'

Lydia let out a small sigh. She was going to have to tell the truth on the flat-hunting front; she couldn't hide it for ever.

'I am still looking but, well… the truth is… they're all so bloody expensive! Even a studio flat is not far off a grand a month. By the time I add on bills, food and travel… I'll barely be making ends meet. I do have savings but I'll burn through those in no time. And they're not enough to put down a deposit on my own place. Not with one-bedroom places coming in around a quarter of a million pounds or thereabouts. I hadn't realised just how expensive London is now. How do people manage to live here?'

'With difficulty, in many cases. I'm so sorry to hear you've been having this problem – it's not fair.'

'Tell me about it.'

'Well... I now have a spare room, if the worst comes to the worst, Lyds.'

She looked at Debbie and realised the reason for the sad, red-rimmed eyes.

'Has Dale moved out?'

Debbie just nodded and Lydia could see her trying to hold back the tears just as she herself had done – by taking deep breaths.

'When?' Grace asked, her tone gentle.

'He told me on Thursday night and was gone by Sunday evening.'

'Bastard!'

'No, no, he's not. He's been really lovely and has left quite a bit of stuff that I would have had to replace – like the television, the toaster, the kettle... He even left me his De'Longhi coffee machine because he knows how much I enjoy my morning cuppa.'

She shared how he'd tried to hide the empty gaps where he'd removed personal items to make their absence less obvious.

'I just can't be angry with him. I know you think I should be, Grace—'

'Damn right I do. You're allowed your anger, Debs, don't invalidate your feelings over Dale's. Yes, I understand that the circumstances are somewhat unusual but when all is said and done, he still cheated on you and abused your trust. You need to take that on board and deal with it otherwise you'll be storing up a whole lot of hurt that could stop you moving on.'

'Hey, Grace, ease up a bit. Lecturing won't help.'

'I… oh shit, I'm sorry, Debbie. I got carried away there. Hang on, let me just clamber down off my almighty big soapbox…'

Debbie laughed at Grace's words and Lydia gave her a small nod of gratitude. The girl had been through enough lately, they just had to let her be and find her own way back to happiness.

'So, anyway, Lydia, as I was saying, I now have a spare room, complete with its own wall-to-wall carpet tile which you are more than welcome to have if it helps you out. The flat's not the biggest but there's no druggies or obnoxious husbands so it does have some benefits.'

Lydia felt the lump reappear in her throat – the damn thing was making a right nuisance of itself tonight.

'Debs, that is really very kind of you. I appreciate the offer and I will keep it in mind once I know what I'm doing. Thank you.'

She leant over and squeezed her friend's hand. She hoped she wouldn't need to take her up on the offer – she'd rather have her own place because forty-two was rather old to begin flat-sharing but it was good to know she now had one option on the table. And one is a hell of a lot better than nothing.

SEVENTEEN

Grace looked at the quality embossed card in her hand while letting out a groan. It was an invitation to an event being held by one of the charities she donated to. The groan was because she knew approximately how much it would have cost to print and send these invites and she would rather have seen the money go towards the people the charity was supposed to be helping.

She turned the card over to find out where the event was being held and saw what looked like a private address in Holland Park. Well, that was okay. At least they weren't wasting money on a suite at The Dorchester or somewhere similar.

Normally, she wouldn't give the time of day to such an occasion and would usually RSVP with a "non-attendance" and a donation enclosed but she knew this particular charity had several affluent patrons and one in particular – Charles Highgate – was a big fish she'd been wanting to reel in and get onto her company's books for quite some time. She'd heard rumours he wasn't happy with the quality of the service he was currently receiving from one of their main competitors and she just needed to find a way to cross his path so she could sell McArthur Forbes to him. This could well be the opportunity she'd been looking for. Unfortunately, there was one other small issue – the card was a "plus one" invite and she had no one to take along with her. Another reason why she so often gave these things a miss – the need to be on someone's arm was generally an annoyance to her.

Mind you... she looked at the invite again. It didn't actually specify she had to take a partner so maybe Debbie could be persuaded to come along. Grace knew she'd barely been out of the shop or the flat for weeks. Apart from their Tuesday nights, she'd been staying holed up alone in her little nest.

Right, no time like the present, she thought. Her mobile was lying on the desk and a second later it was in her hand as she scrolled through to find Debbie's number. Hitting the button, she waited for it to connect.

As it rang in her ear, she wondered how Debbie would feel about this change in their friendship. Would she feel it was an intrusion? That she'd overstepped the invisible and unspoken of boundaries the three of them seemed to have set around their friendship? She'd thought about this before and it came back to her again now.

Well, she'd have to wait a bit longer to find out as the ringing stopped and the call tripped over to voicemail. She left a quick message, simply asking Debbie to call her back when she had a moment.

Ten minutes later, her phone rang, making her jump as she'd been fully focused on the contract in front of her. When she saw it was Debbie, she grabbed it up and rooted around through the papers on her desk to find the invitation which had somehow become buried underneath them.

'Hey, Debbie, how are you? Thank you for calling me back.'

'Sorry about missing your call, Grace. I was with a customer so had to let it go over to messages.'

'Was it a worthy customer?'

'Oh, yes! She bought one of the Chanel dresses that Martha left to me. Fifteen hundred pounds. She got a bargain and I get to pay some bills!'

'Fifteen hundred pounds is a bargain?'

'Oh, yes. I saw a dress from the same collection selling online for over two-thousand pounds not so long ago.'

'So, why didn't you charge over two-thousand pounds?'

'Because I wanted the sale. When people go online, quite often they're actively looking so are already predisposed to spending the price being asked. When they're "just looking" around the shop and then find an item which they fall in love with, they need a little more persuasion to part with their hard-earned moola.'

'As long as you're not underselling yourself.'

'I'm not. Besides, I got the dress for nothing so it was all profit. Anyway, I'm sure you didn't call me to give me business advice, did you?'

'Sorry, was I lecturing again?'

'A bit. Sometimes it feels like having a big sister who keeps handing down her experiences to me. While nice to receive, not always required.'

'Then stop me when I start.'

'Nah, you're good. It means that you care and I'm not so daft as to knock that back. Anyway, I know your time is money, so cut to the chase – why were you calling?'

'I've been invited to a charity bash next week and I wondered if you might fancy coming along.'

'Where is it?'

'Some posh pad in Holland Park.'

'I see.'

Grace heard the hesitancy in Debbie's voice.

'What's the matter?'

'I'm not really a "posh pad" kind of girl. I might let you down or show you up.'

'How on earth are you going to let me down? You know how to hold a wine glass, you don't drag your knuckles on the floor and you always remember to take your curlers out before you leave the house.'

'Oi! I don't wear curlers. Which is probably a good thing as I reckon I probably would forget.'

'Look, put on one of those gorgeous dresses you sell, give your luscious curls a brush, slap on a dash of lippy and every woman in the room is going to wish they looked like you. You ARE a "posh pad" girl, trust me.'

'W-e-l-l…' Debbie dragged the word out, 'I suppose it would be nice to see how the other half live. It's not the kind of invite that's going to come my way all too often.'

'Just one other thing because I don't want to drag you there under false pretences – I'm hoping that one of the main charity patrons will be there as I would like to try and get him to bring some of his business – or better still, *all* of his business – to McArthur Forbes, so you might have to put up with me talking shop for a bit.'

'I think I can cope with that. I'm sure there'll be some expensive piece of art on a wall which I can look at for twenty minutes without ever knowing exactly what it is or what it represents. Or, failing that, a melting ice sculpture which I can wilt alongside.'

'Is that your way of saying you'll come, then?'

'Yeah, go on. It'll do me good to look at someone else's four walls – mine have begun to bore me.'

'Brilliant! Thank you. I'm sure you'll enjoy it. I'll text the details to you when I come off the phone and we can discuss where best to meet up when we're at the pub on Tuesday.'

'Oh, you don't think Lydia will feel left out, do you?'

Grace sat up straighter in her chair. She hadn't even thought of it being something that Lydia might like.

'Ah, I hadn't thought of that. And I would hate for her to think she wasn't welcome. I'll give her a call and ask. If she's up for it, I'll just call the organisers and tell them to add one more beside my name. I donate enough money to them so I doubt they'd say no.'

'Okay, cool. Let me know what she says, yeah?'

'Yes, I will. Catch you later.'

As soon as Debbie had hung up, Grace called Lydia. It was almost four o'clock and she had a memory of Lydia saying the shop tended to grow quieter after that. Something to do with the schools being out…

'Lydia, hi, it's Grace, how are you?'

'Gracie, sweetheart, I'm great thank you, how is it with you?'

For some reason, hearing Lydia's husky tones in her ear, made her smile.

'Oh, I'm good too, thank you. Look, I was wondering…'

Grace filled her friend in on the details, as she had with Debbie, and waited for an answer. Like Debbie, she hoped Lydia would agree to come along because she felt it would do her the power of good to get away from the two male thugs who were supposed to be her family.

'Ah, Gracie, bless you for asking me along but it's really not my kind of thing at all. I can't think of many things that I like doing less than hanging out with a bunch of stiffs in their hand-made suits and women who all look identical with their skinny, toned bodies and bleached blonde hair. Nah, not for me at all.'

Grace let out a chuckle at what she suspected might be a more than accurate description of the evening's attendees. Lydia was considerably sharper than she tended to give her credit for.

'So, I'll take that as a "no", shall I?'

'You absolutely can, Gracie dear, but I love you for thinking of me and asking. That means a lot. Thank you.'

'Hey, it's no problem. Maybe another time.'

'Yeah! And maybe all the pigeons will disappear from Trafalgar Square!'

Grace laughed along with Lydia as they said their goodbyes and hung up. Afterwards, though, she sat looking at the phone in her hand, wondering what was so wrong with her and the way her mind worked. Debbie had immediately thought to ask Lydia and while the woman had declined the invite, her tone of voice had aptly conveyed her happiness at being asked. No way was Grace going to upset her by saying Debbie's kind heart had been behind it and that she herself was a thoughtless, selfish cow.

She let out a sigh and mentally berated herself for a few more minutes, making promises to herself that she must make more of an effort to think of others before returning her attention to the contract she'd been nit-picking her way through.

EIGHTEEN

Debbie gazed critically at her reflection. She was wearing her favourite red dress with its wide shoulder straps, sweetheart neckline, cinched-in waist and ballerina-length skirt complete with a purple net underskirt to give it some body. The colour was perfect against her pale skin and dark hair which had been swept up at the sides but left down at the back to curl around the nape of her neck.

The black, patent, kitten-heeled shoes finished it off beautifully.

When Grace had asked her to join her this evening, outfit planning had been the first thing to fill her mind. This dress was always her number one choice but there had been a concern she may not fit into it for it had always been a little on the neat side and she hadn't worn it for the best part of a year. Her concerns, however, were unfounded. When she slipped it on with the intention of eliminating it from her options, she'd been thrilled to find that it not only still fitted but was in fact a bit loose. Clearly, without Dale's fantastic cooking and her recent lazy efforts of hot dog sausages with steamed mushroom rice, she'd managed to inadvertently drop a few pounds and the dress was now fitting as perfectly as it should.

This gave her a much-needed boost of confidence because she was more nervous about tonight than she was prepared to admit. Grace had said a considerable amount of networking occurred at these events and had suggested she bring business cards to hand out because some of the ladies may be interested in what she was selling. Lydia had backed her up on this which had seen Debbie rushing up the high street at nine o'clock yesterday morning, to the little print shop at the far end, and begging them to do a rush job on a batch of business cards for her.

She hadn't dared to tell her friends that she didn't carry business cards because she knew she should. You never know who you might meet and when, so one should always be prepared. If only she was as good at selling herself as she was at selling her products.

She walked into the kitchen, opened one of the brown paper packages and taking out a small bundle of the new cards, popped them in the clutch bag that matched her shoes.

After a quick walk round the flat to check everything was switched off, especially the curling rod sitting on the dressing table, she pulled on her coat and headed out. She would text Grace when she got on the tube so she'd know to look out for her when the train pulled into Parsons Green station.

Two hours later, Debbie was beginning to wish she'd followed Lydia's example and declined to come along to this soiree. To say she felt like a fish out of water was an understatement. The women were all tall, slim, blonde and wearing varying styles of tight, figure-hugging, little black dresses. Some had flashes of white, silver or gold but the dominant colour in the room was black. The men in their bespoke black tuxedos only emphasised the fact that she stood out like a glaring, garish red, mistake in this sea of quiet elegance.

To make matters worse, she couldn't see Grace anywhere. The room was crowded and it didn't help that Grace, also in her LBD, looked identical to most of the women here. Debbie had only been gone ten minutes, the need to use the loo being the only thing capable of prising her away from Grace's side. She knew Grace had spotted the man she wanted to speak with and Debbie guessed that, in her absence, they had connected and the "friendly sell" which had been carefully planned was now underway. If only she could *see* Grace, she'd be okay. It was this feeling of hanging loose she didn't like.

She spotted a free corner and after taking a glass of wine from the tray of a passing waiter, she made her way over and worked on looking as inconspicuous as possible while watching the ocean of blonde, black-dressed, women flow around in front of her. If she was lucky, one of the ebbing waves might be carrying her friend and she was so busy scanning the crowd that when a voice spoke quietly in her ear, the glass of wine almost jolted out of her hand.

'If you're looking for your friend, she's currently ensconced in one of the meeting rooms off the main hallway. I saw her going in with Charles Highgate and they appeared to be talking in a rather animated fashion.'

'I see, right. Thank you. If you could just point out which room, I'll go and find her...'

'I suspect they may have been talking business – your presence may be an unwelcome interruption.'

'Oh!'

Debbie stopped to think about what to do. She didn't

want to abandon Grace but she didn't want to stand there on her own like a prize idiot, while waiting for her to emerge victorious from wherever she was.

'May I get you a drink?'

'No, I have one, thank you.'

'I think you mean you "had" one. Your glass is empty.'

With a quick glance, she saw her informant was quite correct – the glass she was holding onto for dear life was indeed empty of anything remotely wet and alcoholic.

'Oh! I didn't realise…'

'It's easily done when you're nervous. Would you like me to get you another one?'

She turned to look at the man talking to her. He was taller than her by quite a few inches so she mentally put him at being around six-foot-two or six-foot-three. He had sandy blond hair which was combed forward onto his face – not too dissimilar to the style favoured by Eddie Redmayne in the film Les Misérables although with zero quiff and a chunk of fringe – and she could just about make out his green eyes behind the big, square, black-rimmed glasses he was wearing. The respectful distance he was keeping between them didn't go unnoticed either.

'Do you know, I'm feeling quite hot and rather tired. I think that maybe I'll just go home. I'm sure my friend will understand.'

'Oh, please don't go yet, not when it's taken me nearly all night to pluck up the courage to speak to you.'

'I'm sorry?'

'I saw you arrive. I really wanted to say hello. It's just taken me some time to be able to do so.'

'Actually, if I may be pedantic, you've said a few things but "hello" hasn't actually been one of them.'

'Look, there's a nice garden just at that end of the room,' he pointed over to their left, 'why don't we take a stroll out and you can cool down.'

'I'm not sure…' Debbie didn't know what to make of this person. It appeared as though he was trying to be helpful and kind, but he could easily be some kind of serial killer, trying to lure her outside and away from the safety of the people around her.

'It's perfectly safe – the decking area has been set up for people to go out and smoke so we won't be alone.'

Bloody hell, she thought, the bloke's a mind reader!

'Urm, well… ok, yes, thank you, that would be nice.'

'Follow me.'

He turned and began walking in front of her, cutting a path through the bodies in the room with ease. His hand came back to take a hold of hers but his grip was so soft and gentle, she could break away at any time if she so wished. It was a gesture that, at any other time, would have seen her hackles rise up but with this chap, it felt more protective than intimidating although she almost walked into his back when he stopped suddenly to speak with one of the waiters. She couldn't hear what was said but a moment later, they were on the move again. Soon, she felt the temperature around her begin to drop and when she looked down, she saw they were now walking across wooden decking. A moment later, he stepped to one side and Debbie found herself standing at the top of three wooden steps that led down to a lawn which had tables and chairs dotted around. The tables had little candle lamps fluttering on them and the umbrellas above were laced with twinkling fairy lights. Some of the tables were occupied and the atmosphere felt less intense than that back in the room.

'Would you like to sit over there?'

He pointed to the nearest table and she saw it was in full view of the decking which was crowded with people smoking, drinking and speaking with loud "notice me, I'm here" voices.

'Actually, how about that one? I think it might be a little quieter.'

She was surprised to find herself pointing at the table furthest away from the party but the noise was beginning to give her a headache and she needed some respite.

When they reached it, her rescuer – as she was now beginning to think of him – pulled out the chair for her, picking a fur-lined throw off the seat first and gently draping it around her shoulders once she'd sat down. He then turned to face her, gave her a small bow and holding out his hand, said, 'Good evening, ma'am. My name is Allan and it's my pleasure to meet you.'

Debbie grinned as she shook his hand, once again noticing the gentleness of his grip, and said, 'Good evening, sir, I'm Debbie. It is also my pleasure to meet you.'

They exchanged smiles as he sat down on the chair opposite. When her powers of observation caught up with her, she saw that he'd engineered their sitting positions to be side-on to the decking area, thus ensuring they were both in full view and neither was being obscured by the other.

She was about to speak when the waiter Allan had spoken to on their way out arrived.

'Sir, I have here the unopened bottle of champagne as requested and also the unopened bottle of water. Would you like me to open and pour?'

'Yes, please, but could I ask you to give the glasses a polish before you do so.'

'Of course, sir.'

Debbie worked on keeping her face neutral throughout this exchange but her mind was working overtime. What on earth? She'd gotten it all wrong – he *was* some kind of a nutter. Of course, he was. There was no chance of her ever attracting anyone who was just simple and ordinary.

When the waiter left them, he only went as far as the first decking step where he stopped, put his tray down on the planter behind him and stood to attention like a soldier outside Buckingham Palace.

She was unable to keep the confusion off her face as she turned back to look at Allan.

'What's going on?'

Her confusion was echoed on his face.

'I'm sorry?'

'The waiter over there, the glass polishing and stuff? What's your game?'

He gulped. 'Err, there's no game. I'm trying to make you feel safe and unthreatened.'

'You what?'

'In the office, I hear the women talking about men being overbearing, being rude with the words they say to them, treating them like they're stupid and behaving in ways that make them feel unsafe. I've also heard them saying things about drinking from unopened bottles to make sure they've not been tampered with and had drugs put into them. That's why I asked for unopened bottles – so that you knew you were safe. The glasses were polished so you knew they hadn't been laced with anything and I've asked the waiter to stay close so you don't need to worry about being alone with a man you don't know.'

'Right! Wow! That… this is…unexpected. Thank you for being so considerate.'

'Have I done it wrong? I'm sorry… I'm not very good with people. I'm just a nerdy computer geek. Give me a computer and I will make it sing in twenty different languages all at once. I can create a plethora of programs and win almost every computer game created. But when it comes to dealing with human beings… with people… well, they scare me. And I don't do it so well. That's why I noticed you tonight – not only do you stand out with your beautiful red dress, but you also looked a little scared and I thought that maybe two scared people might be able to talk to each other.'

Debbie saw the earnest look on his face and her reserve drained away. He'd observed what she hadn't been fully aware of until now – she had been feeling scared and out of her depth. Her dress that wasn't black had made her stand out like a beacon and she could still feel the eyes of everyone upon her. She was also sure she'd heard a few sniggers too, as she'd walked through the rooms, and had felt what little confidence she'd been able to cling on to, shrivel-up and die. He was right, she was, in her own way, a nerdy little geek.

'So, you noticed me because I wasn't tall, blonde and willowy like the women over there.'

'Too right I did.' He leant across the table towards her. 'You had the courage to arrive here and be yourself. You didn't try to fit into the mould the way they've all done.' He inclined his head in the direction of the party people. 'See how boring and unexciting they are. Look at them, Debbie, really look at them. They're sheeple – so worried about what people will say if they dare to do something that their so-called "friends" might disapprove of. It's all about being seen in the right places, wearing the right clothes, sending their kids to the right schools. They never stop to think that what's right for one person may not be right for them.'

She followed Allan's gaze and made herself see them as he did. It didn't take long. Suddenly, all the blonde became bland – there was so much of it. Occasionally, a redhead or brunette could be spotted but they were rare creatures. The tight, tall, willowy bodies became shapeless and dull. No womanly curves among that lot.

'You, Debbie, were the beautiful ruby in among the grains of black dirt. You weren't a clone and that was why

I wanted to meet you.'

Debbie felt herself blushing so to hide it, she picked up her – safe – glass of champagne, leant across the table and clinked it against Allan's.

'Here's to being real, geeky and nerdy. Long may we be a thorn in the side of the clones.'

Their laughter rang out, floating across the lawn, and when she sneaked a little glance at their waiter, she saw he was smiling too.

NINETEEN

Lydia hurried from the station to the pub. It was bucketing down and she wanted to get indoors before her newly straightened hair went all frizzy from the damp.

She also wanted to hear about the charity event on Thursday night. While it hadn't been the sort of occasion she'd have been comfortable attending, she did want to hear everything about it – right down to who was wearing what, were there any celebrities and how exotic was the "posh pad" where it had been held.

The dry warmth of the pub hit her as she walked through the door and upon arriving at their usual booth, she saw she was the first to arrive. Her coat had barely landed upon the newel on the edge of the booth when the door opened and Debbie arrived bringing a gust of damp air with her.

'Hey, Lydia, how are you? Blimey, it's wild out there. No sign of Grace yet?'

Lydia gave Debbie a hug and waited for her to hang up her coat to dry before moving into her usual seat in the corner of the booth.

'No, but she is on her way. She sent a text letting me know there were delays on the tubes.'

'Oh, that's good.'

'What's the matter, Debs, you seem a bit agitated. Is everything alright?'

As soon as they'd sat down, Debs had picked up one of the cardboard coasters which lay on the table and had already shredded nearly half of it.

'Err, I think so but I'm not sure.'

'Did something happen on Thursday?'

'Maybe. The night turned out quite different from what I had been expecting and… well… you'll hear more on that once Grace gets here. I'm just worried that she might be angry or annoyed with me.'

'Well, now I'm really intrigued.'

Just then, Grace came in and rushed to the table.

'Sorry, I'm late, ladies. The Underground system was down to its usual crappy standard. Are we both well?'

After taking her coat off, she scooched into the booth next to Debbie and grabbed the menu.

'I am starving. What's looking good tonight?'

The three of them pondered the menu and had just made their choices when the waitress came over.

'Oh, no Alyson tonight?'

'No, she's on holiday this week but she left me strict instructions to look after her Prosecco ladies in her absence. So, the barman is sorting out your drinks while I take your food order and then I'll be right back with your bottle of wine.'

'Ah, now that's what you call good service. Thank you.'

Grace flashed a smile at the waitress but Debbie sat nibbling her thumbnail, a small pile of ripped coaster pieces on the table in front of her. She was definitely nervous about something and Lydia wanted to get to the bottom of it before the food arrived. She came here to get away from the bad atmosphere at home, she didn't need it seeping into the few hours of peace she got each week.

Once their orders were given and the wine had been delivered, she sat back and gave both Grace and Debbie what she called her "Paddington hard stare"!

'Right, you two, before we go any further, what went down on Thursday night that has turned poor Debbie here into a nervous wreck?'

'It's my fault, I'm to blame.'

Lydia watched as Debbie looked to Grace in confusion.

'No, Grace, I shouldn't have gone home without letting you know. I'm sorry.'

'Er, no, Debbie, I was the one who left you. When Charlie Highgate suggested we speak in a more private environment, I should have said I was with someone and arranged to meet him the next day or something. I'm so sorry you ended up going home alone. I looked for you when we'd finished talking but I can understand why you didn't hang about. It wasn't the best place to be when you were alone and didn't know anyone.'

'Grace, how long were you talking with him because I was there until almost midnight waiting for you?'

'What? Midnight? I left just before eleven. I searched everywhere for you and when I couldn't find you, figured you must have bailed. I felt so awful for deserting you.'

'I'm guessing you didn't check the garden because I was out there talking to someone called Allan for ages.'

Grace palmed her forehead. 'The garden! The only place I didn't think to look.'

'Erm, at the risk of sounding like the old farty voice of reason, but why didn't you both just text or phone each other?'

'Because my phone was out of juice. I'd used it several times that day and had forgotten to give it a boost as I was getting ready to go out. I only noticed when I was waiting for Debbie's text to let me know she was on the train.'

'And I didn't text or call her because I knew her phone was dead.'

Lydia looked at them and shook her head.

'So, you've both been beating yourselves up over this since Thursday?'

'Yeah. I texted Debbie the next day to make sure she had got home okay but I wanted to apologise face-to-face, not over the phone.'

'And I thought you were mad at me because I had left without you. I thought you were still in that room with your Charlie-bloke and didn't want to interrupt you so just left because I was shattered by that point.'

'I think this is the bit where you both hug and make up, yeah?'

Lydia felt the tension in her shoulders ease away. The problem may not have been hers but these were her only friends and she didn't want any bad feeling between them. Not now that her Tuesday nights had become the only thing left for her to look forward to these days.

'Anyway, this guy, Allan, tell us more, Debs. What was he like?'

'Yes, give us the full work-up. We want to hear more. What does he look like? Is he hot?'

'Oh, Lydia, trust you to ask that!' Debbie laughed as a soft, pink blush rose in her cheeks. 'As it happens, he has a kind of cuteness about him but I don't think he'd be what you'd call "hot".'

'So, what does he look like?' Grace asked, a hint of exasperation in her voice.

'He's tall, maybe about six-foot-two-ish, slim built, sandy hair all brushed forward onto his face so not easy to actually define his features, and green eyes which were doing a great job of hiding behind a pair of *massive* glasses.'

'Excuse me – did you say hair on his face and big glasses?'

'Er, yeah, Grace.'

'Oh-em-gee! I think you met Allan Ross.'

'Who?'

'Allan Ross. Arty!'

'Arty? What are you talking about? His name was Allan – where are you getting Arty from?'

'A.R.T.I – Allan Ross Technical Industries. Known to the world at large as ARTI. Hang on…'

Lydia and Debbie waited as Grace pulled her phone from her bag, did some swiping, tapping and more swiping until a moment later, she turned it towards Debbie.

'Is this the bloke you were talking to?'

'Oh, wow! Yes, it is.'

She took the phone off Grace, looked at the picture for a few seconds before passing it to Lydia who also studied it then handed it back to Grace.

'He looks nice,' she said, 'although I don't think he was comfortable having that photograph taken.'

'You're probably right there, Lyds, he told me that he's rather shy and doesn't like people very much.'

'You've got that one right, Debs. He's known for being quite reclusive.'

'But who is he, Grace? I've never heard of him and yet you seem to know a lot more.'

'Actually, I don't. I know *who* he is but not much more than that. There's not a lot of info out there on him. He's some sort of gadgety, computer-coding kind of whizz-kid who started off in computer gaming before moving onto greater things. There's speculation that he's branched out into defence and has contracts not only with our MOD but also with a few other countries. Which, if that is the case, would explain the secrecy around him.'

'Or, he just hates being a public figure. He described himself as a nerdy geeky dude who can talk to computers but not to people.'

'I reckon he's possibly had an awkward childhood – people who are as brilliant as this bloke appears to be are often outcasts among their peers at school because they're mentally so far ahead of them. This forces them into spending more time on their computers which compounds the problem.'

'How come you know about this kind of thing, Lydia?'

'One of my customers has a grandson with a similar issue. Her son and his wife are trying to find solutions that will enable him to have a normal childhood without impeding his abilities. It's not easy and that's *with* all the awareness we have these days. Can you imagine what it must have been like for Allan, say twenty, twenty-five years ago? No wonder the poor sod hides behind a computer screen.'

'I don't think I'd be using the word "poor" when talking about Allan Ross, Lydia – he's worth billions if these articles are to be believed. More zeros on his bank account than you or I could probably count.'

'Then it looks like our Debs has bagged herself a good one.'

'I haven't "bagged" anyone. He kindly came to my rescue when Grace disappeared with her bloke. We sat chatting for ages and then he sorted out a taxi to take me home. Nothing more.'

'What? No exchange of phone numbers? No hot dates planned?'

'No, Grace. Nothing like that. He gave me his number and told me to text him when I got home so he knew I'd arrived there safely. He was very conscientious about ensuring I felt safe at all times.'

Lydia looked at Grace who looked back at her and they

both burst out laughing.

'What?' Debbie looked from one to the other in obvious confusion.

'Do you want to tell her, Lydia, or shall I?'

'You can do the honours, Grace…'

'Debbie, did you text him when you got back to your flat?'

'Of course I did.'

'Then he has your phone number. Just as you have his otherwise how could you let him know you were home. You have exchanged numbers but it was very subtly done.'

'Oh!' Debbie sat back as the realisation sank in.

'Which means you are also probably one of a handful of people whom he trusts to have it. That's a big deal, Debbie.'

'Well, I won't be doing anything with it, Lydia. I mean, come on, I didn't even know who he was, for goodness' sake!'

'That was probably the appeal. You didn't fawn over him or try to impress him. And of course, the fact that you're a gorgeous, lovely lady won't have been lost on him either.'

'Have you heard from him since?'

'No, don't be silly, Grace. We were two ships who anchored alongside each other for a while before moving off into the night in opposite directions. Besides, I'm not ready to get involved with anyone yet – I'm still too tender and bruised right now. Allan Ross was a pleasant experience and one which I will share with my grandkids many years down the line. The night I met a multi-billionaire. Now, less about me… Lydia, how are things with you?'

'Erm, well—'

'Here we are, ladies. One steak pie with veg over here, one lamb and mint with chips over there and a steak and kidney with peas and mash just here. If I can help you with anything else, just let me know.'

'Thank you, this all looks lovely.'

Lydia gave the waitress a brighter than necessary smile because she'd intervened at exactly the right moment and taken the attention away from her. She was not in a good place right now and didn't want to burden her friends with her troubles. She met with Gracie and Debs to get away from her problems, not to bring them out with her.

TWENTY

The following morning, Debbie stepped into the shop, opened the shutters and the door and as she walked back inside, a stray sunbeam came in through one of the bay windows and highlighted the dust around the sill.

'Oh, bugger! Looks like some spring-cleaning is needed in here,' Debbie said to the mannequin standing at the side of the counter. While it was lovely to see sunlight again after the long, dark days of winter, it was less fun eliminating the dust from the sills and the dust-bunnies under the counters and shelves. But it needed to be done and the sooner she started, the sooner she'd be finished.

Although, she thought, looking down at the pretty floral print skirt she was wearing, not in this outfit. She quickly locked the door, stuck up her little sign which said she'd be back in five minutes and ran up to the flat to change.

When the shop reopened barely six minutes later, she was sporting a pair of baggy dungarees, pulled in at the waist with a wide belt, a yellow t-shirt underneath and a pair of yellow tennis-shoes to match. To stay in keeping with the vintage theme of the shop, she'd wrapped a yellow and blue scarf around her head in the style favoured during the forties and fifties.

While the kettle boiled in the little kitchen through the back, she dragged the mannequins from the windows along with the shoe and handbag stands. Soon, she was up to her elbows in mucky water as the windows, sills, paintwork and floor were scrubbed down, dried off and polished up.

She was down on her hands and knees, scrubbing at a stubborn stain in the corner of the second window – where on earth had that come from – when she heard the little doorbell tinkle.

'Please have a look round, I'll be with you in a moment,' she called over her shoulder while picking up the cloth to dry the area she'd been cleaning.

'It's okay, no need to rush,' replied a soft, gentle voice.

Surprised, Debbie looked swiftly over her shoulder, lost her balance and ended up landing on her bottom on the floor, just narrowly avoiding tipping over the water bucket. She looked up at Allan as he leant forward and extended his hand to help her up.

'I'm sorry, Debbie, I didn't mean to startle you. Are you okay?'

'Yes, yes, I am. Thank you. You just surprised me, that's all.'

'I'm sorry.'

'No, it's a nice surprise. No need to apologise.'

'You're not hurt, are you? From your fall?'

'No, my pride maybe but not physically. And it was only a little tumble, not a fall.'

'Oh, good. Here, I brought these for you.'

He picked up a beautiful, large, bunch of yellow tulips, tied with blue string, from the countertop and thrust them towards her.

'I thought you would like yellow because it's such a bright, cheerful colour and looking at your top, I can see I was right. You both match.'

'Oh, Allan, these are gorgeous. Thank you so much. May I ask, did you get these from the stall at the top of the mews?'

'Yes, how did you know?'

'Colin uses different coloured twine to tie his flowers as it's more environmentally friendly.'

'He was a very nice man. Quite chatty actually.'

'Is that so? Did you tell him the flowers were for me, by any chance?'

'I did! How do you know that?'

'Because he knows I love tulips and he knows I love yellow. Did he recommend you buy the yellow ones?'

'No, but when I said I wanted yellow and that they were for you, he told me I had made a good choice.'

'You most certainly did, thank you. Just let me empty this bucket and put some fresh water in. I'll put them in here for now. Would you like a drink – tea or coffee?'

'A coffee would be very nice, if it's not too much trouble and if you're not too busy that is.'

'I was cleaning. Any excuse to stop is always welcome.'

She threw him a smile before dipping her head to take in the lovely scent of the flowers. She could feel herself blushing and the flowers helped to hide it.

'Have a nosy round, while I get your drink, although mind your step, it's a little more cluttered than it would normally be.'

She dived into the kitchen, placed the flowers on the draining board and opened the back door to pour the mucky water down the drain. She then filled the kettle, put it on to boil and cleaned the bucket out before putting some cold water in to keep her flowers fresh. As she straightened up, she caught a glimpse of her reflection in the little mirror behind the door and just about died when she saw the streaks of dirt dotted about her face!

'Oh, no!' she groaned, quickly grabbing a piece of kitchen roll and wetting it to scrub the offensive marks away. She dreaded to think what must have gone through Allan's mind when he saw her. She couldn't have looked any more different from the smartly dressed woman she'd been last week if she'd tried.

The kettle clicked off and she poured the water onto the granules in the mugs on the worktop. She'd been thinking about getting one of those pod-type coffee machine things for ages and now she really wished she'd done so because she was about to give a cup of Tesco's basic instant to one of the richest men in the world. Talk about embarrassing! He probably drank that really expensive Kopi stuff which was pooped out of some wild cat's bottom.

She stuck her head out of the kitchen door.

'Er, Allan, do you take milk or sugar?'

'Both, please. Two sugars.'

When she stepped back onto the shop floor, it was to see Allan holding a flowery woman's blouse up in front of him and checking out his reflection in the mirror.

'Do you like that one?'

He grinned as he turned around and returned it back to the rail.

'No, not at all but I know men wore stuff like that back in the seventies and I was wondering how I would have looked back then.'

'And, what did you think?'

'To use Del Boy parlance, I would have looked "a right plonker"!'

He burst out laughing and Debbie could only join in because he was absolutely right about that.

There was silence for a moment or two afterwards until Debbie asked, 'Allan, how did you find me?'

'Oh, it was easy. You mentioned you ran a vintage

clothes shop and you told the taxi driver to take you to Putney. A quick search on the internet brought me here. I walked down to peek in the window first though, to make sure it was you before going back up to get the flowers, as I didn't want to come empty-handed. Can you imagine if I'd just walked into the shop and presented them to some strange woman – she'd have been calling the police to lock me up!'

'Hmm, I don't think she'd have done that but you may have had some explaining to do.'

They were chuckling over the possible outcomes of his actions when the doorbell tinkled and the postman walked in.

'Hey, Pat, how are you today?'

'Oh, can't complain, Debbie. The sun is out, it's warm but not too hot and it's not raining. In my profession, that's a winning combination.'

'Pat? Seriously?'

The postie turned to Allan and gave him a glare.

'Yes, I'm a postman and my name's Patrick, Pat for short. What of it?'

'Oh, nothing, nothing at all.'

Debbie could see Allan was doing his best not to laugh and knowing how sensitive Pat could be, she thought it best not to keep him hanging about.

'Thank you for the post, Pat. Have a good rest of the day.'

'Yeah, see you, Debbie.'

He gave Allan another glare through the glass as he closed the door behind him.

'Don't you dare… he'll hear you,' she admonished Allan.

'I can't, Debs, I can't…'

'Quick, get in there.'

She pushed him into the kitchen just as the first giggle

left his lips. A second later, he was bent double, tears pouring down his face and the words, 'Postman Pat...' came out in gasps.

After a minute or so, he finally began to quieten down.

'Are you quite finished now?'

'I... I think so.'

She handed him a square of kitchen roll for him to dry his face and when he took off his glasses, she couldn't hold back the gasp of surprise.

'What?'

He looked at her as he wiped his face.

'Urm... it's... it's you look so different without the glasses on. It took me by surprise.'

'Oh, right.'

He quickly pushed them back on and pulled his hair forward again with his fingers.

'Hey, stop!' She stilled his hand and pushed his fringe off his face. 'Why do you wear your hair like that? And why do you wear such big, unbecoming frames? Surely you could find nicer glasses than those – they don't do anything for you.'

She was shocked to see Allan's face turn bright red.

'Can I tell you a secret?'

'Of course you can.'

'I don't need the glasses, they're not real. They're props – to help me face all the attention I get. I... I kind of hide behind them.'

She looked at him for a moment before saying, 'Just like the kid in the film "Big Daddy"?'

'Yes, exactly. That's where I got the idea from. I know it sounds silly but I feel like they stop people seeing the real me.'

'And the same with the hair – you wear it forward to hide behind.'

He nodded, a look of chagrin on his face.

'I've told you I don't do well with people and I worry that I'll look like a fool if they could see deep inside me.'

'Why would they think that?'

He shrugged. 'I don't know. When I was at school, the kids were mean to me and that sort of stays with you. Even though I know my success could now outstrip anything they've achieved combined and multiplied by ten, it doesn't change how I feel inside. I still feel like the loser they called me back then. I'm fully aware I'm – what is called – socially awkward, which makes me worse and doesn't help. And I *REALLY* don't know why I feel comfortable sharing this with you when I've never told another soul in my life!'

'Then I thank you for trusting me. I promise I won't ever tell anyone else. Your secret stops here. Now, tell me what was *so* funny about Postman Pat...'

She made her way to the shop counter and Allan followed behind her although he moved around to the front of it when she stopped and began flicking through the envelopes Pat had placed there for her.

'I don't know, it just made me laugh. Childish, I know. I think it was the fact he was SO serious that did it for me. If he'd laughed it off, I don't think it would have amused me half as much.'

'I suppose he's sick of hearing it after all these years.'

'I suppose he probably is. If I see him again, I'll be sure to apologise.'

Debbie smiled as she picked up the white envelope from the middle of the little pile but it soon dropped when she saw the post mark on it.

'Oh, shit!'

Allan straightened up in front of her.

'Hey, what's up?'

She waved the envelope in front of him.

'This can only be bad news. Do you mind if I open it?'

'No, go ahead. Do you want me to leave? I can go if you'd rather have privacy.'

'I think I'd rather you stayed. I might need you to bring me round if I keel over in a dead faint.'

'Okay. I've done my first-aid courses, I'm ready and primed to put those lessons into action so, open away.'

Closing her eyes in trepidation, Debbie ripped open the envelope, felt around inside and pulled out the paperwork within. When she'd unfolded it, she opened her eyes, quickly scanned through it, let out a quiet expletive and then read the contents again.

'Bastards!'

She threw the papers on the counter.

'May I ask what's wrong?'

She pointed to the letter.

'It's from the management company who own the lease for the mews. They've just put up the ground rent again. This is the third time in eighteen months. It's getting ridiculous.'

'But, how can they do that? I thought they could only do it once a year.'

'Or when the lease is being renewed. Which, in this case, is now every six months! This new company took over the lease about four years ago and has been putting up the ground rent every time. They then changed the yearly leases to short-term six-month leases which means they can now increase the ground-rent twice a year. We either suck it up or move out. So far, we've all managed to suck it up but this last one might be a step too far. It's just not fair.'

'May I?'

Allan pointed to the letter.

'Sure, knock yourself out.'

He picked it up and Debbie watched as his eyebrows disappeared under his fringe when he saw the new costs.

'Now you understand why I'm pissed off!'

He put the letter back down.

'Yes, I sure do. I'm sorry. If there's anything I can do to help…'

She gave him a wan smile. 'If you can stick one of my cards up in the office canteen so the ladies you work with can see it, that might help because, unless sales pick up, I'm going to be in a very sorry pickle.'

'I can most certainly do that for you.' He picked up the whole pile of business cards she'd placed on the counter from the batch she'd bought last week and put them in his pocket. 'In fact, I won't put a card in the canteen, I'll put one on the desk of every woman in the building.'

'Tell them that, if they mention they work with you, I'll give them a ten-percent discount.'

'Oh, that'll definitely get some of them over your doorstep, for sure. Now, is it too early for lunch? The smells coming from that restaurant over the way are making my stomach rumble. How do you manage to work with that level of temptation every day?'

'You get used to it although some days it's not so easy.'

'Is the food good?'

'The best Italian food I've tasted.'

'Then can we go eat, please?'

'Sure, we can. Give me a few minutes to change.'

'Oh, do you have to?'

'I'm sorry?'

'Allan pointed to her outfit.

'You look so pretty in your dungarees, why do you need to change?'

'Okay, let me just take this scarf off and brush my hair.'

'Cool!'

Debbie couldn't help but smile as she ran up the stairs to the flat. There was something so natural and guileless about Allan. He said what he was thinking and she found it rather refreshing. It made his company enjoyable and after that letter, enjoyable company was exactly what she needed!

TWENTY-ONE

Lydia took her time walking from the bus stop to the flat. She was getting home later and later these days although her family didn't care enough to notice. All they cared about was how delayed their dinner was but she'd managed to get around that by finally sorting out the timer on the oven. Luckily, they both loved pies, pizza and lasagne and hadn't noticed the frequency of them lately.

Since she'd found the stash in Davie's bedroom, she hadn't felt comfortable being in the house when he was there. She had a constant bad feeling in her gut and simply couldn't relax. Maybe it was her own fault – she'd read far too many novels where drug gangs and drug wars were at the centre of the plot and watched too many TV dramas of the same which were now making her imagination work overtime even though she was sure they hyped these things up for dramatic effect. She didn't, however, fancy being around to find out if that was the case or not.

She was also concerned about Davie's personal use of drugs. There was no denying that he was getting high on a regular basis now and unlike some druggies who could be quite merry when they were stoned, he was mean and nasty. She'd tried to speak to Dave again but he refused to see any harm in it and just wouldn't take her concerns seriously. Even when she'd told him that Davie had asked her for money a couple of weeks before and when she'd refused to give it to him, he'd pushed her rather viciously, hard enough to bruise her back where she'd hit the door jamb. Dave, however, had just laughed it off saying she was being overly sensitive. She'd reached the point where she was desperate to get out but still couldn't find anything affordable and wished now that she'd accepted Debbie's offer to share her place although at the time, it had felt more like a nice gesture on Debbie's part rather than a sincere offer. The fact it hadn't been mentioned since only emphasised that.

She sighed as she turned the corner towards the flat – a sigh which was quickly followed by a groan as the heavy thump-thump-thump of loud music assaulted her ears once again. She picked up her pace and almost ran the remaining distance, knowing that the neighbours were now getting really pissed off and threatening to report them to the council.

The front door slammed against the wall as she flung it open, dropped her bags and ran up the stairs. When she entered Davie's room, it was empty like before so she headed straight for the hi-fi in the corner and turned it off.

'Oi, I was listening to that!'

She turned to see Davie coming out of the bathroom.

'And, as I've mentioned before, so was half the neighbourhood. Are you trying to get us evicted because that's what's going to happen if you don't stop doing this! We'll be reported and then we'll be out on our ears! The neighbours have had enough of your behaviour and so have I.'

'The neighbours are a bunch of nosey, interfering

arseholes and so are you! You think you can come in here and tell me what to do like I'm a child. Well, I'm not a child anymore and you can't boss me about. I'm my own boss, yeah! I'm my own boss.'

'You say you're not a child anymore so why don't you act like the grown-up you profess to be, huh? When are you going to take responsibility for your actions? You're smoking these drugs all the time and you've lost touch with the real world. What I want to know is – are you just smoking weed or are you taking something stronger because your behaviour suggests that you are?'

'What I do with my life is none of your business.'

'I'm your mother, your life *is* my business.'

Lydia walked over to the doorway and took a good look at her son. He was standing just under the landing light and she could see the effects of the drugs beginning to show on his face. His eyes were bloodshot, his skin was pasty looking and he'd put on weight. While never slim-built – he'd always liked his food – he was now carrying some serious bulk. No doubt from the munchies he'd be experiencing as he came down.

'Look at yourself, Davie. Can't you see the harm you're doing?'

'Oh, stop pretending you care. You don't care about me.'

'That's not true, I've always cared about you, you're my son.'

'Yeah? Well, why don't you act like my mother? You're a crap mum! You wouldn't lend me money when I asked.'

'You work full-time, Davie, you earn a good wedge and you don't pay a penny towards your keep so the last thing you need is a loan from me.'

He stepped forward and yelled right in her face.

'I NEEDED MONEY AND YOU WOULDN'T GIVE

IT TO ME!'

Suddenly, her cheek was throbbing, her eye felt like it had exploded and her head was ringing. Davie had punched her and it looked like he was coming in for seconds. She tried to duck and he caught the top of her head, slamming it off the wall.

'YOU DON'T TRY TO HELP ME! YOU HATE ME! YOU'D BE HAPPIER IF I WAS DEAD! WELL, GUESS WHAT! I'D BE A LOT HAPPIER IF YOU WERE DEAD!'

He kicked her leg and caught her on the back of the knee. Losing her balance, she dropped down onto the floor where she rolled up into a ball, trying to prevent Davie's kicks from hitting her vital areas. Just as she thought he'd worn himself out, he leant over and spat in her face.

'You disgust me, you bitch. Just die and let Dad and I enjoy our lives.'

After uttering these final words, he gave her a push and she felt the brief sensation of hanging in thin air before the hard edge of the top stair hit her back. She rolled down the staircase, coming to a halt by the front door which was still open and she felt the cool air of the night on her face before everything went dark.

How long she lay there, Lydia didn't know but when she came to, she'd been pushed against the wall, the front door was closed and silence surrounded her. With difficulty, she was able to open one eye and could see the clock in the kitchen. Just after eight p.m.

A low groan escaped from her swollen lips as she worked on moving herself upright, trying not to feel the pain that roamed through every part of her body.

Once she was in a sitting position, the wall helping to keep her there, she felt along the floor to where she'd dropped her handbag. She slowly unzipped it, her arm sore and her shoulder screaming in pain when she moved it, and managed to find her phone which she pulled out and dropped onto her lap.

For a few minutes, she remained as still as possible, taking shallow breaths as the pain rolled up and down her body in waves. Eventually, she took a deep breath, wincing at how much it hurt to do so, unlocked the phone and scrolled through until she found the name she wanted.

She hit the connect button and waited.

'Hi, Lydia.'

'Hi, Debbie.'

'Are you okay?'

'No... no, I'm not. Debbie... can I... can I take up your offer of your spare room. And can I move in tonight?'

TWENTY-TWO

Grace was just walking out of the tube station, thinking
about her new sofa and how she couldn't wait for it to be
installed, when she felt her phone vibrate in her pocket.
She pulled it out and smiled when she saw Debbie's
number on the screen. It would seem that their friendship
was growing and this gave her a lovely warm feeling
inside. She had to stop being such a loner – it wasn't good
for her.

'Hey, Debbie, how's it going?'

She spotted a gap in the traffic and quickly ran across
the main road.

'Hi, Grace, are you at home?'

'On my way there now. I've just come out of the
station.'

At that moment a bus went by, honking its horn at a
bloke on a bicycle and she couldn't hear Debbie's reply.

'Debs, hang on a second. The traffic is chronic and I
can't hear you. Give me thirty seconds till I turn into my
road.'

She picked up the pace and soon turned down into her

street. She walked a little further until the street noise was a muted hum behind her.

'Hi, Debs, sorry about that. What were you saying?'

'I said we need to get to Lydia's now! Something's happened, I'm not quite sure what but she needs us. Can we go in your car?'

Grace felt her heartbeat begin to race.

'Of course we can. Let me quickly jump into my jeans. I'll be five minutes and then I'll head down towards you. Is that okay?'

'Absolutely! Pick me up at the train station, it'll be quicker. In the meantime, I'll let Lydia know we're on our way and ask her to text over her address. She's asked if she can stay at mine so we may be bringing back some of her belongings.'

'That's not a problem. There's plenty of space. I'll see you very soon.'

Grace was already halfway up her stairs as she ended the call and, after performing the fastest change known to man, was running back down them barely ninety seconds later. She was still wearing her work blouse but that didn't matter, it was the jeans that were important if there was a likelihood of carting suitcases or holdalls about.

For once, the traffic was on her side and it wasn't long before she was giving the horn a parp when she saw Debbie pacing up and down on the pavement.

'Hey, any more news?' she asked as her friend got in. She was already moving off again before the seatbelt had been done up.

'No. All I know is she had some kind of fight with Davie and she sounded awful. I've got her address here.'

'Can you put the postcode into the satnav for me please? That'll save us driving around trying to find her.'

Debbie did as she was asked and Grace was pleased to see they weren't too far away.

'It might be worth letting her know we're together and on our way. If she's really upset, it will help her to stay focused.'

'Good idea.'

Debbie quickly fired off a text and a reply soon came back.

'What does she say?'

Debbie read it out loud, "Thank you. So sorry to be a bother."

'Oh, the daft mare. It's not a bother at all. She's our friend and she needs us. Honestly!'

They were soon turning into the estate and it took a couple of U-turns for them to find where they needed to be.

'It looks like it's along that path there. We'll need to park up here and walk.'

Grace pulled into the nearest space she could find and had barely cut the engine before the two of them were out and running along the path.

'There it is!'

Debbie pointed up a flight of stairs.

A moment later they were knocking on the door.

'Lydia, are you in there? It's Grace and Debbie. We're here now, please open up.'

There was silence for a few seconds and then they heard a faint shuffling noise followed by the sound of bolts being pulled back and a key being turned.

The door opened a crack and Lydia peered out before opening it wide enough to let them in. As soon as Grace had crossed the threshold, it was slammed closed behind her and one of the bolts pushed back across again.

When Lydia turned round, sagging against the door-frame, Grace saw the mess her face was in and stumbled back with shock. One of her eyes was so swollen and bruised, she couldn't open it. The other was slightly less so

– just enough to allow it to be marginally opened. There was blood under her nose and both lips were split. She could actually see finger marks in the bruising on Lydia's cheek. She was also holding her left arm across her middle and Grace didn't know if it was her arm or her stomach she was nursing although given how damaged she was, it was most likely both.

'Oh, Lydia, what's happened? Who did this to you? You need to go to the hospital.'

'No, Grace, not the hospital. Just… just away from here, please. Now!'

'But you need to be checked over.'

'Later. Just get me away, please. Help me to leave… now!'

'Okay. Where's your bedroom? I'll go and pack your clothes. Debbie, are you okay getting Lydia's toiletries from the bathroom?'

'On it! Lydia, are you able to show us, or just tell us, where we need to go and where we can find suitcases or bags to put your stuff in?'

'Follow me.'

She limped slowly ahead of them towards the stairs and behind her back, Grace and Debbie exchanged a look of horror. Grace gave a small shrug and mouthed, 'later' to Debs. Debs nodded her head in agreement.

As Lydia pulled herself up onto the first step, a moan of pain slipped out of her bruised lips.

'Lydia, why don't you stay down here, tell us where to find stuff and what you want.'

'No! When I leave this place tonight, I am never coming back, so I want to make sure I take it all now or else it'll be gone forever.'

'Okay. Well, look, put your weight against me and let me help you up.'

She put one hand under the elbow of Lydia's good arm,

the other around her back and the three of them slowly made their way up the stairs.

'You'll find suitcases in there.' Lydia gestured towards a door in front of them. 'There's the bathroom and this is the main bedroom.'

The lawyer in Grace noticed that she didn't say "our bedroom" – so much said by omission. She led Lydia in and sat her gently on the bed while Debbie went into the other room to find the cases.

'Right, you direct me. Where are your things?'

'Here we go, one suitcase and I noticed another in there which I believe we'll need, Lydia, because if you're adamant about never returning,' Debbie turned towards their friend, 'then we do need to try and take away everything that we can tonight so there's absolutely no requirement for you to come back. Are you sure you're okay with that?'

Lydia nodded and tried to give a smile but her grimace of pain wasn't missed by either of them.

'Oh, result, I've got a holdall in here,' said Debbie, picking it out of the suitcase she'd placed on the bed and opened. 'I'll pack up everything in the bathroom that is feminine. I'll come and ask if there's anything I'm not sure of.'

'Which wardrobe is yours, Lydia?'

'The left one,' she whispered, her voice breaking.

'Hey,' Grace knelt down in front of her and very gently pushed her blood-matted hair back off her face. 'I know this is shitty right now and I can't even begin to imagine how, or what, you're feeling but eventually, this is going to be a small moment in your life although it's the moment from which better things will grow. I get that it doesn't feel like that right now but you need to trust me on this. And you won't be alone. Debbie and I will be right here with you.'

'Too damn right we will be,' Debbie smiled as she walked back in the door. 'Now, this dressing table – I'm guessing the straighteners and makeup belong to you, or is there something about Dave you've omitted to share with us. Do you call him Davina on the weekends?'

Lydia let out a bark of a laugh followed by a groan of pain as she hugged the sides of her ribs.

'Oh, don't make me laugh, Debbie, it hurts.'

Above Lydia's head, Grace gave Debbie a little smile and a wink. They had to keep their friend's spirits up to help her through whatever was to come.

Fifteen minutes later, the three women stood looking around the room. Every cupboard had been checked and every drawer rummaged through or emptied. It was only the soft décor that suggested a woman had ever occupied the room.

'Let's get this lot down to the car. Do you want to check the other rooms, Lydia, for any other personal pieces you want to take?'

'I'll check the lounge and kitchen when I go down – there may be a couple of items. Oh…' She stopped and looked back at the room where the suitcases had come from. 'My sewing machine… would it be possible to bring that? Will there be space in the car? My mum and gran gave it to me for my sixteenth birthday.'

'We'll find space for it.' Grace gently patted her hand.

'Yeah, even if it has to sit on my lap, Lydia, it's coming with us.'

'Thank you both so much for this.'

'Don't mention it. Debbie, can you help Lydia down the stairs while I grab the machine.'

'It's a bit heavy, Grace, so mind yourself.'

'Thanks, Lydia. This can be my gym workout for the week,' she smiled, although the smile soon slipped when she lifted the machine from the corner it was occupying.

'Bloody hell!' she muttered, 'You're no lightweight, are you?'

Once she'd managed to get a better grip on the old Singer, it wasn't so bad and she eased down the stairs sideways in order to watch her step.

'Is that everything now?' She looked at the luggage by the door.

'Yes, I've got what really matters to me.'

'Okay. Then, if you're quite sure, let's get you down to the car, we'll take the suitcases with us, settle you in and then Debs and I will come back for what's left.'

It was a slow walk to the car and Grace helped Lydia into the front passenger seat while Debbie put the suitcases in the boot. As Lydia went to put on her seatbelt, Grace stopped her.

'Hang on a wee tick.'

She leant in and opened the glovebox. After a quick shuffle, she pulled out a bulldog clip which she then clipped to the top of the seatbelt.

'There, that'll stop it being tight on your sore bits. Let me know if it needs adjusting.'

'No, it's fine. Thank you, Grace.'

'No need to keep saying thank you, lovely, we're all good on that front. Now, I need your door key.'

'Put it through the letterbox when you're done. I won't be coming back.'

'Okay, will do.'

No, I damn well won't, she thought as she gestured to Debbie to follow her back. There was no knowing what the next few months would hold for Lydia but she should still have access to what was still her home. Just in case.

Soon, they were backing out of the parking space and turning onto the road out of the estate, the sewing machine sitting on Debbie's lap, just as she'd predicted. While waiting to exit the junction, Grace saw that Lydia was sitting rigidly in her seat, staring straight ahead. As she moved out into the flow of traffic on the main road, she gave Lydia a sideways glance and noted that her friend never once looked back.

TWENTY-THREE

'Okay, if you take a right turn here...' Debbie directed Grace to the mews, completely forgetting that Grace and Lydia had helped her home the night she'd gotten drunk after Dale moved out. 'Just follow the road around the bend and I'm there on the right.'

When the car came to a halt, Debbie opened the door and wriggled out from under the sewing machine, placing it down on the back seat.

'Here, I'll show you both up to the flat and then come back for the stuff. Let's get you inside first, Lydia, and make you comfortable.'

She led the way down the alleyway with Lydia behind her and Grace bringing up the rear, pulling one of the suitcases behind her. They came into a small courtyard with a little seated area and plant pots scattered around. The outside solar lamps had come on and it all looked very cosy.

'We need to go up these stairs, Lyds, let me give you a hand.'

'Thanks, Debs, sitting in the car has caused me to

stiffen up.'

Debbie felt her heart contract at seeing her friend walking like an elderly lady and not the vibrant woman she usually was. She'd managed to keep her emotions in check when they'd arrived at Lydia's because she hadn't wanted to cause more upset but she'd been absolutely seething with anger at what had happened. Davie was *so* lucky he hadn't returned home while they'd still been there as she wouldn't have been responsible for her actions if he had!

When they reached the top of the external staircase, Debbie pointed Lydia to the left and slipped past her to open the door. She stepped inside and headed straight for the lounge, glad she'd put the heating on before going out as it was still nippy at night and the flat felt lovely and snug. She flicked the light switch as they walked in and over to the chair which wasn't as soft as the sofa and would give Lydia more support while she was sore.

'Here, sit yourself down.'

When she was seated, Debbie carefully put a throw around her shoulders.

'Would you like a tea or coffee?'

'I could murder a coffee.'

'Where will I put this?'

Debbie looked over her shoulder to see Grace pointing towards the suitcase.

'Oh, through that door just there please.'

She inclined her head towards her own bedroom. There was no way Lydia was in a fit state to be clambering up and down the miniscule space in the spare room.

'I'll ask Grace to sort out drinks while I go and bring up the rest of your stuff.'

'I'll go, Debbie.'

'You did the driving. I'll only be a couple of minutes. You can have the coffees ready for my return.'

Grace handed over the keys and she ran back down to

the car where she opened the back door and began hauling out the sewing machine.

'Right, ya brute, let's get you sorted first.'

'Talking to inanimate objects, Miss Debbie, that's a guaranteed way to get yourself locked up.'

'Oh, Cedric, you gave me a shock there.'

She smiled at her neighbour. Cedric was a lovely man – always so polite and kind. He had a gentle Caribbean lilt to his voice and Debbie could listen to him talk until the cows came home. She reckoned he was in his late forties to early fifties.

'Here, let me carry that for you.'

'Oh, there's no need, I've got it.'

'Now, Miss Debs, what kind of man would I be if I were to let you cart that heavy thing up the stairs all by yourself?'

'I can manage.'

'I'm sure you can but my mother would come right down out of the heavens above and give me a slap if she thought I'd allowed a lady to carry a heavy object while I had nothing but fresh air in my hands. Please allow me to help.'

'Thank you, that's most kind. If you can take the machine, I can manage the suitcase and holdall.'

Cedric waited while she emptied the car and locked it then followed her along the alley.

'So, what's this, Miss Debs, taking up sewing to put me out of business?'

His deep, throaty chuckle echoed down towards her.

'Haha! No, definitely not, you're quite safe there. My friend is staying with me for a while; the machine is hers.'

'Ah, bringing in a labourer to put me out of business.'

Debbie glanced round at him and chuckled, 'I reckon it would take more than that to move you out, Cedric. I can't compete with your skills.'

On that score, she had no doubt. She'd once asked him to put together a shirt for Dale for a fancy-dress bash they'd attended and she'd been astonished by how perfect his seam work had been. She'd been very impressed.

'If you can just pop the machine on the table in the lounge, that would be most helpful.'

He walked into the lounge behind her and the startled look on Lydia's face had her mentally kicking herself.

Stupid woman! The last thing Lydia needed was a stranger seeing her like this. Bugger! Knowing it was too late to do anything now, she exchanged a small look with Cedric, thanked him for his help and showed him out, locking the door behind him.

She dashed back into the lounge.

'Oh, Lydia, I'm so sorry, I simply didn't think. Cedric lives next door and offered to help me carry up your stuff. I'm such a doughball!'

'It's okay.'

Grace was walking in with their coffees, one mug with a straw in it for Lydia, when there was a gentle tap on the back door. She looked at Debbie, who looked back, gave a small shrug and then closed the lounge door before going to answer.

'Oh, Cedric…'

Her neighbour handed over a carrier bag.

'For your friend,' he said in a soft, gentle voice. 'Cider vinegar. It's excellent for helping with bruising. A couple of cups in a warm bath will help to ease her aches. Also, if you soak the cotton wool with neat vinegar and hold it against the bruises, it helps them to disperse quicker. Let me know if I can be of any further assistance. My van is available should you need it.'

'Cedric, you are too kind. Thank you.'

'You're welcome, Miss Debbie.'

He stepped away and she closed the door.

'Who was it?'

Grace looked up as she walked back into the lounge with the bag.

'It was Cedric, he was passing on some treatment advice for bruising and gave me some cider vinegar.'

Lydia let out a snort.

'Oh, great! I'm going to smell like a chip shop again!'

'Again?' Debbie looked at Grace before they both turned to look at Lydia.

'My gran used to do the vinegar remedy on me when I was little and bruised my shins or whatever. From memory, it does work quite well. That was very kind of your neighbour to be so helpful.'

'Cedric is a lovely man. You'll get to meet him once you're feeling up to it.'

'Debbie, I won't be in your hair for long, just until I find somewhere.'

'Lydia Beaumont! You can stay here for as long as you want to. You're not in my hair, in my way or in anything else you can think of! Okay? Now, are you up to telling us what happened or would you prefer to leave it for the moment?'

'Would you be offended if we put it off for now? I'm aching and sore and even talking is painful.'

'Of course, we're not offended although I'd be happier if you would let us take you to hospital to get checked over. You could have broken ribs or a concussion or anything. You said you blacked out, didn't you?'

'Grace, I'll be okay. My ribs are bruised but I doubt they're broken.'

'How do you know? You're not a doctor.'

Lydia was able to give them a ghost of a smile.

'I'm just sure.'

'Very well but there's something I would like to do, Lydia, and you may not be agreeable, and it could be

148

painful, but I want to photograph your injuries.'

'Oh, I couldn't.'

Debbie sat down on the arm of the chair and took Lydia's hand.

'Lyds, Grace is right, we need to document what's happened. I'm not saying,' she held up her hand as she saw Lydia was about to speak, 'that there will ever be a need to use them but it's better to have the pics and not need them than to need the pics and not have them. You don't know what's going to happen next, it's merely a precaution.'

'I can tell you exactly what's happening next. I'm getting a divorce and if I never see either of them again, it'll be too soon!'

A thought suddenly hit Debbie and she voiced it without thinking, 'You don't think Dave will come looking for you, do you?'

Both Grace and Lydia turned to look at her and both with expressions of concern.

'I… I don't think he would but… I don't know, I really don't.'

'Tell you what,' Grace leant forward, 'I have an idea…'

Thirty minutes later, once Lydia had lowered herself into a warm, vinegary bath, Grace sent a couple of the photographs she'd taken to Dave along with the words, "This is what YOUR son is capable of! Try to find me and I will go to the police. My solicitor will be in touch in due course. Lydia".

She then sent copies to her own phone, to Debbie's, and also synced them to her Cloud account.

'Just in case!' she said with a grim look on her face. 'Just in case!'

TWENTY-FOUR

Lydia slowly opened one eye and then equally slowly, opened the other. With great care, she turned over onto her back and lay looking up at Debbie's bedroom ceiling.

It was Saturday and her third day of being at Debbie's place. She'd slept most of Thursday and Friday, her body doing its best to heal while she was out of it. The swelling and bruising had really come out over that time but she felt a little less achy this morning. Cedric's vinegar had definitely helped and she must be sure to thank him when she was in a position to face him.

She looked at the clock on the bedside table and saw it was after ten o'clock. Normally, on a Saturday morning, she'd be up to her elbows in soapy hair and perming lotion. She couldn't remember the last time she'd taken a Saturday off. Thank goodness Heather had stepped up and was happy about filling in during her absence. Grace had called her on Wednesday night telling her that she'd fallen down the stairs – an abridged version of the truth – and had asked if she'd be okay to cover for the next week or so. Lydia had just about collapsed when she heard Grace say this but

Grace had motioned to her to be quiet and explained, when she came off the phone, it would take at least that long for her body to heal enough to take the strain of the constant standing that doing her job entailed.

She grimaced to herself. At the time, she hadn't believed her friend but now, still feeling like she did, she was glad Grace had been a bit bossy and taken the matter in hand if, for no other reason, than if she had she turned up at the shop with a face looking like it had done a few rounds with Muhammed Ali, there would have been questions galore and she just wasn't ready to face up to those yet. She still hadn't told Gracie and Debbie the full story. All they knew was that Davie had been high and attacked her. She was planning to tell all tomorrow. Debbie had invited Grace round for Sunday lunch and it was the perfect time to bare her soul to them.

A big sigh slipped out from between her lips. If she hadn't been so damned proud and had taken up Debbie's offer of the spare room sooner, this could have been avoided. She knew she was lucky to have come away with nothing more than some extreme bruising and a headache. It could have been considerably worse.

There was also the silver lining to be found – something her gran had always insisted she looked for when faced with bad times – and in this case, it was knowing she was definitely doing the right thing by leaving. Had Davie not attacked her, and she'd just left as she'd intended, a little part of her would always have wondered if she'd done the right thing, had given in too easily or should she have tried harder?

Now, however, those worries would never surface because if she'd stayed, she could have ended up dead. Dave wasn't prepared to listen to her when she'd told him about Davie's escalating drug use so now, he could deal with the consequences.

Grace had turned off and hidden her phone after she'd sent the text to Dave so Lydia didn't know what his response had been to the photographs. She'd check it out at some point but she wasn't strong enough for that today.

What she was strong enough for, though, was getting up and getting dressed. If the swelling in her face had gone down, she might even put a little makeup on to cover the worst of the bruising and go down to the shop to sit with Debbie for a while. A change of scenery would be just the ticket.

Two hours later, she wandered down the internal stairs to the shop and quietly slipped out the connecting door, not wanting to disturb Debbie if she should happen to be with a customer but when she walked round to the shop floor, she found Debbie alone at the counter, putting some items on hangers.

'Hey, Debbie, got some time for a visitor?'

'Lydia! Of course I have! Welcome to my little slice of heaven. How are you feeling today?'

'Back on track to being human again. The bruises are still livid under the clothing but Cedric's cider vinegar has certainly helped on my face which is not so easy to hide.'

'You've done a good job with your makeup. You can barely see them unless you look really hard. Was it sore putting your face on?'

'There were a few "ouchy" moments, especially covering up the splits on my lips, but I got there. The swelling has also subsided a little although I still resemble a battered football. Anyway, I hope you don't mind me popping down – I just needed to see something different for a little while.'

'Don't be so daft! I'm thrilled you felt up to coming down. It's been busy this morning but has eased off in the last ten minutes which is why I now have the time to replace these goodies back onto their hangers and get them out on the rails again.'

Lydia leant across and picked up a blouse which was sticking out of the pile.

'Oh, this is a beauty.'

'Ah yes, it's not a big name – just Next – but I believe it's from the early nineties which makes it desirable now.'

'Thanks, Debbie, make me feel old, why don't you?' she laughed.

'You're not that old?'

'Debbie, I was a kid in the nineties, so yes, I am!'

'Well, you don't look it and you certainly don't act it.'

Lydia held the blouse up. It had slightly puffed sleeves with long cuffs and six little pearl buttons on each. The bodice was fitted and the bottom was fluted all the way round. It really was a pretty little number.

'You should try it on, I think it would suit you.'

'Oh, I couldn't…'

'Why not? It's your size. Look, I'll pop it behind the door and you can take it up with you. Try it when you feel up to it.'

'But I'll never go anywhere to wear it.'

'But you might.'

She was about to reply when a girl came in and began mooching through the rails.

'If I can help you with anything, please ask. We also have a fitting room if you'd like to try on any items you like the look of.'

The girl smiled her thanks and carried on browsing.

'I'll go back up and get out of your hair. You don't need me getting in your way.'

'No, please stay. Well, if you feel up to it. It's nice to have some company. I used to have a Saturday girl but she went off to college and I've not got around to replacing her yet.'

The customer came over just then with a dress in her

hand and Debbie took her to the fitting room. A few minutes later she came out to ask their opinion. Lydia could see straight away that the colour did her no favours whatsoever. With her strawberry blonde hair, the shade of yellow made her look washed out which was a pity because the style of the dress was perfect on her. She held her counsel, however, and let Debbie run the show. She was interested to hear what she had to say.

'Well…' Debbie tilted her head to one side as she assessed the situation. 'That is totally your style – it looks amazing – but the colour is letting you down. It's not for you at all.'

The girl's shoulders slumped in disappointment.

'That's what I thought too but wanted a second opinion in the hope I was wrong. As you say, the style is bang on but the colour is way off. I don't suppose you have it in green, do you?'

'I'm sorry, it's a one-off.'

'Damn! It's for a wedding and I just can't find anything suitable. I've been searching high and low for the right outfit.'

'Where are you on the guest list?'

'First cousin. Not close enough to be in the main wedding party but close enough to be in more than one photograph. We're a tight-knit family. Ah well, back to the drawing board.'

The girl went back into the changing room and when she came back out, Lydia was sure she'd been crying. She replaced the dress on the rail, shot a smile in their direction and had her fingers on the door handle when Lydia suddenly called out, 'WAIT!'

The girl turned around to look at her and Debbie followed suit.

Swallowing hard and taking a deep breath, she asked, 'When's the wedding?'

'A month away but the hen do is next week and I've got other commitments after that. This is my last chance to find something.'

'Then why don't I make you a dress?'

Debbie's eyes widened at this but she kept quiet and let Lydia take the lead.

'You could do that?'

'I think so. Here, bring the dress over and let me have a closer look.'

The girl grabbed the hanger and almost threw the dress across the counter. Lydia looked closely at the cut, the seams, the darts and the component parts which when all put together, made this lovely item. Once upon a time, she would have been confident enough to take this on board – heck, she'd been making her own clothes and copying designs since she was in her early teens. It had just been a while and she was worried she may have lost the knack. She was on the verge of retracting her offer when Debbie gave her a little nudge, a smile and a small nod. She'd guessed where her head was at and that gave her the boost she needed.

'Right, well, it all looks fairly straightforward. What you need to do is find the material you like and I'll do the rest.'

'Oh, thank you so much. You're so kind.'

'Oh, it's okay. First though, I need to take your measurements and then I can work out how much material you'll need to buy. Oh…'

'What's the matter, Lyds?'

She turned to Debbie. 'I don't have a measuring tape.'

Debbie smiled brightly at her. 'But I know a man who does! I'll be right back.'

She ran out of the door, leaving a bemused Lydia and customer behind. A moment later she was back.

'Here, Cedric said you can keep it, he has plenty.'

For the first time in many years, Lydia felt a blush creep up her cheeks and she hid it by busying about, writing out a list of requirements, while the girl, whom she now knew was called Meghan, returned to the changing room to remove her outer clothes.

When Meghan left the shop thirty minutes later, she had a list of exactly what she had to buy, right down to the zipper length, and had a big smile on her face.

'You look pleased with yourself.'

'Oh, Debbie, I didn't step on your toes there, did I? I'm sorry, I didn't think… I just saw how disappointed—'

'Lydia, stop. I think it's fantastic! I was watching you while you discussed it with Meghan and you looked so happy. Vital, is the word. It was wonderful to see.'

She stepped away to sort out some shelves, leaving Lydia to think about what she'd said and realising that that was exactly how she felt! Excited! Something else that hadn't happened to her in a very long time!

TWENTY-FIVE

Debbie was humming quietly to herself as she replaced hangers on the rails and straightened shoes and bags on their stands. It had been a busy afternoon and she'd had some good sales. She wondered how much of it was down to Allan handing out her cards. No one had asked for the discount, however, so maybe it was just one of those lucky days when everyone decides they want something old and unique.

She walked back over to the counter. Lydia had returned upstairs an hour earlier after holding the fort while she'd popped out to the little stationers on the high street to pick up a roll of brown paper for Lydia to cut her pattern from. It had been lovely to see the change in her demeanour as she'd talked to Meghan whilst taking her measurements. It had been "darts this" and "tucks that" along with "a bit of lace here" and "some ribbon there" – she was glowing like a beacon by the time the girl walked out of the shop. Debbie had never seen her so animated before. It was clear she had a passion for dressmaking and it would be interesting to see the finished product.

The bell above the door pinged and Debbie had to stifle a groan. It was almost closing time and she was looking forward to joining Lydia over a bottle of wine – customers were wonderful but she did like to close on time, especially on a Saturday.

She mustered up a smile, plastered it onto her face and turned around.

'Allan! Hi!'

The plastered smile was immediately replaced with a genuine one.

'Hey, you, how are things? Had a good day?' He gave her one of his little shy smiles, his head tilted slightly downwards and his voice quiet, almost as though he was apologising for being there.

'I have actually! One of the best for a long time.'

'Ah, that's great to hear! You sell quality stuff; it's good for people to know that.'

'Did you have anything to do with it? Were you handing out my cards on Piccadilly Circus? Or did you just promise your ladies a pay rise if they popped in?'

'Oh!'

His face fell and he suddenly looked totally forlorn.

'Hey, what's the matter? What did I say?'

'It's just... well... you know who I am now, don't you?'

'Er, yes! I knew who you were when you were here on Wednesday. So? What's that got to do with the price of cheese?'

'You'll be different now.'

'No, I won't!'

'Yes, you will. Everyone always is.'

'Did I seem different towards you three days ago, when you were upsetting my postman? Or when we went for lunch?'

'No, you were just you.'

158

'But I knew all about you then. Grace filled me in on Tuesday night, unable to get her head around that I wasn't aware of your "presence" shall we say, when I met you.'

'But—'

'No "buts", Allan, to me, you're still the nerdy geek I met at a charity bash who kindly sat in the garden with me until it was home time. All the other "stuff" holds no interest for me.'

'Prove it!'

'I'm sorry? What?'

'Prove it! Prove that you still like the nerdy geek by going out with him tonight. There's a small cinema in Soho doing back-to-back showings of the first three Star Wars films and I have tickets.'

'When you say "first three" you mean…'

'The originals from the seventies.'

'Oh, that does sound good but I'm afraid I can't.'

'Oh! Of course! It's Saturday – a lovely lady like you is already going to have plans. I'm sorry. I didn't think.'

'Will you stop blooming apologising all the time.'

'Sorry.'

'Seriously?'

'Sor— force of habit'

'We're going to have a conversation about that at some point, however, the reason I can't come ou—'

'Debbie, sorry to be a bother but do you happen to have a pencil I can borr— Oh, I'm sorry, I didn't realise you had company.'

'Hey, Lydia, you're fine. This is Allan, come and say hello. Allan, this is my friend Lydia who I told you about. She's just moved in with me on Wednesday and we were planning to spend our first Saturday night chewing the fat over a bottle of wine. You know, the kind of getting to know your flatmate better sort of thing.'

Debbie didn't miss the disappointment on Allan's face.

159

Blimey, did this bloke ever wear his heart on his sleeve or what?

'No, no. I understand. Silly of me to ask. Impulsive at times.'

His stilted speech alerted her to the fact that Allan was now feeling anxious. It was something she'd sussed out the first night they'd met and it had popped up a couple of times when they were having lunch on Wednesday.

'Actually, Debbie, I'd be more than happy to do the wine thing tomorrow. I've got the bit between my teeth on this dress and I'd love to spend a few more hours on it.'

'But you'd be on your own.'

'Debs, my love, I know you mean well but I've been home alone many times and, do you know what, being here on my own would be lovely. I can really relax without wondering what's going to walk through the door and upset me. Please, go out with Allan and have a wonderful time.'

Debbie looked between the two – it would appear the decision had been made for her and she could appreciate Lydia's desire for a little solitude. She'd been through so much and now she was feeling stronger, she needed time to process all that had happened.

'Okay, I'll do the cinema but there are conditions.'

'Which are?'

She didn't miss Allan's look of cautious suspicion.

'I need a large bucket of sweet popcorn which is all mine – no sharies! An equally large bucket of Coke, at least two bags of Maltesers and two hot dogs with onions and tomato sauce.'

'Just a small snack, then?'

'Look, we're talking the best part of six hours and sixteen minutes of celluloid plus breaks in between. That's a long night, so plenty of sustenance will be required.'

'Debs, trust me, when you see what I'll be eating, yours

will seem like a small snack. Put me in a dark room with a big screen movie and my stomach gets the idea that we've been plunged back into the Dark Ages and demands a constant supply of food!'

'Well, it sounds like you two are going to have a whale of a time so I'm going to head upstairs and possibly treat myself to a pizza.'

'I'll come up with you and get changed. I'll show you where the takeaway menus are. Allan, are you okay to wait here for ten minutes?'

'Of course. I can't wait to see your outfit.'

'Allan, I am not wearing a Princess Leia outfit.'

'You're so boring!'

'Be that as it may, it ain't happening.'

'Fine.'

He pretended to grumble but she'd spotted the little smile on his lips and as she walked up the stairs, she found herself looking forward to the night ahead.

TWENTY-SIX

Grace gave a wide yawn and stretched out the length of the bed. Her clock said eight thirty and she felt quite decadent still being in bed at that time. She had, however, worked from seven till seven the day before so she'd earned her Sunday morning lie-in.

A sudden impulse struck her. She jumped out of bed, went down to the kitchen, made some coffee along with a few slices of toast and marmalade, put it on a tray and took it back upstairs. She stopped along the way to pick up a book she'd been meaning to read for months and snuggled back between the sheets to treat herself to a few hours of reading and chilling. It dawned on her, as she plumped the pillows up behind her, that she hadn't done this kind of Sunday chilling since she'd left uni. It was long overdue.

Two hours later, she dragged herself out of the wet, windswept woods and the serial killer stalking her in the dark, put the bookmark in its place and went for a shower. She could easily have stayed where she was until teatime, however she had not one but two engagements today. The first was with Jake to see her new sofa in all its finished glory and the second was a late Sunday lunch with Debbie and Lydia. Although she'd made a point of speaking with both of them every day since she'd gone to Lydia's rescue with Debs, there hadn't been the opportunity to visit and she found she was looking forward to seeing them. Their friendship had moved onto a new level although she'd have preferred for it to have happened without Lydia being half beaten to death.

When she was ready to leave the house, she picked up her car keys but then hesitated. The tube was the quicker option for getting to Jake's place and if there was wine with dinner, she'd have to stick to soft drinks. The tube was only about ten minutes from Debbie's place and she could get a taxi back after that. Decision made, she put the keys back in the drawer, grabbed her handbag, Oyster card and a jacket and headed out the door.

As the tube gently rocked her back and forth, Grace felt a frisson of excitement in the pit of her stomach and she was honest enough to admit it wasn't all reserved for seeing her sofa. She'd enjoyed her unexpected dinner with Jake and had surprised herself by thinking about it several times since as she'd found being in his company relaxing. They were able to talk about things without it feeling like a competition. Most of the men she'd spent time with in the past were city professionals in one guise or another and there was a constant feeling of one-upmanship. It didn't matter what she'd done, who she'd seen, or where she had been, they always had to have done it just that little bit better or a little more impressively. It was exhausting and was one of the reasons why she'd gradually stopped dating. Jake, however, had listened intently to whatever she'd been sharing, laughed in the appropriate places and asked further questions, showing that he was genuinely interested. It had made a pleasant change.

When she alighted from the tube, she had to stop herself

from jogging down the road. It was only the fact that arriving all sweaty, with a shiny face and puffing like a steam train, would not have been a good look, that stopped her. To compensate, however, her speed walking was of a rate that had her thinking about applying for the Olympics. Soon, she was at his gate and just managed to stop herself redoing her lippy. Heck, she was not about to show herself as trying too hard. He was a lovely man – he probably had female clients throwing themselves at him all the time. Well, she wasn't going to be one of them!

She pushed the button on the intercom and when his voice welcomed her through the little speaker, she made a point of ignoring the fluttering in her belly.

No! She was *not* going there!

He was waiting by the door of the workshop and beckoned her over as she came down the covered walkway.

'Hello, Grace, how are you today?'

'Hey, Jake. I'm good, thank you. Very excited to be here again.'

'Oh, yes?'

'Err, yes, excited to see my sofa. It feels like a lifetime since I was here, telling you what I was hoping you could create.'

'Of course. I'm sorry about the delay in completion but I wanted to get the correct material for upholstering and felt it was worth the wait to get it perfect. I hope you understand.'

'Jake, like I said at the time – this is your masterpiece and I trust your judgement. You know what I was looking for and I'm sure you're about to deliver in spades.'

'Hmm, we'll see.'

'You doubt yourself— Oh!'

A sudden nudge on the back of her leg had her losing her balance and grabbing a hold of Jake otherwise she'd have gone flat on her face.

'What the hell?'

She looked round and saw a black cocker spaniel, tongue hanging out and its mouth wide open as though it was laughing at her.

'Was that you?' she asked in a stern tone. 'Are you a cheeky dog?'

She hunkered down and was rewarded with a big, sloppy lick which had her bursting out laughing. She ruffled the fur behind the floppy ears and scratched under its chin.

'Okay, you're a cutie and you know it. What's your name?'

'He's called Perfectly Frank. Frank to his friends.'

'Perfectly Frank?'

'Yes, because he's perfect and he's Frank. So, he's Perfectly Frank.'

She laughed again at the silly but, dare she say it, perfect name.

'I love it! That's so clever.'

'We think so, don't we, boy?'

Frank replied with a woof before picking up the ball which he'd previously prodded her with.

'I'm guessing he wants me to throw it for him.'

'He does but I can tell you now, if you do, your arm will drop off before you tire him out so I suggest you don't.'

'Sorry, handsome chap, not this time, I'm afraid.'

'Are you still talking to Frank?'

'Err…' she turned round to see the cheeky grin on his face and the twinkle in his eye. 'Yes, I am. You should be ashamed of yourself, trying to steal your dog's compliments. Shame on you.'

'Hey, a bloke has to grab all the compliments he can when he gets to my age. I wasn't about to let a good one like that go to the dog.'

'Well, tough. It's his. However, if you show me a very nice sofa, I may well be showering you with compliments of your own.'

'Well, when you put it like that, what are we hanging around here for? Follow me.'

He led her inside and walked over to the other side of the shed to where a large dust sheet covered whatever was underneath.

She caught a tantalising glimpse of a walnut-coloured leg but nothing more. Suddenly, it felt like her heart was in her throat and she began to grow scared, worried that, after all this, she wouldn't like it.

'Close your eyes.'

She did as she was told and found herself holding her breath as she listened to the light rustle of the covering being removed.

'Okay, open them.'

Grace couldn't bring herself to respond immediately. A few seconds passed and her heart was thundering while her palms grew clammy. Knowing that the longer she waited, the worse it would be, so, counting to three, she threw her eyes open and stared at the large piece of furniture in front of her.

And stared.

And stared.

And stared.

Eventually, Jake broke the silence.

'Err, Grace? Care to say something? Anything?'

'Jake… it's… it's… it's beautiful. It really, truly is. It's even nicer than the one I saw in the shop. This is total perfection. It's amazing.'

And it was. The sofa had one static arm, to the left as she faced it and it was as high as she'd wanted it to be. There was a nice cosy corner to burrow into. The back of the sofa was the same height all the way round the corner

166

and the other end was finished off with a large footstool. What really had her almost crying tears of joy was the colour. It was the darkest shade of red, almost burgundy, but he'd used Damask fabric which meant there were deeper and lighter shades across it. The pattern gave the sofa a kind of vibrancy and made it appear more than just an item of furniture. She couldn't understand how he'd managed to make it more of a statement than just a place to park your butt, but he had and it was why every interior designer within the M25 was after his work.

'So, you like it, then?'

'Oh, it'll do, I suppose. When all you've got is a sofa with no legs to sit on, one doesn't have the right to be too fussy.'

'I suppose, when you put it like that…'

'Jake, it's stunning. I'm messing with you. I love it. I've never had a piece of furniture that has left me breathless before. In fact, thinking about it, there's not been much in my adult life that's left me breathless but you've managed it today.'

'I've managed it or the sofa has?'

'Honestly? Are you at it again? Trying to steal the sofa's compliments now – just how desperate are you?'

'Terribly! I'm a needy individual – what can I say?'

'Well, you do make a decent sofa, I'll give you that. Can I sit on it?'

'Of course you can bloody sit on it – that's what it's for! Go on, try it out.'

She gently lowered herself down, hoping it would be as welcoming as the one in the shop had been and was thrilled beyond belief to find it even cosier. Despite having a rigid back, it supported you yet cuddled you at the same time. She was going to have to ration her minutes on this sofa because if she didn't, she'd be spending most of her nights on it. Although, she supposed, that was kind of the point;

to create a home she wanted to be in and which relaxed her. This sofa was going to go a long way towards doing just that.

With more than a touch of regret, she pushed herself back onto her feet.

'Okay, it's official. I love it to bits. How soon can you get it into my house? And, more to the point, HOW are you going to get it into my house?'

Out of the blue, this thought hit her hard! She lived in a little terraced house. The doors were not the biggest on the planet and the thought of having to take the window out terrified her. One of the blokes at work had had to do that when his wife hadn't taken the door width into account when she'd bought a new sideboard. They'd had to take the window out to get the sideboard in and then they'd had some right fun and games getting it back in again.

'Hey, don't you worry about that. It all comes apart in a certain way that'll get it in without any problems. It does mean, however, that I will need to come over to assemble it in your room. Will that be a problem?'

He was standing close to her, close enough for his aftershave and woody scent to make her feel lightheaded again and she was sure she swayed – swooned? – ever so slightly.

'Erm, no, no… that wouldn't be a problem at all.'

He walked away, over to a desk in the far corner, and the air where he'd been standing suddenly felt chilly. His body heat had been keeping her warm and she only noticed it now that he was no longer by her side.

'When would it suit you to take delivery? I have a firm who'll bring it to you and then I can pop round and put it all together.'

'Let me see…'

She took her phone out of her bag and checked her diary, resisting the temptation to take a sneaky snapshot of the sofa. After all, Jake had specified she was to invite people round to see it, photographs would be cheating. Or it felt that way to her.

'I could get away early on Thursday if your firm is happy to do a late afternoon delivery – say just after four?'

'That'll be fine. They're very flexible – I give them a lot of business.' He threw her a small wink and she could feel little prickles akin to small electric shocks darting around her body. It seemed the longer she was in his presence, the more Jake Valentine was affecting her.

'And the assembling?'

'If Thursday evening works for you, I'm more than happy to put it together then.'

'That would be perfect, thank you. And, if you fancy, I could make dinner as a thank you. You know, for working out of hours.'

Eh? Where on earth had *that* come from? She didn't invite people to dinner, it wasn't her thing at all. Hell, *cooking* wasn't her thing either!

'Why, that would be very nice. Thank you. I'd like that.'

'Great. Sorted. Well, I'd better get a move on, I've got a lunch date with my girlfriends and they'll be wanting to hear all about my visit here. Err, to see the sofa of course.'

'Don't forget to tell them about the handsome man who practically swept you off your feet?'

'Huh?'

Shit, did he really have mind-reading skills? Was her poker face slipping?

'Perfectly Frank. He'll be devastated to know you've forgotten about him already.'

'Oh, I hadn't forgotten – after all, how could I forget someone so perfect?'

'Indeed, how could you?"

His soft brown eyes held her gaze and it took all the

willpower she possessed to step back, turn around and begin making her way to the door. He followed her down to the outside gate and as he opened it for her to walk through, he whispered, 'Till Thursday. I'm really looking forward to it.'

She turned around in surprise but he'd already closed the gate behind her, leaving her standing in the lane, gawping like a goldfish.

Blimey, she thought, as she walked down the lane to the main road. I know I've heard about animal attraction before but I never realised until now that it really did exist. Wait until I tell the girls this one.

TWENTY-SEVEN

'Are you telling me, Grace Mitchell, that you sat on this juicy gossip all day Sunday and never mentioned a word? Not even the tiniest hint of a whisper?'

Due to Lydia's still tender and delicate state, they were having their Pie & Prosecco night in the flat. Debbie had popped up to the pub, explained about Lydia's "fall down the stairs" and they'd sorted out takeaway boxes for their extra special customers.

'Sunday was your day, Lydia. Given the severity of what you were telling us, it didn't seem appropriate to share. Besides, it was kind of nice keeping it to myself for a few days, just while I got my head around it.'

'So, is this the start of a beautiful relationship?'

'I don't know, Debs, maybe…'

Lydia watched her friend talking and saw the hint of hope on her face. There was clearly an attraction to this Jake fella, she just prayed it was mutual and it wasn't mindless flirting on his part with a female client. After all, some people will do anything for a sale although this one was a done deal so perhaps the man was being genuine.

'You said he was coming round on Thursday evening to put the sofa in place – what's happening after that? Do you think he'll ask you out for dinner again?'

'Well, that's the bit I haven't shared yet – I've offered to cook dinner for him!'

'You've done what?'

Lydia felt like shaking her head to check her ears had heard correctly.

'Grace, by your own admission, you don't cook. If you learnt how to use your cooker, M&S Food Hall would see a drop in their share price!'

'I know, Lyds, you don't need to tell me what a faux pas I've made there.'

'What on earth possessed you?' The look on Debbie's face spoke for all of them.

'I didn't think. It just popped out. I was as surprised as you guys are.'

'How do you propose to get around it?'

'I figured maybe steak and chips? I've got one of those air fryer things in a cupboard somewhere and a few women in the office rate them. They say the chips come out a treat. As far as I know, they use frozen ones. And how difficult are steaks to cook? I've seen a few cooking shows – if I buy them tomorrow, they can marinade overnight in some steak flavouring stuff which I've seen on the shelves.'

'Hark at Gordon Ramsay here!' Lydia rolled her eyes in despair. 'Steak flavouring stuff! Honestly! Look, I know a quick marinade recipe, I'll write it down for you before you leave. You might also want to pick up some salad bits, perhaps some dips to pick at while the main course is cooking. Just to make it look like you've been in your kitchen for more than coffee and toast.'

'And pizza.'

'Huh?' Lydia looked at Debbie who was grinning like a good 'un.

'Pizza. We know Grace is good at reheating left-over pizza in her microwave. I thought you were being unfair by reducing her repertoire to just toast and coffee.'

'I suppose you both think you're hilarious!'

Lydia and Debbie were too busy laughing to be able to reply.

'Fine. So, that's steak and chips with dips and salad on the side. Pudding? Do I add that?'

'Why not grab something simple like a cheesecake. Serve it up with a dollop of extra thick cream.'

'Yes, I like the sound of that. Again, fairly simple.'

'Just a quick question – have you seen the cooking scene in the film "Bridget Jones's Diary"?'

'Oh, will you two just sod off!'

Grace smiled good naturedly as Debbie leant against Lydia, the pair of them cackling like two old witches.

'Anyway, Debbie,' Grace looked pointedly to her left, 'from what I've heard, I'm not the only one with a budding romance going on. You were also rather quiet on Sunday.'

'Only because I was blooming knackered! I hadn't planned a Stars Wars marathon when I rolled out of bed on Saturday morning. And it had been an especially busy day in the shop.'

'I forgot to ask; did you get to the bottom of that – did Allan have anything to do with it?'

'In a roundabout way, Lydia. He mentioned the shop to a work colleague who looked up my pathetic excuse for a website. She liked what she saw so tagged it, along with pics of the stock, on social media. Apparently, she's a bit of an Instagram guru with a load of followers and Saturday was the result of that. I have to say they're still coming in so I'm not going to complain about the free publicity.'

'But what about Allan? What's the story there? That's the second date you've been on together.'

'Well, lunch at Luigi's wasn't exactly a date and I

wouldn't class Saturday night as one either.'

'I would. Lydia, would you?'

'Darn right I would. He asked you to join him, didn't he?'

'Yeeeeees...'

'Then that sounds like a date to me! I'm sure you agree, Grace.'

'Yup! That was definitely a date.'

'I'm not sure Allan would see it that way.'

'Did he kiss you at any time?'

'Nope.'

'Put his arm around you?'

'Nope.'

'Hold your hand?'

'Nope! There was no physical contact so it wasn't a date.'

Lydia looked over at Grace. 'She might have a point.'

'Or maybe he's just biding his time. Does he know about Dale?'

'It came out while we were talking at the charity thing, when he asked me how I'd ended up being there.'

'Then he's definitely biding his time.'

'To be honest, ladies, I don't think he is. He's not that kind of bloke. His face always reveals what he's thinking – or I think it does. I don't believe he has many friends although that's an assumption on my part which I've deduced from his insecurity around people. I could be wrong. I mean, you don't get to be the head of a massive conglomerate without a few tricks up your sleeve.'

'When are you seeing him again?'

'I don't know – he didn't ask.'

'Perhaps, Debbie, it's your turn,' Lydia said softly.

'How do you mean?'

'Well, the lad has turned up twice at the shop to see you and mustered up the courage to invite you to the cinema with him. It's your turn to let him know this thing, friendship or otherwise, is not one-sided. You need to give him something back.'

'Yes, you're right. I hadn't thought of it like that. But what can I do? He's got the billions to do anything he wants – how can I come up with something that he'll find interesting?'

'Debs, I don't think two tickets for the cinema put any kind of dent in his bank balance. You went for lunch at the little trattoria over the street. I get the feeling Allan doesn't have expensive tastes so why not keep it simple. Does he like museums? There's plenty of them in London. Or maybe a boat trip down the Thames to Greenwich followed by a picnic in the park there. Or, one of my favourites, is to play tourist for a day. Go and see all the sights we take for granted because we grew up with them on our doorstep.'

'You're right, Grace, I've been letting his corporate persona colour my judgement a little which I vowed not to do. I need to stay focused on the person behind that.'

'Debs, you do like him, don't you?'

'Yes, Lyds, I do, quite a bit, as it happens. I suppose I'm still adjusting to being in the company of someone different. It does feel strange after three years with Dale although I've enjoyed the time we've spent together so far and I'd be happy to spend more time with him.'

'Then come up with something to do and let him know.'

'I will. So, that's Grace and I sorted on the romance front at the moment, what about you, Lydia? We need to find you someone nice.'

Lydia let out a laugh but inside her stomach did a nauseating flip. Quite frankly, the thought of being in a relationship again made her feel sick. She couldn't even entertain the idea. The last week had been blissful, despite her aches and pains, and she was quite happy to keep it like that for now.

'Thank you for thinking of me, Debbie, but let's wait till I'm unshackled from my current incumbent before we go down that road.'

'Well, now that Grace has found you a good lawyer, hopefully it won't be too long.'

'Hmm, hopefully.'

Grace must have sensed her discomfort for she subtly drew Debbie's thoughts back to Allan and possible things for them both to do. Lydia gave her a small, grateful smile. Maybe one day she'd feel comfortable being in the company of a new man but not now and not in the foreseeable future. In fact, even the distant future wasn't looking good at this time!

TWENTY-EIGHT

Grace looked at the pile of stuff in her front room. Everything was bubble-wrapped and it currently looked like the beginning of a zorbing festival for eight-year-olds! She'd pushed the old sofa, which now looked rather insipid when compared to its replacement, against the opposite wall to give Jake room to work in when he arrived. She'd ask him to help her carry it outside to the front garden so the council could come and take it away.

She looked at her watch and walked back to the kitchen to take the steaks out of the fridge. She'd read on the internet that it was better to cook them from room temperature and, given her lack of skills in that particular department, she wasn't leaving anything to chance.

The bowl had only just clanked down on the marble worktop when the doorbell rang. As she walked through the dining area, she paused for a second to check her reflection in the mirror over the fireplace. A quick smoothing of her bob ensured every hair was in place and she ran her pinkie around the edge of her lips to remove any smudging of her lipstick. Satisfied she looked presentable, she gave herself a sharp nod and then hurried to answer the door.

'Hi, Jake, please come in.'

She moved back to give him and the tool bag he was carrying space to manoeuvre past and then closed the door behind him.

'Good evening, Grace, I'm hoping the delivery boys have been and gone.'

'Yes, they have. Please go through.'

She pointed him towards the lounge and followed in behind him. He placed the bag on the floor and began counting the items on the pile. She kept quiet so as not to distract him and when he'd finished, he seemed happy with the total.

'Okay, Grace, first things first. We need to remove your old sofa – are you okay to help me take it to my van?'

'Oh, yes, sure! I was planning to ask the council to remove it.'

'Oh, no, you can't do that. It'll likely end up in some landfill site somewhere – I'll take it away and recycle it in one way or another. I never let anything go to waste if I can help it.'

'I see. Then, sure, fine – I'll help you carry it.'

She walked over to the piece of furniture, placed her hand on it and then stopped. She'd had this faithful old thing for many years and it was now suddenly a wrench to let it go.'

'Hey, Grace, you alright?'

'Uh, yeah, yes... just need a moment. I got this old thing when I moved off campus into digs in my second year at uni. I picked it up in a junk shop – it was probably third or fourth hand by the time it came to me – and I've spent a lot of time on it. It saw me through my studies and more than once I woke up with a book splayed over my face when I'd fallen asleep while swotting. This stain here is from when I graduated and came home more than the worse for wear after celebrating into the night. I fell asleep and drooled like a toddler. I never was able to remove it. When my mum died, I couldn't face going to bed to sleep and this sofa was my comfort space while I dealt with the grief. It's been a part of my life for a long time and it now feels difficult to let it go.'

The tears gathered in her eyes, blurring her vision.

'Hush now, it's alright to feel sad at saying goodbye. At least you know that by coming with me, it will have more to offer. Now, you grab that end and I'll get it from here.'

Jake's no-nonsense tone helped and she did as he'd asked. Ten minutes later, it was in the back of his van, he was in the lounge and she was in the kitchen having been told in no uncertain terms that he'd call for her when he was finished.

To keep herself occupied, she set the table, opened the patio doors to let in the warmer-than-usual April evening and wiped down the table and chairs on the outside deck, just in case they were enticed to sit out there after dinner. She then walked around checking the plant pots she'd placed around the little courtyard to see how they were doing now that spring was well and truly underway. Grace didn't consider herself to be a gardener of any kind but hoped that the few attempts she'd made would make it and she was therefore pleased to see green shoots pushing up through the dark soil.

As she stepped back into the kitchen, she could hear a lot of rustling going on and the click of the front door.

'Everything alright out there, Jake?'

'Yup! Nearly done. I'm just going to the van – no peeking while I'm gone.'

'Okay.'

'Promise?'

She rolled her eyes.

'Yes, I promise.'

It was only a few minutes later that she got the call.

'Okay, you can come in now.'

Excitement skipped in her chest as she walked to the lounge door. There was a brief moment of hesitation and then she threw the door wide and walked in.

'Wow! Just… wow! Wow! Wow!'

The sofa was now in situ and the room looked cosy and very inviting. Jake had moved about the few pieces of furniture which had been there so the tall, standing lamp was by the side of the sofa as you walked into the room and the matching lamp was on the little side table over in the alcove. By some miracle, it just managed to fit in against the bookcase. Then she realised – Jake had already "dressed" her room when he'd come to measure up. It was no miracle at all, he'd planned it like this from the off.

'It looks good, even if I say so myself.'

'Jake, it looks amazing. Thank you so much. I could never have imagined it would look like this.'

'It's what I do. I see the things others don't, I look beyond the obvious and find the potential. I'm glad you like it.'

'Like it? I LOVE it! I think my days at the office just became shorter now I know I have this gorgeous haven to come home to. Thank you.'

In a completely impulsive move, she threw her arms around him, hugged with all her might and placed a resounding kiss on his cheek.

'Oops! Sorry! I… er… I…'

She felt her face burning up as she stepped back.

'It's okay. That's the kind of thanks I can live with.'

Jake's easy smile and gentle expression helped her to compose herself.

'If you're hungry now, I'm all ready to begin cooking dinner.'

'Now that sounds good to me. Lead the way.'

'May I ask, if it's not too personal, when did your mum die?'

Grace looked down at the empty plates on the table. Her cooking hadn't been a disaster and the evening had been easy and relaxing. They'd been exchanging small snippets of themselves and it had been nice.

'Ten years ago, now.'

'But you still miss her.'

'Yes, I do. We were a close family – there was only the three of us.'

'No siblings, then?'

'No. In fact, there shouldn't even have been me.'

'I'm sorry?'

'I was the miracle baby. The baby that shouldn't have been but somehow was.'

'I don't follow.'

'My dad had mumps when he was a kid and... well... it was a severe case which led to the ultimate side-effects including infertility.'

'Ah! I get you now.'

'Against all the odds, however, I was created. My mum always said the determination of that little tadpole was very evident in my personality. If I want something, I won't stop until I have it.'

'Do you look like her or your dad?'

'Both. I have her blonde hair and blue eyes with his height and slender build.'

'At least you still have your father.'

'Hmmm...'

'Oh, not so good?'

'Mum's death hit him really badly. It was so sudden you see – she had a heart attack. Silly woman thought it was indigestion. Apparently not unusual in women. Did you know heart attacks kill more women than breast cancer? No? Neither did I. Anyway, Dad took it hard, floundered about for a few years and then started dating women half his age. Some have been younger than me. I try to keep my own counsel on it but he knows I don't approve. It's created a distance between us.'

'Do you know why he's doing this?'

'I've got a pretty good idea – he doesn't want to become too involved and risk being hurt again. He's choosing inappropriate women because he knows they're not long-term. I totally get it but it's not what Mum would have wanted. She only ever wanted us to be happy and she'd want him to make another woman as happy as he made her.'

'What about you, though? Are you happy?'

'I will be when I'm made a partner at work.'

'Is that your only goal?'

'It's my main one and the one that keeps me focused.'

'But when that moment comes, and I have no doubt that it will, who are you going to share the joy with? Who's going to be by your side celebrating with you?'

'My friends.'

'Really? Because when we first met, the day you ordered your sofa, I got the distinct impression that you're not much for socialising.'

'You're right, at that time I wasn't but I've been working on changing it. I have two friends, Debbie and Lydia, and we've been growing closer over the last few months. Different events in our lives have given our friendship more meaning and it's nice. Not necessarily the actual events themselves, some of those have been horrible, but the deepening camaraderie between us is good.'

'Ah, that's nice to hear. So, my creation in your lounge will be admired by other people as I requested.'

Grace couldn't help the wide smile that crossed her face.

'Yes, it most certainly will.'

'Excellent. And, since you seem to be all in on this new "friendship" thing – may I ask you out on a date? Would that be acceptable?'

'Oh? Erm... do you always date your clients?'

SHUT UP! the voice in her head screamed loudly. The bloke who'd been giving her hot flushes whenever she'd thought of him over the last two months, had just asked her out and she was trying to put him off – what on *earth* was her problem?

'Well, as of...' Jake looked at his watch, 'one hour and forty-three minutes ago, you are no longer a client. The commission has been paid for, installed and, therefore, complete. In which case, I can now ask you out.'

Come on, girl, what you waiting for? Say yes, ya dumb broad!

'That... that would be nice. Thank you. I would like to go on a date with you.'

She managed to ignore the whooping and hollering going on inside her head.

'Great. Are you into art?'

'I don't mind it, why?'

'They've got a Canaletto exhibition going on at the National Gallery. I was thinking we could maybe pop in, take a look, and then have dinner afterwards. Would that work for you?'

'Canaletto? He's the bloke who did all those fabulous Venetian pieces, isn't he?'

Jake laughed at her description.

'Yes, that's the bloke.'

'Then I would love to see them. Thank you.'

'Great! I'll look into the dates and we can sort one out. Now, I'd better get on – Frank will be sitting with his legs crossed.'

'Oh, I forgot about him. You should have brought him with you.'

'Not the done thing when visiting a client. Not everyone likes animals or wants them in their homes.'

'Weirdos!'

'Possibly.'

'Well, if you happen to visit again, he's more than welcome to come along.'

She followed Jake out into the hallway and towards the front door.

'I'll be sure to let him know. I suspect he'll do everything he can to see you again.'

With those words, he leant in towards her, placed the gentlest of kisses on the side of her mouth, flashed his soft easy smile and then left, pulling the door quietly closed behind him.

Grace stood for a few seconds, slightly dazed as the spot where his kiss had landed tingled. Then, with a small shake of her head and a smile that ran from ear to ear, she stepped forward, locked and bolted the door and then went back to the kitchen to tidy up.

She was still smiling when she walked into the lounge and sat on her new sofa for a few minutes before turning off the lights.

She floated up the stairs, got ready for bed, brushed her teeth and switched off the bedside lamp. As she fell into sleep, the smile was still there, helping her towards happy dreams containing soft brown eyes and a dog called Perfectly Frank.

TWENTY-NINE

'Here we have Braidwood Street which is named after James Braidwood who was the first Superintendent to what has now become the London Fire Brigade. Before he came along, the firefighters were employed by different insurance companies. If your house was on fire and the firefighters who turned up worked for a different insurance company than who you were insured with, they wouldn't help and your house burnt down.'

'Get away! I don't believe you!'

'It's true, Allan, I kid you not. That's how it used to be.'

'How do you know this?'

Debbie grinned up at him.

'To be honest, I used to work with a girl who was his great, great grand-daughter. There may be another great or two in the number, I'm not quite sure.'

They turned and Debbie led the way along Tooley Street towards Hay's Galleria. For her "date" with Allan, she'd gone with the "tourist for a day" option and they were walking through the city, finding all the different, lesser-known, bits of history that were on offer. She'd spent several nights trawling the internet, making notes and working out a route, all the while hoping that Allan wouldn't think it was a lame idea.

Fortunately, when she'd asked him if he fancied playing tourist with her, he'd been all for it and here they were. The weather was also on their side. More often than not, the May Day Bank Holiday brought rain and foul weather but not this time. The sun was bright in a cloudless, blue sky and all the buildings were shiny and stunning. The good weather had also brought out the crowds but they simply added to the atmosphere.

She slipped a sideways look at Allan as they strolled along and saw a small happy smile on his face.

'Having fun?' she asked.

He didn't answer immediately but when he did, the little smile had grown into a big one.

'Yes, I am, thank you. I've never properly taken in London. It feels like I kind of landed here and all of this is alien to me. It's like I know London but don't actually *know* it at all. Does that make sense?'

'It does to me. You're saying you know what's on the surface of the city – the stuff that almost everyone knows – but you don't know its secrets, the depths of its history and the things that actually made it the city it has become.'

'Yes, that's it exactly. I knew about The Tower of London but had never walked around it. I've seen a ton of pictures of Tower Bridge but never walked across it. You know, that kind of thing.'

'Did your parents not bring you to visit when you were a kid?'

She glanced round as she asked the question and was shocked to see the joy drain away and be replaced with a closed, blank expression.

'No, that didn't happen.'

The reply was short and stated in a bland tone.

'Allan, did you have a difficult childhood?'

When Lydia had made mention of her client whose grandson had an off-the-scale IQ, it had set Debbie wondering about Allan's own upbringing and the problems he may have encountered. Up till now, there hadn't really been the opportunity to bring it up but she wanted to know more about him without feeling like she was prying. She liked him, more than she'd thought she would after that first night, and having never met a genius before – or dated one for that matter – she felt that having a better understanding of what had brought him to this point in his life would help her to make the right choices going forward.

They turned a corner and she spotted a pub over by the river.

'Come, let's take a load off for a bit. We can sit outside and watch the boats going by.'

Once they'd managed to secure a couple of pints of cider in the very busy establishment, they pushed their way back outside and onto the decked area which looked down onto the water. They leant against the railings, not talking for about ten minutes until, out of the corner of her eye, Debbie saw the people at a nearby table preparing to leave.

'Quick, table!' she hissed before striding across to secure it and receiving a dirty look from another couple who'd been making a beeline for it.

Allan sat down opposite her and she could see the happiness he'd been feeling earlier had vanished completely. Part of her was kicking herself for this but another part was saying that there was never going to be a good time for this conversation so better to get it over with sooner rather than later.

'Allan,' she laid her hand gently on his, 'what were you like as a kid? When did you find out you were so amazing?'

'Amazing? No, I don't think so.' He shook his head

vehemently. 'It felt like I was cursed. I don't know about "finding out", I just remember always being different. I read all the time and had no interest in going outside to play like other children did. My mum would send me out but I just didn't fit in. I would try to join in with the neighbourhood kids, to keep Mum happy, but couldn't make it work. I'm not into sport, I really don't like football, and when you grow up in Manchester, not liking football is as big a cardinal sin as it can get!

'To make matters worse, I was disruptive in class – not because I was naughty but because I was bored. The thing is, back then, no one thought to look for reasons behind it all – I was merely a disruptive kid who didn't fit in and nobody liked. My mum and dad argued over me. He thought I needed a tougher hand, Mum disagreed and said there was more going on than anyone realised. She was the only one who seemed to have some kind of inkling of the issue but with the internet still being in its infancy at that point, the information she needed wasn't available and she had to rely on the so-called expertise of my teachers who, it turns out, knew nothing. The arguments grew more intense as I grew older until, eventually, my father began ignoring me and by the time I reached senior school, he'd left us. Said I was too much trouble and he wanted nothing more to do with me.'

'Oh, Allan, he didn't actually say that, did he?'

'Not to me but he did to my mum. You see, I heard all the arguments and fighting and I was always at the centre of them. It reached the point where I stopped talking to people, stopped joining in in class, kept my head down and tried to be invisible but that *still* caused problems. I was either disruptive by being too boisterous or disruptive by being too quiet – it felt like I couldn't win. The irony was that even though I was so "disruptive"', he made quote signs with his fingers, 'I was getting top marks in all my

188

subjects. I mean, how stupid were they that they couldn't see the issue?'

Debbie couldn't answer this. All she could do was give his hand a small squeeze.

'What happened next?'

'Well, senior school was even more of a nightmare. That's when the bullies came along and life grew almost unbearable. I'll be honest, Debbie, there were several occasions when the idea of nicking Mum's pills and a bottle of whisky was far too appealing. When I read now about kids who go down that road, I empathise with them and understand what no one else does. Until you've been the kid on the outside and experienced the pain your peers are inflicting on you, you simply can't get it.'

'What drew you back from the edge? What stopped you from going over?'

'Computers. Or computer games. At that point in my life, they were beginning to really improve, become more sophisticated and I loved them. I would immerse myself in them for hours and, sometimes, days on end. When it was possible, I would skip school just to get lost in a game because in there, no one bullied me. No one ignored me. I had the control. I was *in* control. If I could've gotten away with it, I'd never have gone back to school again. Unfortunately, my mum got into trouble with the authorities because of my truancy and it broke me to see her upset so I made a point of going back.

'Was it any better?'

'Actually, it was. For a time. And it was all down to Grand Theft Auto.'

'Excuse me?'

'It was now a big deal in computer games and I'd been playing it for several years despite being younger than the target market for it.' He gave her a little shy grin. 'Anyway, I was good at it and a lad in my class began hanging out with me. It was nice. He was my first proper friend and we had lots of fun playing the games and stuff. That was until I found out he was selling the game hacks I'd discovered to people and making a nice pot of money from it. It wouldn't have been so bad if he'd told me his plan and at least split the proceeds but there was none of that. He'd friended me purely to make money.'

'Bastard!'

'That's as good a name as any. I dropped out of school as soon as I was old enough to leave but by this time, I'd begun to develop my own computer games and shared them over the internet. They proved to be popular and some developers came asking to buy them. I declined but it gave me the idea to form my own company, which I did. I never at any time thought it would become what it is today and I certainly never thought I'd have foreign countries asking me to design their cyber-security systems. You see, I'm not interested in all of that – the thrill for me lies in having these way-out ideas and turning them into a reality. All these new apps you can get which monitor your fitness, or you can share videos on, or doing your banking while you're out paintballing or whatever – that's where I get my fun.'

'But friends, Allan, you must have friends, surely.'

'I told you, Debbie, people are too scary. After my dad and the school stuff, well… I just find it hard to connect.'

'Yet you connected with me. Why?'

'Because you're like me.'

'How do you figure that one out?'

'You wore a red dress when everyone else was in black.'

'That's because I didn't know there was a dress code.'

'There wasn't. It's just what all the sheep did because being different scares them.'

'But…' She tried to come up with an answer but didn't

have one. For whatever the reason was, in Allan's head she was someone he felt he could reach out to. She couldn't begin to comprehend how lonely his life must have been and if she was being honest, she was more than a little flattered that after all he'd dealt with over the years, he'd picked her to be his friend.

'You know, I've never told all of that to anyone before.'

'Seriously?'

He stared at the table as he shook his head.

'Never.' He suddenly looked up. 'You won't tell anyone, will you? It's our secret.'

'I promise I will never tell. Ever!'

'Great.' The smile that had been on his face earlier reappeared. 'Now, what's next on the agenda? It's time we went back to being tourists.'

'Then let's get to it.'

As she picked up her handbag, Debbie couldn't help but wonder what sort of relationship she had with Allan. Did he see her simply as a friend or more than that? It wasn't the sort of thing she felt she could ask and right now, after what had happened with Dale, she wasn't altogether sure she was ready for a relationship anyway. Probably best, she decided, to just go with the flow for a while and see where it takes us.

THIRTY

'Good morning, Debbie.'

'Hi, Lyds, how are you feeling today?'

'Good, thank you. Most of my bruises have gone and the few remaining ones have almost faded away. There's no more pain and that in itself is a blessing.'

'Aww, that's great to hear. So, what brings you down to the shop this early?'

'Meghan Gibbons is due in today to collect her dress. I've brought it down ready for her.'

'Oh, do I get to see it now?'

'No, you don't. You'll see it when Meghan tries it on.'

'Spoilsport!'

'If you say so.'

Lydia's smile dropped as she walked into the little kitchen to put the kettle on. It was three weeks since she'd foisted herself on Debbie and now that she felt so much better, it was time to sort out what to do next. She was actually enjoying sharing with Debbie even though the space was cramped and her bedroom was tiny. It was nice not to have the constant stress that had become the norm in her marriage.

So much had happened in the short time since she'd left Dave. Grace had contacted an old friend from uni who specialised in family law and she'd agreed to handle Lydia's divorce for a fraction of her usual costs and Dave, having seen sense for once, had agreed not to contest it which meant it should go through fairly quickly and smoothly.

She was also giving serious consideration over what to do with her hairdressing business. She hadn't been back since this had all kicked off and she wasn't missing it in the slightest. She hadn't missed standing on her feet for eight hours or more, she hadn't missed feeling totally exhausted, and she definitely hadn't missed the sore throats she often got from talking to customers all day and inhaling the fumes of the chemicals they worked with. She had, however, really enjoyed creating the new dress for Meghan and helping Debbie out in the shop when it was busy, which it had certainly become since Allan's marketing guru had name-dropped them. She'd be more than happy to continue working with Debs if she would have her. However, it was how to bring that up in conversation…

'Have you gone to Brazil to get the coffee, Lyds?'

'Cheeky bugger! I'm just coming!'

She quickly stirred the milk and sugar into Debbie's beverage and took the two mugs out. They sat behind the counter, chit-chatting about the drama they'd watched the night before and Lydia worked on plucking up the courage to bring up the subject of her presence here. She'd just opened her mouth to speak when the doorbell tinkled and Meghan walked in.

'Hi, ladies, how are you both? Today's the day and I'll be honest, I'm more than a little nervous.'

'Hey, Meghan. Your dress is ready for you to try on and if it's any consolation, I'm nervous too.'

Lydia smiled but she spoke the truth. In her eyes, the dress was perfect. It was almost identical to the original the girl had tried on but she'd also embellished it here and there to give it its own style. She just had to hope that Meghan agreed.

'Well, let's get on with it and, hopefully, put us both out of our misery.'

Meghan walked into the changing room as Lydia went to get the dress for her.

'Debbie, close your eyes, please.'

'What? I'm not even allowed to see it at this point?'

'Nope!'

'Geez!'

She let out a big, exaggerated sigh but did as she was asked. Lydia sidled by, keeping the dress on her other side just in case Debbie peeked. She slid it through the curtain to Meghan and then walked over to stand in front of the counter, her heart thumping wildly as she waited on the verdict.

'Can I open my eyes yet?'

'Oops, sorry, Debs, yes you can.'

Just as Debbie blinked, a squeal came from behind the curtain. Lydia glanced at Debbie who looked back at her with concern.

'Was that a good squeal?' she whispered.

Lydia's heart was now in her mouth as she replied, 'I really don't know!'

Just then, the curtain was flung back and Meghan stepped out with the biggest smile on her face.

'Lydia, you angel! This is absolutely perfect. And it's even nicer than the original dress I tried on.'

A huge sigh of relief escaped silently through her lips as she stepped over to Meghan to check the dress fitted as well as it should.

'You're happy with it?'

'I most certainly am. Thank you. It's amazing.'

Meghan turned this way and that as she admired her reflection in the mirror. This time, the colour was perfect – the shade of green she'd chosen brought out the rosy bloom in her pale cheeks, the specks of green in her hazel eyes, and made her hair look stunning. The style was perfect for her shape and she looked gorgeous. Lydia was beyond thrilled and pleased to see that she hadn't lost her touch after all this time. Okay, there had been a few occasions where she'd had to do some unpicking but that was only to be expected when she hadn't sat at a sewing machine for more years than she wanted to count.

'Meghan, you really do look beautiful and your cousin is going to be quite jealous as I suspect you'll be outshining her on her special day. Lydia has done a wonderful job.'

'She absolutely has, Debbie. I am so grateful to you both. Now, I'm going to take this off very carefully. Oh, Lydia, I was telling a woman I work with that you were doing this for me and she was interested in coming to see you – apparently her first grandchild is being christened next month and she wants something really special to mark the occasion. I suspect it's more to do with the fact she wants to outshine her daughter's mother-in-law… anyway, would it be okay if I gave her your number?'

'Erm…' She looked at Debbie who nodded vigorously at her.

'Yes, Meghan, I would be happy to help.'

'Smashing. I'll let her know when I see her later.'

After she'd paid up and left, Lydia turned to Debbie, concerned about how she would feel over this development.

'Debbie—'

'Oh, Lyds, isn't that fantastic? Another commission for you. Your needlework is beautiful but I told you that before when you wore that skirt you'd made to the pub. I could see you were nervous earlier but you had no need to be. You've still got it.'

'So, you don't mind? That I could have another job?'

'Of course I don't. I'm thrilled for you. I've seen how much you enjoyed working on Meghan's dress these last few weeks – you clearly love doing dressmaking.'

'I do, I've just remembered how much I do.'

'Look, I need to ask, do you intend to return to hairdressing?'

Oh blimey! This was it. The conversation she'd been dreading.

'Erm, cards on the table, Debbie, I don't want to. This prolonged break from it has made me realise that I actually don't like it anymore. In fact, I'd go as far as to say I detest it.'

'Then may I make a proposition? I've so loved having you here these last few weeks and really appreciated your help when it's been busy. Is there any way I could persuade you to stay on in a permanent position but with a side-line in alterations thrown in? I tried to get Cedric to help me out with those but he wasn't interested and I do lose business at times because people don't want the hassle of finding someone to take up a hem or put in a tuck. Having you here would be a real bonus.'

Lydia blinked and gulped at the same time. Was she hearing right? Had Debbie just said what she thought she'd said?

'Are you… are you offering me a job here?'

'Oh no! I've put my foot in it, haven't I? I've offended you. You're used to being your own boss – why would you want to work for someone else? I'm really sorry—'

'No, Debbie, stop. I would love to work here with you. I just can't believe you're asking me. I've enjoyed being here so much and to know I can carry on doing so would make me incredibly happy.'

'I can't offer a massive wage but hopefully you'll get enough seamstress work to compensate. Obviously, whatever you earn from it is yours to keep. That'll be your own business to grow and develop.'

'Great. Now, while we're talking about "stuff" – how do you feel about us continuing to share the flat upstairs? I want you to be honest – if it's too much of a squeeze for you, I will try to find something as soon as possible.'

'Lydia – the room is yours for as long as you want it. I've never flat-shared with another woman before and it's a lot of fun having you around. I know it wasn't what you had in mind so you need to promise that when it's too much for you, you will let me know.'

'I promise I will do that. So, how much wages and how much is my share for the flat?'

Debbie did a few calculations and presented her with the final figures.

'Is that okay?'

Lydia felt a bit light-headed when she saw the numbers – they were more than okay. The wage was more than she'd been awarding herself from the shop all these years and her share for the flat was a fraction of what she'd been looking at when she'd been searching.

'Debs, it is absolutely perfect. Thank you.'

'Cool!' Debbie gave her a big grin and a hug. 'Welcome aboard the vintage ship! So, what about your business? What will you do with that? Sell it?'

'I'm not sure but I don't think I will. I'm considering asking Heather to manage it full-time and she can take on a junior to fill the space I'll be leaving. That way, I'll still have an additional income if I need it and I've got a safety net should things go pear-shaped at any time.'

The doorbell tinkled just then and Pat walked in with the morning's mail.

'Here you are, Debbie, not too many brown envelopes

for you today.'

'Thanks, Pat, that's how I like it. You can come back again tomorrow!'

'Shall I get us another cuppa?'

Debbie was looking through the envelopes but stopped when she came to a large A4 one in the middle of the pile. She went quite pale when she saw the postmark and muttered, 'Oh no, what now?'

'Is there a problem, Debs?'

'I think there's about to be. This is from the management company who own all the leases for the buildings in the mews. Hearing from them is never good.'

She ripped the envelope open and Lydia hovered at the side, not wishing to be nosy but wanting to be there if the news was as bad as Debbie was anticipating.

'Oh!'

'What is it? Is it really bad?'

There was no mistaking the look of shock on Debbie's face.

'Hang on, let me read this again. I just want to be sure I'm understanding it correctly…'

Lydia waited as her friend's eyes scurried across the pages. Eventually, she placed the letter on the counter and turned, her face glowing with joy.

'You are not going to believe this! The management company has been bought out and is now under new ownership. Apparently, while performing due diligence, it has come to the attention of the new owners that the rates on the leases for the mews have been increasing at an unacceptable level over the last three years, so we'll all be receiving a rebate and our rates have been revised down to what they hope is a more agreeable charge.'

'And is it agreeable?'

'Oh, yes! Very much so! Now, where's that cuppa you promised? Today has just turned into the best one I've had for a long time and I need a drink to celebrate!'

'With a cup of Tesco instant?'

'With whatever comes to hand – I really don't care!'

THIRTY-ONE

Debbie hummed to herself as she straightened the rails and tidied up. The sun was shining and a few rays had managed to climb over the roofs of the buildings across from the shop and sneak their way in through the window. It was just over three weeks since she'd sorted everything out with Lydia and they had been three weeks of fun. Her new flatmate and herself were beginning to form a routine and she enjoyed having the company during the day in the shop. The initial increase in business following the shoutout on social media hadn't abated and was continuing to rise. New customers were also tweeting about their visits and purchases and thus the interest in her little shop kept creeping up. Her own social media pages had attracted a hefty number of new followers and several of her Instagram posts which highlighted new stock just arrived, often had phone calls coming in asking for a dress or jacket to be put aside. Lydia's needlework skills were the icing on the cake and she was finding her own little business beginning to flourish.

   She was about to call out to her colleague if she fancied

a cuppa but stopped herself just in time as she remembered that Lydia had taken the morning off to go to the salon. She was confirming Heather's new position and taking two final interviews for the new stylist. Debbie had become used to her presence so quickly that it now felt strange to be in the shop alone.

The doorbell tinkled as she walked out of the kitchen with her coffee and she saw Pat drop some mail on the counter.

'Alright, Debs?'

'Yup, all good, Pat. You?'

'Same. See ya.'

She gave him a wave through the window as he headed down the mews to his next delivery and, placing her mug on the counter, picked up the post to see if there was anything other than bills to excite her.

She stopped when she came to an envelope with Dale's name on it. She turned it over and seeing that it was just some junk mail, she deliberated on whether to forward it on or not. After a few seconds, she decided she would, so put it in the drawer under the counter to be dealt with later. She was flicking through the remaining bits and pieces when she suddenly stopped for a second time.

What the h—

She opened the drawer, took out the envelope and looked at it again, waiting for the pang of loss, which usually accompanied anything related to Dale, to kick her.

Except... there was nothing.

She prodded around in her memory banks and came up with the moment Dale had proposed to her. That one was guaranteed to bring on the trembling lip and waterworks except it would seem as though the guarantee had expired because she wasn't feeling anything. Not even a hint of a wobble.

As an experiment, she moved her thoughts over to

Allan. They'd been spending quite a bit of time together between sightseeing which had become a Sunday afternoon regular and visits to the cinema. They'd also had a go at bingo and had thoroughly enjoyed themselves. They were going ten-pin bowling the following night and the thought of that caused a little frisson of excitement to skip through her.

Really?

She thought some more of the time she'd been spending with Allan and a number of little things came to her – such as his small shy smile which doubled in size when he realised he'd made her laugh, and how she now knew if he was stressed or relaxed simply by his speech pattern, or that he preferred his Big Mac without the gherkins but he still ordered them so she could have them instead. These were only small instances but going over them in her head made her feel quite happy and, she had to be honest with herself, a little giddy.

It would seem that, totally unexpectedly, Allan had managed to find a way into her heart and she wasn't in the least upset about it. She wondered how he felt about her and if there was a way of finding out without the hazard of upsetting their friendship. Should she just let things progress as they were or should she give it a little push? After all, she didn't want to risk that thing happening where you stay friends for too long that eventually the thought of being romantically involved is weird.

Debbie was ruminating over this when the doorbell tinkled. She looked up, her welcoming smile already on her lips but when she saw two men walking in, it faltered. Instantly, and for no good reason that she could put her finger on, she felt threatened and unsafe. They both gave off an air of intimidation even though they smiled at her and walked around the shop floor, flicking at the rails and feigning an interest over the shoes and bags on the shelves.

The first man was of medium height but solidly built. He had dark hair, small, mean-looking dark eyes, a bulbous nose and a large bushy moustache. His companion was taller but skinny and lanky with beady little eyes and a sharp, pointy nose. Debbie would have put him down as being a rat in a former life.

'C...can I help you?' She forced a smile to accompany her words.

'No, thank you. But I believe we can help you.'

The sentence slipped out from under the moustache and was spoken in an accent she couldn't place. The tone had her surreptitiously sliding closed the bolts under the countertop so it couldn't be lifted.

'Err, how would that be?'

'We've heard there has been some trouble down here and have come to offer our services to help it go away.' Moustache looked right at her but Ratty kept his face diverted, intent on looking out of the windows from his position behind a rail of coats.

'I think you must have heard wrong because everything in the mews is fine. There has been no trouble.'

The two men exchanged a look and the one who was doing the talking stepped towards the counter. Debbie's first instinct was to move back but she forced herself to stand her ground.

'I don't think you understand – if you accept our services, there will be no trouble. You won't have to worry about removing any graffiti, replacing smashed windows, repairing damaged stock or maybe even walking on broken legs.'

An unpleasant smell, a combination of musk, body odour and bad breath, seeped towards her across the countertop. His words, spoken in a low, menacing tone, confirmed what she had begun to fear was happening. She'd read enough gangland thrillers in her time to know these men were trying to get some kind of extortion racket going. Well, it wasn't going to work on her. She'd put too much of herself into this shop to start giving her small profits away to a pair of thugs. It was a rare event for her to lose her temper but this was too much. Her anger rose with a hot, molten, force.

'Get out of my shop, NOW!'

She pointed towards the door, hoping that the action of her left hand would distract them from her right hand which was currently dialling 999 on her mobile underneath the counter.

'I don't think we want to do that—'

'Oh, I think you do!' She stepped away from the counter, beyond his reach and held up her phone. 'You have got five seconds to get off my property or I'll be hitting the call button.'

'That would be a very big mistake.'

'No, the mistake will be yours if you don't piss off and take your skanky worm of a friend with you.'

She held up the phone and her thumb hovered over the call button.

'You will regret this choice,' Moustache growled.

'Not as much as you'll regret your choice not to move it.'

Her thumb came down on the screen and Moustache did a quick about turn, said something to Ratty in his mother tongue then moved towards the door. They stepped outside and as he turned to close it behind them, he flashed a sinister smile in her direction.

Debbie quickly cancelled the call on her phone, unlocked the counter and dashed over to the door where she locked it and threw the bolts home. She then staggered back to the counter just as her trembling legs gave way and she slid down onto the floor. As she sat shaking, her nostrils were once again assaulted by the heavy, thick stench of musk, sweat and halitosis that still hung in the air.

THIRTY-TWO

Grace walked up the lane towards Jake's place. He'd invited her over for Sunday lunch and she was looking forward to being with him. There had been a number of meals out and a theatre visit over the last few weeks but this was the first time they'd be truly alone together since the night he'd installed her sofa.

She was not, however, forgetting the other young man who would be present. Not only had she brought along a nice bottle of wine for Jake but there was also a new ball and a chew toy in the bag for Frank. After all, it was no secret that getting the four-legged member of the household on your side was always a good start.

She pressed the intercom button and a few seconds later, the gate buzzed open. Jake hadn't spoken to check it was her which meant he must have cameras situated nearby. She glanced around as she turned to pull it closed behind her but couldn't see any.

Jake was already at the side door when she arrived and without giving her a chance to speak, he drew her into his arms and kissed her. Once again, his gentleness sent sparks flying through her. His kisses were always soft and slow and it was beginning to drive her insane. She wanted him to hold her tight against him and kiss her with deep, hard passion. She also wanted him to do a lot more than that and was hoping that maybe this would be the day when they'd finally take the next step.

Once all her senses were scattered to the wind and she was at risk of swooning in his embrace, he released her and stepped back to allow her to walk inside. Grace drew in a deep breath as she crossed the threshold and held it inside, willing her spinning head to sort itself out. For goodness' sake, she was an independent professional career woman with her own home and bank balance and yet here she was, behaving like the never-been-kissed heroine in a five-hundred-page bodice-ripper!

Get a grip, she told herself just as a black bundle of fur came flying in her direction.

'Frank! Oh, come here, you gorgeous, gorgeous boy!'

She dropped the carrier bag onto the kitchen table and knelt down to greet the daft, soppy beast.

'How come you never greet me like that?' Jake asked in amusement.

'Babes, the day you come bounding up towards me bearing the gift of a drool-drenched tennis ball in your mouth, I promise you I will.'

'Hmm, if that's what it takes, I think I can wait a bit longer.'

Grace chuckled as she buried her face in Frank's soft, silky fur. 'Your daddy has no sense of adventure, does he? No, he does not!'

She rose up, took the wine from the carrier and passed it over to Jake.

'I do have a tennis ball here if you'd rather have it,' she grinned.

'Tempting but I think I'll pass, thank you. Besides, if I

took that, you'd have to give Frank the wine and he's a right pain in the arse when he's pissed. You really don't want to go there.'

'Mean drunk?'

'And the rest!'

She looked down at the dog sitting by her side, his eyes staring at the ball in her hand.

'Frankie, baby, your daddy's saying not nice things about you. I think you need to go and poop in his favourite shoes.'

'As if he hasn't done that already. Like I said, mean drunk!'

Grace laughed as she passed the ball and the chew toy to the dog and he trotted off out of the room with both in his mouth.

'Is there anything I can do to help?'

She slipped off her jacket and hung it up on the coat hooks she'd spotted behind the kitchen door.

'Not really, thank you. Although… could you just check the veg to see if it's near to boiling yet?'

'Sure.'

When she lifted the lid, her eyes widened at the large amount of Brussel sprouts in the pan and grew wider again as she checked the others. Blimey, how much was Jake planning to eat?

He walked back into the room just as she placed the last lid back on the pot.

'Nothing's boiling yet but they're pretty close. Another few minutes, I think.'

'Perfect. Thank you.'

'I have to ask, though, are you prepping your veg for the coming week? There's enough in those pots to feed an army!'

'Well, I always worry about not cooking enough and with there being four of us, I didn't want to run short.'

'Four of us?'

Damn! So much for getting fruity and burning off the calories later.

'Yes—'

Just then a bell rang.

'Oh, great, they're here. Back in a sec…'

He left the kitchen but returned within a few seconds and went to the side door. He opened it wide and she caught a brief glimpse of a red-haired woman before she was swallowed up in Jake's embrace. When she was released, he moved out of the way to allow her to walk into the kitchen. Before Grace could say anything, Seb Andrews walked in behind her.

'Hi, Grace, how are you?'

'Erm, hi, Seb. Good, thank you. How are you?'

She tried to swallow down her surprise. Jake knew his brother wasn't up there on her list of favourite people so why on earth had he invited him here today?

'Grace, this is my fiancée, Mel. Mel, this is Grace Mitchell whom I have the pleasure of doing daily battle with at the office.'

'Hi, Grace, I'm delighted to meet you at last. Seb talks about you a lot. If I didn't know better, I'd almost be jealous that you were the other woman in his life.'

'Nice to meet you, Mel. Seb, I didn't know you were engaged.'

Grace worked on making small talk while her head spun around Mel's comment. Seb talked about her a lot? Jake had mentioned that when they first met but she'd later put it down to him being polite. For Mel to say the same thing, however…

'We're keeping it quiet for the moment but we'll make an announcement when we feel the time is right.'

'Oh, don't you want to shout it from the rooftops? Surely an engagement is a cause for celebration, not something to keep hidden.'

'It sure is... when your mother isn't as hard-hearted as mine. Mel's not something wonderful in the legal world and therefore my mother will not be interested.'

'Oh, Seb, surely not?'

'Surely yes. She has illusions of me marrying a fabulous, well-renowned barrister so we can create some family dynasty together.'

'And I'm guessing, Mel,' she turned to the girl by her side, 'that you're something fabulous elsewhere?'

'You've got that one right. I'm a primary school teacher but I'm definitely fabulous with it.'

Grace found herself laughing along with Mel. She gave her the quick once-over, as you do, and the auburn, shoulder-length hair with a soft natural wave suited her pretty oval face. She was a touch shorter than Grace and not at all the willowy, stick-insect type she'd always imagined Seb would date.

Boy! She pulled herself up short! She really did have a rather poor opinion of Sebastian Andrews and it was time she put it to one side and actually got to know the bloke properly. If not at least for Jake's sake, given their brotherly relationship and the fact that she wanted her own relationship with Jake to develop into something more. Having a downer on his brother wasn't going to do her any favours there.

'So, have you been together long?'

'Here, let me show you ladies through to the dining room where you can get comfortable. Seb and I will finish off in here.'

'We will?'

Before Jake or Grace could respond, Mel grabbed a bottle of wine and said, 'Yes, Sebastian, you can help your brother in here. Grace and I are going to have a nice long chat and there's every chance that you are going to feature in it strongly as I encourage her to tell me all the things you get up to in the office.'

'Grace, I promise to do all your photocopying and filing for a month if you don't say anything…'

'Sorry, Seb, I have to tell her everything. It's part of the Sisterhood Code. Besides, I have a secretary to do my photocopying and filing.'

'Oh crap! That's me screwed!'

'Yup, I would say so!'

Grace grinned at his mock dismay before following Mel down the hallway.

'Oh, I shouldn't have eaten that!'

'Why, did it taste that bad?'

Grace smiled at Jake's pretend look of concern.

'No! And that was the problem, it tasted tooooooooo good. Trifle is my downfall and sherry trifle is a temptation I simply cannot resist. Those two massive helpings are going to see me rolling back up the road to the train station!'

'Now that I need to see!'

'What, and have you telling the whole office, Seb Andrews? I don't think so!'

Amidst more laughter, Jake pushed back his chair.

'How about we all retreat to the conservatory and soothe our bulging bellies with some coffee?'

'That sounds good to me.'

Grace rose and was about to gather up the empty bowls when Seb stopped her.

'Er, Grace, would you mind if I had a word with you? In private…'

'Urm…'

She looked at Mel and Jake in confusion.

'Why don't you guys go out into the garden while Jake and I clear up in here. We'll see you in the conservatory when you're ready.'

'Ah, sure, okay. Thanks, Mel.'

She gave the other woman a small smile before following Seb up the hallway and out the side door. He walked halfway down the garden before stopping and turning towards her.

'First of all, Grace, I want to apologise for gate-crashing your lunch with Jake today. When he mentioned you were coming over, I'm afraid I invited myself and Mel along.'

'Oh! Why? I'm sure it's not because you felt the need to bathe in my sparkling company.'

'Your company has been sparkling and I have enjoyed our meal very much but no, you're right, it wasn't the reason for me being here today.'

'So, what was?'

'I want to speak to you on a confidential basis and needed it to be away from the office. What I'm about to share really must stay between us.'

'Right.'

Grace was now beginning to feel a touch apprehensive – what on earth could Seb have to say that required such a cloak-and-dagger approach.

'Okay, here goes.' Seb looked down at his feet and kicked a tuft of grass before continuing. 'A couple of weeks ago, I had an appointment to see Alistair Forbes but I arrived early. The Bulldog wasn't around so I just hung about outside the office, waiting until my appointed time. You know what a stickler he is for punctuality.'

She smiled. Yes, she did know and she also knew that had Pam, Alistair's fierce secretary, been at her desk, Seb would have been sent away and told to return at the appropriate time.

'Anyway, the door was closed when I arrived so I knew he had someone in with him. I saw movement through the blinds on the windows and stepped away so as to avoid detection. The door opened but whoever was about to come out stopped and began talking again. It was David McArthur.'

'Well, that's not unusual, Seb. They are our bosses. You know, McArthur Forbes is the name of the company.'

'Ha ha! You're so funny... not! Anyway, what made me prick my ears up was the mention of our names.'

'Oh! Were they extolling my virtues over yours?' She grinned as she spoke to ensure he knew she was joking. While Grace was confident in her abilities, she was also aware that Seb was very much her equal. Hence why they bounced off each other the way they did.

'They were... but not in a manner that either of us should be happy about.'

'What do you mean?'

'Grace, it's no secret around the office that both of us are vying with each other for a partnership and we're putting in an awful lot of hours to try and make sure we're shining brighter than the other. That would be a lot of *unpaid* hours... yes?'

'Well, yes. You have to show willing if you want to get on.'

'Yes, you do. Unfortunately, our not-so-illustrious leaders aren't seeing it that way. The gist of the conversation was that they'd be stupid to make either of us a partner while they're making so much money off us with the extra time we're putting in and the amount of business we've been clearing. Those unpaid hours we're doing are still paid hours being charged to the clients and the company is the only one benefitting because we're certainly not. The last word of the conversation was that neither of us will be getting even a sniff of a partnership for some time to come.'

'You… you… please tell me you're kidding me.'

With her head swimming at this news, Grace leant against a nearby tree to help keep her upright. How dare the senior partners behave in this manner! She'd worked bloody hard for this promotion and that was their opinion – that she and Seb were just cash cows?

'Trust me, Grace, this is as far from kidding as it gets.'

'How do I know you're not just saying this for your own gain? Some people will stop at nothing to get onto the next rung on the ladder.'

'Because my brother would kill me if I did something like that. He's more than a little fond of you and I would never do anything to hurt him.'

'So how come you're so calm about it?'

'Because I've had the best part of two weeks to get my head around it. Try to imagine how difficult it was for me to have the meeting with Forbes afterwards and act as if I knew nothing. What I really wanted to do was impale the conniving bastard on that bloody trophy which sits on the window ledge behind him.'

Despite her state of shock, this comment managed to elicit a giggle from her. She knew the trophy Seb was alluding to and right now, she'd pay good money to see it sticking through the chest of Alistair Forbes.

'I just don't know what to say… I'm… I'm speechless.'

'I'm sorry to break this to you but I felt you had a right to know. It's our careers they're messing with.'

Her career.

The one thing Grace had spent her life focusing on. She'd known since her early teens that she wanted to be a lawyer and she'd had her eyes on that prize ever since. Sacrifices had been made – so many sacrifices; the Christmases she should have spent with her parents but hadn't, choosing instead to remain in her dorm, her digs, her flats where she'd studied and studied in order to achieve the highest grades possible. She knew the top firms in the City took only the highest one percent of the qualifying students; she'd finished in the top point-five percent and had thought it was all going her way when McArthur Forbes had selected her to join them.

She slowly raised her gaze to Seb and was annoyed to feel tears pricking her eyes. She didn't want to appear like an emotional woman but right now, she just wanted to kick, scream and lash-out at anyone and everyone. Knowing that she couldn't, her anger was finding another escape route.

'Have you given any thought to what you're going to do next? Will you consider leaving?'

'The temptation to tell them where to stick it has been overwhelming and it's only Mel's calm thinking that's stopped me going ahead. I'd most likely be waving my P45 in the air by now if it hadn't been for her.'

'She's lovely. I really like her.' She gave him a sideways look. 'I like how she doesn't take any of your crap and stands up to you. Not what I expected at all.'

'She's been the best thing to happen in my life, Grace, I have to be honest. She's also made me see that all this working and not much playing is a bad thing. She came up with an idea and since she mentioned it, it's been growing stronger and stronger.'

'Really? What is it?'

'Rather than moving to another company where it's going to be more of the same – you know, the long hours trying to prove yourself and some other bugger reaping the rewards, why not set up my own practice.'

'Wow! I did not see that one coming!'

'Yeah, it threw me for a doozy too but the longer I've had to dwell on it, the more attractive the idea is. Just think, the freedom to choose the cases you want; shorter working hours; all the profits are yours… what's not to like about it.'

'Sounds like you *have* given it quite a bit of thought.'

'I have. You see, Mel and I plan to have kids and I want to be a part of their lives. My mother was barely present in mine except to tell me to work harder and study more. I don't want that for my children. This way, I'd be my own boss and I could set my time how I want it to be.'

'It does sound good when you put it like that.'

And she meant it. These last few months, since she'd begun to take back a little bit of time for herself, had been really nice, and she was enjoying spending more days and evenings with her friends. And, of course, Jake.

'Which brings me to the next thing…'

'There's more?'

'Yeah. I want you to join me. I want us to set up a practice together.'

'You what?'

Grace felt her mouth drop wide open and she quickly closed it. At this moment, she didn't know what had been the bigger shock – the betrayal of trust by her employers or Seb's barking mad suggestion. Both of them were bonkers.

'I don't know what to say to that. I'm flattered, obviously, but…'

'Look, don't say anything just now. Take the idea away with you and mull it over. See how it's fitting on you in a few weeks or so.'

'I don't get why you're asking me though. Okay, you've kept me in the loop regarding the lack of partnership but I'm sure Jake will still talk to you without us going into business together.'

'Oh, I know that he would but this is nothing to do with Jake and everything to do with you being one of the best solicitors I know. It's one thing vying with you when we're both on the same side but I never want to come up against you on the opposite side. I think our respective talents would complement each other nicely and would enhance the services we can offer.'

She stared at him for a moment as she let the idea sink in. Sure, she would need to give it more thought but, and for all the reasons Seb had already voiced, it was certainly worth giving it some headspace to develop.

'Thank you for asking. It's a compliment and I really am flattered. Let me mull it over for a while. I don't plan to rush into anything so I'll get back to you at some point. Now, I'm going back to join the others and I really hope Jake has made Irish coffees because, after all that, I need something very strong. Very strong indeed!'

'Well, if he hasn't added alcohol, I will be!'

Seb gave her a conspiratorial wink followed by a wide grin which left her thinking, as she followed him down the path, that she should really give the bloke a break. After all, if she was being truly honest with herself, he'd never actually done anything to cause her dislike. It was his easy outgoing personality that she'd found annoying and she'd now come to realise she'd been jealous. Jealous that he had the ability to put people at their ease and make them laugh. Her own uptight nature, along with her ambition and intense focus on the partnership, had been the root of the problem but she'd finally learnt to relax in recent months so maybe now was the time to accept that Seb wasn't, and never had been, a problem.

THIRTY-THREE

Debbie had only just popped out of the shop barely a moment before, to get a meat pie for dinner from Bait's Bakery on the corner, when the bell over the door tinkled. Lydia looked up and saw the shape of a tall man walk in. The sun was behind him and it wasn't until he was closer to the counter that she saw him properly.

Slim built, with cheekbones to die for, deep brown eyes, skin the colour of polished walnut and a smile that really did light up the room – he was a joy to behold and the increased speed of her pulse told her she was definitely beholding the joy!

His crisp white shirt, beautifully cut tan trousers held up with matching braces and shining brown leather shoes gave him an old-fashioned debonair look and it suited him perfectly.

'Good morning, you must be Miss Lydia.'

'Err… urm… yes, I am. How…'

'I'm Cedric from the tailors next door. Miss Debbie told me she had a new work colleague who was also a magnificent seamstress.'

'Oh, gosh, no, I wouldn't go that far—'

'Ah, if Miss Debbie says you are, then you are. That young lady has a good eye.'

Lydia felt the blush begin to creep up her cheeks and she lowered her head to hide it.

'Anyway, it's lovely to meet you.'

His hand came across the counter and as she slipped hers into it, the smallest of tingles skipped up her arm. His grip was firm but gentle and when he let her hand go, she felt a little bereft. However, before she could question the sensation she was feeling, he said, 'I've brought this in for Miss Debbie, the postman delivered it to me in error,' and he slid an envelope over the counter towards her.

'Oh, right. Thank you.'

'It's no trouble. The pleasure was all mine.'

He began walking towards the door when Lydia suddenly said, 'Cedric…'

He stopped and turned.

'Thank you for the cider vinegar and your advice that night when I first arrived. It worked a treat and I'm very grateful.'

'I'm glad I was able to help. Women as beautiful as you should be treated with care; it saddens me that you were not. I hope you are in a better place now.'

'I am. Thank you.'

He flashed his smile again, gave a small incline of his head and walked out the door.

Lydia was still staring at the space he'd occupied when Debbie trotted back in, holding their dinner aloft in her hand.

'We were in luck – it was the last one. Some bloke in front of me was after it but I'd signalled to Bait when I walked in that I wanted it so she had to fob the chap off with something else.'

'Great news.'

'Did I see Cedric leaving when I turned the corner?'

'Yes, he was dropping off a letter which had got caught up in his post.'

'Ah, that was nice of him. He's such a lovely man. If only he was a little bit younger…' She winked and gave Lydia a nudge.

'Really? And what about Allan? Are you tired of the poor boy already?'

'Absolutely not. Although where we're heading is still a mystery to me.'

'Sometimes the not knowing is part of the fun.'

'For sure. Anyway, I'll run upstairs and pop this in the fridge.'

For the next few hours, the shop had a steady stream of customers but that didn't stop Lydia thinking back to her morning encounter. It had been such a long time since she'd felt anything which could be construed as attraction – Dave may have once been the boy of her dreams but he'd grown up into the man of her nightmares – and she was still in a state of surprise.

'Lydia, can you come over a moment please?'

She turned to see Debbie standing with a lady outside the dressing room.

'Hi, how can I help?'

Debbie stepped to the side and Lydia immediately saw the issue. The lady had a spinal defect which caused her to lean to one side. This meant the dress she was trying on did likewise.

'Is there anything you can do that would make the dress sit better?' Debbie asked.

Lydia smiled at the customer. 'I'm sure I can help, let me see.'

She knelt down and inspected the way the skirt of the dress was falling. Trying to pin it was going to be awkward. She sat back on her heels and looked up.

'I really need a hemming marker – it would give me a proper line to work with but I don't have one.'

'You could ask Cedric if he has one you could borrow.'

'Oh, yes… I suppose I could…'

'I'm sure Claire would be happy to hang on while you go next door and ask.'

The customer nodded her assent so Lydia clambered up onto her feet and went to see Cedric. Her heart picked up the pace when it realised where she was heading and Lydia was nothing short of relieved that it wasn't bouncing out of her chest like something from the cartoons as she walked in the door of the tailors.

She had a quick look around and was impressed to see a nice line of suits, jackets and trousers all hanging up smartly on built-in rails on the wall. The store was very smart and spacious – quite different from Debbie's cluttered, homely atmosphere.

'Ah, Miss Lydia, how can I assist you?'

Cedric stepped out from a door in the corner of the store and caught her unawares.

'I… erm… I… I was wondering if you might have a hem marker I could borrow for a few moments. It's an awkward hem to pin and a marker would be so much easier.'

'Hmm, it's not something I use – not much of a need for such a thing on gentlemen's trousers but…'

He stopped and seeing that he was having a think, she kept quiet and stole the opportunity to gaze at his handsome face.

'Ah, yes! I think I might just be able to help. If you don't mind holding the fort for a couple of minutes, I need to go upstairs.'

'Of course. Thank you.'

He smiled, inclined his head to her again and went back through the door he'd appeared from earlier.

A few minutes later, he was back carrying a rather old, wooden, hemming marker.

'Sorry I was so long – I had to wipe the dust off it. It was tucked away at the back of the cupboard. It belonged to my mother – I remember her doing the hems for all the local ladies and she swore by this as the best means of getting a good straight line.'

'Oh, I hope she won't mind me borrowing it.'

'I'm afraid she's no longer with us but she would be thrilled to know it was back in use once again.'

'I'll return it as soon as I'm finished with it.'

'No need, Miss Lydia. You hold onto it. It's a shame for it to be gathering dust when it can be put to good use. No, you keep it.'

'Cedric, that's very kind of you. You must let me pay you for it, at least.'

'Absolutely not! I won't hear of it.'

'Oh! I…' Lydia didn't know what to say and felt a little embarrassed by this second act of kindness from this man she barely knew.

'There is one thing I would like to ask you, Miss Lydia, if I may?'

'Er, of course.'

'If it would suit you, would you like to join me for a glass of wine over in Luigi's this evening? He has a lovely little garden area on the other side of the wine bar.'

'I'm so sorry, Cedric, I'm afraid I can't.'

'Of course. I understand. It was presumptuous of me.'

'I'm not busy tomorrow night though, if that could work for you?'

If she'd thought his smile that morning was bright, it was nothing compared to the one he bestowed upon her now.

'Miss Lydia, tomorrow night would be perfect. I will call for you at seven-thirty.'

'I look forward to it.'

With a parting smile, she left the shop, hem marker in hand, and while her brain was asking 'What the heck do you think you are doing?', her heart was shouting, *'You go, girl!'*

THIRTY-FOUR

Debbie twirled in front of the mirror, checking her outfit looked as good on her as she'd imagined in her head. She'd managed to drop a few more pounds over the last few weeks and the wide belt sitting above the glorious emerald-green circular skirt cinched her waist in beautifully. The pale lemon jumper and cardigan set was a perfect match. Harold, the cobbler next door, had done a fabulous job of dying the mucky gold-coloured suede shoes she'd found to almost the exact shade as the skirt. Her hair was clipped up on one side and she felt great.

'Oh wow, look at you. You look stunning.'

Lydia stood in the doorway of the bedroom, a big smile on her face.

Debbie looked at her through the mirror.

'You don't look so bad yourself. I love your dress. Another one of your creations?'

'It is. Now that I've started sewing again, I don't want to stop.'

'At this rate, we'll be giving you your own rail in the shop. I'd be happy to sell your items – I think they'd go down well.'

'Aw, shush!'

She grinned as Lydia blushed at the compliment.

'Well, bear it in mind. The offer's there for whenever. Are you out with Cedric tonight?'

'I am.'

'Venturing far?'

'No, not yet. I'm still happy just going to Luigi's.'

'I'm sure you'll both have a great time.'

'We will. By the way, have you asked Allan to Grace's party on Saturday?'

'Not yet, I'm asking him tonight. Have you asked Cedric?'

'Same as you – asking tonight. Anyway, I'd better go and finish getting ready.'

Lydia went to walk away but then turned back.

'Debs, did Grace seem a bit out of sorts to you last night?'

'Yes. I couldn't quite put my finger on it but she certainly wasn't herself.'

'Hmm, that's what I thought. And she wasn't for sharing either.'

'No. I got the impression that, if pushed on it, she might have been a bit snappy.'

'I hope everything's okay with her and Jake – it would be a shame if it wasn't, as she certainly likes him. Anyway,' Lydia gave a small smile, 'standing here chewing the fat won't get either of us ready in time for our respective dates.'

She walked away as Debbie picked up her earrings, popped them in and then stood debating which perfume to wear. She picked up a couple, had a sniff and then put them back down. When she picked up the third bottle and inhaled its scent, the smell had her recoiling back in horror. The lid was quickly put back on and the bottle was thrown into the bin. The heavy musky base had rushed back the memory of the day those heavies had tried to intimidate her in the shop. For a whole two weeks after their visit, she'd hardly relaxed, constantly looking over her shoulder and jumping every time the bell tinkled on the shop door. Lydia had noticed her being skittish but when she'd asked why, Debbie had laughed it off, making up some silly excuse about lack of sleep. After what Lydia had been through, Debbie hadn't wanted to drop any further worries upon her.

As the days and weeks had rolled on by without further incident, she'd gradually forgotten about her unwelcome visitors, putting it down to a couple of geezers just chancing their luck. The smell of the perfume, however, had brought it all right back like it had happened only yesterday, which just went to prove that smells were one of the most evocative elements for memories.

She made a concentrated effort to push the memory from her mind and finally selected the light floral perfume that she preferred, gave a couple of skooshes around her neck then picked up her handbag. Allan was going to be here any moment; she didn't want to keep him waiting.

'So, good surprise?'

'Oh, Allan, the best surprise ever! That was truly amazing, thank you so much.'

'No need to thank me, seeing you this happy is all the thanks I require.'

Debbie grinned at him before turning to look out the window of the chauffeur driven car Allan had arranged for the night. She adored seeing the streets of London when they were all lit up and driving through the West End was something that had always been a thrill for her and still was.

She let out a little happy sigh of contentment. Allan had treated her to a night at the ballet – Sadler's Wells nonetheless! They'd put on a special charity event which was a one-off performance of Matthew Bourne's Swan Lake production and it had been every bit as glorious as all the reviews she'd ever read had said it was. Somewhere, in one of their many long talks, she must have mentioned to Allan that she'd longed to see this particular version of the famous ballet and he'd made it happen. She slipped a sneaky glance at him and thought again of how incredibly handsome he looked in his tuxedo. She'd just about managed not to gasp aloud at the sight of him when he'd stepped out of the car earlier in the evening, having arrived to collect her in a chauffeur driven limo. He'd also ditched the big black glasses tonight and looked so much better for doing so. She'd noticed he wasn't wearing his glasses quite so often these days but she didn't want to say anything that might make him self-conscious. If he was growing more confident and didn't feel the need to hide away behind his "disguise", then she was more than happy for him.

'How do you think the ballet worked with male swans?'
She twisted in her seat to face him.

'Really well, actually. It actually made a lot more sense of the story. For the prince to fall in love with a male swan, and for that love to be forbidden, was more realistic to me. The anguish and pain the prince experiences at not being allowed to be himself was heartfelt. This version is considerably more thought-provoking. Did you enjoy it?'

'Surprisingly, yes I did.'
'Surprisingly?'
'I'm not a lover of ballet.'
'Then why were we there?'
'Because I knew it would make you happy. I knew you

wanted to see it and I was prepared to sit through three hours of boredom if the experience gave you many more hours of a happy memory. As it happens, however, it was a spectacular show and I enjoyed it immensely.'

Debbie took in the pleasure on Allan's face. He really meant what he'd said. All of this had been for her. He was prepared to sacrifice his own enjoyment for her. She couldn't remember anyone ever doing that for her. Even Dale, sweet as he was, had only done things which they'd both had an interest in.

'Thank you.' She leant over and gave him a kiss on the cheek. He took her hand, gave it a squeeze and they remained holding hands until the car drove down into the mews. He got out with her and stood at the mouth of the entry down to the back door to the flat.

'Let me walk you to your door.'

'Oh, there's no need for that. I can find my own way from here.'

Allan hadn't been inside the flat yet and remembering the state of it as both she and Lydia had scrambled around getting ready to go out, tonight wasn't the night for him to get his first glimpse of it.

'I should really walk you to your door, that would be the gentlemanly thing to do. You're short-changing me on my duties here.'

'I promise not to tell anyone if you don't.'

'You're determined, aren't you?'

'Yes.'

'Very well, I will leave you here, at your insistence.'

'Thank you so much again for a truly amazing night. I will never, ever forget it.'

She leant in to give him a hug and as he went to kiss her on the cheek, she quickly turned her head so that their lips met. She felt him stiffen in her arms and she held herself completely still, waiting to see what he would do. A second or two passed by and then he relaxed, pulled her slightly closer and kissed her a little more strongly.

The relief she felt quickly took second place to the other sensations coursing through her body. Every part of her felt like it was melting and turning to liquid and she found herself holding him even tighter.

Eventually, they parted, but the light was too dim to see the expression on his face.

'Goodnight, Debbie.'

He stepped back and slipped back inside the car. As it pulled away, her heart was palpitating in her chest. Had she pushed it too far? Was her friendship all he cared for? After what had happened with Dale, her insecurities came rushing to the fore.

She watched the car slowly move up the mews but as it turned the bend, Allan looked out of the window, waved and blew her a kiss.

She sagged against the wall with relief – everything was okay.

With a spring in her step, she all but skipped down the entry and was so busy looking in her bag for her door key that she didn't notice the wheelie-bin until she almost fell over it.

'What? Eh? What are you doing there?'

The bins lived over in the far corner of the yard and Cedric put them out whenever it was bin day. She could never remember which bin was supposed to go out when, so Cedric had taken command of the weekly chore. He never, however, left one sitting right in the way of the entry.

Just as she was about to move it, a shape launched itself from the shadows beside her and the next thing she knew, a hand was clamped firmly over her mouth while an arm wrapped itself across her chest, holding her tightly.

She struggled against the person holding her, aware of

them trying to drag her across the yard. Their grip was strong and her squirming was only making them hold her tighter. Her stomach clenched tight with fear and the sensation rushed through her like ice-cold shards stabbing at her skin.

She tried to scream but the sound was lost behind the hand covering the lower half of her face. Panic began to dull her brain and she had to force it away. She needed to stay calm. She had to focus.

With a herculean effort, she managed to draw in a deep breath through her nose, hold it and felt the fear ebb slightly away. Not a lot but just enough to give her clarity. Her eyes closed, Debbie quickly thought back to the YouTube videos she'd watched on self-defence for women. From the deepest, darkest corner of her mind, one came back to her.

She knew she had to act now – there was no time to mull over if it would work. She stopped fighting against her assailant, stiffened her body and pulled up both her legs until they were sticking straight out in front of her. This sudden shift in weight distribution pulled the attacker off balance and the hand fell away from her mouth.

With as much volume and energy that she could muster, Debbie yelled into the night.

'HELP! HELP ME!'

THIRTY-FIVE

Lydia smiled at Cedric over the small candle sitting on the table as she played with the glass of wine in her hand. Cedric was telling her about his life growing up in London with his two sisters, and their St Lucian parents. His parents had been young children themselves when they'd arrived in this dark, dank part of the world but they'd grown up within a tight-knit community of fellow Caribbeans in Peckham and he and his sisters had also shared a similar upbringing. She could tell, some from what was said and also from what was not said, that it hadn't been an easy life but it had been filled with love and laughter and that always helps you through the worst of times.

'Are you okay there, Miss Lydia? You're very quiet.'

'I love listening to you talk. You make everything sound so colourful and lively, even those times when your lives must have been so difficult.'

'My sisters and I were lucky – it was considerably harder for my parents. We were second generation and while there were – and still are – many obstacles to cross, our spaces here had been carved out to some small degree.'

'You still haven't told me why you refer to all ladies as Miss Whatever.'

'Do you dislike it?'

'Actually, no, I don't. I think from some men, it would come across as patronising but you can tell you mean it respectfully. It's perhaps more about the tone rather than the word itself.'

'In England, children tend to refer to non-relative adults who feature frequently in their lives as aunts and uncles despite there being no blood shared. My mother always felt that was a bit strange but did agree that children calling adults by their Christian names alone was disrespectful, so we had to add Miss or Mister first. It was a sharp clip around the ear if we didn't.'

Lydia nodded at this.

'Yes, I remember all the "aunties" I had who came to my grandmother's salon when I was a child. They often used to give me ten pence "for a sweetie". It never occurred to me at the time how strange it was that I only ever saw these women in the shop. I was such a naïve child!'

They chuckled and she took another sip of her wine.

'I have to say that I really do enjoy these nights out we have.'

She gave a small sigh as she tilted her head back and looked up at the stars in the sky above. Despite the light pollution of the city, they could still be seen and she had always found a small sense of comfort in their existence.

'It is one of the nicer aspects of the summer – being able to eat al-fresco. It won't be long until the nights begin to cool and we'll be begging Luigi to give us a seat closer to the fireplace.'

'I'll bet you wish you were in St Lucia when winter arrives. Do you go back often?'

'The last time I was there was for my honeymoon. My

mother maintained the communication between our family here and the family there. Since she died, I haven't been so good. Marcie's death barely eighteen months later didn't help either as I was only just getting over one level of grief and then thrown back into an even deeper one.'

Lydia didn't reply to this. She already knew his wife had contracted a case of measles which had led to complications resulting in her death from encephalitis. That was when Cedric had closed up the family tailoring shop in Peckham and moved all the way over to Putney. The memories had been everywhere and too many people were intent on keeping Marcie's memory alive and while he didn't want to forget her, he needed space to allow himself to heal. The mews, with its old-fashioned cobbler and a clothes shop that hadn't been vintage back then, had been the perfect place to restart his life.

'Well, maybe one day, eh?' she smiled.

'Maybe.'

She looked at her watch.

'I suppose we should head back. Tomorrow's a school day after all. I'm surprised Luigi hasn't been out to tell us to sod off!'

'We've become his regular customers – he doesn't want to scare us away! Although, it would be nice to venture a bit further afield one night.'

'We will. Very soon. Another couple of weeks and we can go out and trip the light fantastic. I promise.'

'I will hold you to that, Miss Lydia.'

She smiled at him again but it slid off her face as she turned to pick up her silk scarf and handbag. There was only two weeks to go until her divorce was finalised and her marriage to Dave was over. The Decree Nisi had come through and she knew the Absolute was merely a formality but she didn't want to be seen out with another man, even though she and Cedric were nothing more than friends, until the Absolute had been signed, sealed and delivered. She wouldn't have pegged Dave as being a vindictive man but he had been possessive and wouldn't take kindly to his "wife" being out with a gentleman friend, no matter how innocent the relationship was. She had no intention of giving him any kind of excuse to stick a spanner in the works. She'd got this far – two more weeks wouldn't kill her!

They walked through the restaurant, said thank you and goodnight to Luigi and stepped out into the quiet of the street.

Cedric crooked his arm and she placed her hand on his elbow. He had such old-style manners but she liked them.

'I wonder if Debbie's home yet – I'm desperate to find out what the surprise was that Allan had for her. I hope it was a good one because she was so excited.'

'I've seen the way that young man looks at Miss Debbie – I can't see that he'd have done anything she wouldn't have enjoyed.'

'Do you think—'

Her words were cut off as a scream rent the air.

'HELP! HELP ME!'

With barely a glance at each other, they ran down the entry into the backyard and almost tripped over a bin blocking the way. Cedric pushed it aside and when the security lights didn't come on, Lydia pulled her phone from her bag and quickly flicked on the torch to light their way. She saw Cedric run across the small courtyard and raised the phone higher, trying to spread the pale beam further, when a dark shadowy shape jumped onto the remaining bins and threw itself upwards over the wall.

Just then, Cedric crouched down and her eyes fell on Debbie, lying on the ground at his feet.

'Ouch!'

'I know, I know, it hurts but I need to clean the dirt out.'

'The police are on their way.'

'Oh, Cedric, I said not to call them. I don't want any fuss.'

'Debbie, you've just been attacked. You need to let the police know. While you may have gotten away with a nasty gash on your arm, some other woman might not be so lucky. It has to be reported. Now will you hold still and let me clean this.'

'Sorry, Lydia, you're right. I just… I just… Oh, I don't know!'

'Here, let's get you out of these clothes and into your cosy onesie. You're beginning to shake which will be the shock setting in. We need to keep you warm.'

Debbie got to her feet and Lydia helped to ease off the little short-sleeved cardigan, keeping it away from the blood on her friend's arm. As she began folding the pretty top, a nasty smell emanated from it.

'Urgh! That is disgusting.' She couldn't help wrinkling her nose.

'What is?' Debbie's head appeared from beneath her jumper.

'The smell on your cardigan. Something nasty must have fallen out of the bins and you've rubbed against it when you fell.'

'Let me sniff?'

Lydia passed the item of clothing over and waited to see the same look of disgust on Debbie's face. However, it was a look of fear that appeared instead.

'Debbie, what's wrong?'

Her friend began to tremble and she knew this was nothing to do with being in shock.

'I… something happened… in the shop… I never told you…'

She began to cry and Lydia quickly gathered her in her arms.

'Hey, hush now, you're safe. It's okay. Come, finish getting dressed and we'll go and sit by the fire in the lounge. The police will be here in a minute, you don't want to greet them in your undies, do you?'

Lydia tried to lighten the moment but her insides were flipping in fear. What on earth had happened that had Debbie feeling so scared?

THIRTY-SIX

Grace walked over and checked the platters on the dining table for the umpteenth time. She already knew everything was as perfect as it could be but she was still nervous. Not only was today her birthday, but it was also her first social gathering in her home. The gathering she'd promised Jake she would have to show off her beautiful new sofa. She'd put it off long enough and she was growing tired of his nagging. This had seemed the ideal opportunity to finally get him off her back.

Mind you, getting him off her back was one thing but when was he ever going to get on her front? She didn't have a problem with taking things slowly but at this rate, she'd be dragging him up to her bedroom on her Stannah stairlift!

In other areas, their relationship was moving along nicely. He knew she'd wanted to be a lawyer since her early teens and had been a serious, rather boring teenager and young adult as a result of this desire. Apart from her one holiday abroad each year, which was always somewhere new to enhance her experience of the world, she'd done nothing of any merit outside of her career. She'd once done an abseil for charity, not long after she'd left uni – it had been organised by the company – but that was probably the most "out there" thing in her life. She hadn't even been in love... until now.

Jake had shared himself with her. How he'd discovered his love for carpentry and how it had become the safe spot in his life. When things were bad, his woodworking eased his soul and helped him to face his life again. Moments such as his dad leaving and his marriage breaking up... The last one had been a bit of a shocker but the man was forty-one years old – just because she was an old spinster didn't mean everyone else followed that path. He'd met his wife when he'd been working in America but the marriage hadn't lasted long. Three years later, they were divorced but had remained good friends. In a way, she respected him more for that. It takes a mature approach to understand that sometimes being good friends doesn't guarantee they'll make good spouses.

Sometimes, in an unguarded moment, she found herself wondering what it would be like to be married to him. She would daydream for a few minutes before giving herself a shake and snapping out of it. Marriage was something she just didn't fancy.

Her eyes glanced around the room again and came to rest upon Frank's spare bed and food bowls sitting in the corner. Honestly, she sighed, the dog was far better placed for a sleepover than his master was. A small grunt left her lips as she finished checking everything was in its place. Her gaze came to a halt on the clock. Time to get changed into her party dress.

She was just sweeping a second layer of gloss over her lips when the doorbell rang and when she rushed down to answer it, Debbie and Lydia were standing there with wide smiles on their faces. Allan and Cedric stood behind them.

She threw the door open wide and ushered them in.

'I'm so happy you're here, thank you for coming.'

Hugs were exchanged and birthday greetings voiced as she led them through the kitchen and out into her courtyard where the patio table and chairs were set up, ready for everyone to sit down and chill.

'What can I get you to drink? Or, if you would rather help yourself, all the glasses are on the breakfast bar along with the drinks. Chilled stuff is in the fridge. Please just relax and make yourself at home.'

Whenever she'd visited Debbie and Lydia at their flat, it was always a very laid-back atmosphere and no one stood on occasion. She knew where their fridge was, along with the tea and coffee cupboard and she was regularly encouraged to just help herself. She really wanted to extend that same feeling of homeliness to her friends.

The doorbell rang again.

'Oops! I suppose that solves that one – you're helping yourselves!'

She grinned before rushing off to let Jake in. She knew it was him because he was the only one of her guests not yet here.

She pulled the door open and had to quickly work at not letting the welcoming smile on her face slip as she saw Seb and Mel standing behind him. Luckily, Frank came bounding straight at her and she was able to use the moment of giving him some fuss to school her face back into a wide smile of happiness by the time she stood up.

'Hi… err… hi! You guys are a surprise.'

Jake gave her a hug and a kiss as he walked in with Mel and Seb doing the same although they made sure to place their kisses on her cheek.

'I brought Seb along because getting your birthday present in on my own would be difficult and as he comes with a plus-one, Mel is here too. I didn't think you'd mind.

The more the merrier, eh?'

'Of course, of course. You're both very welcome. Thank you for coming. Please, through there...'

Grace pointed them towards the kitchen but hung back in the hallway for a moment to gather her thoughts. She genuinely didn't have a problem with Seb being here but they hadn't spoken outside of the office since that day when he'd filled her in on the conniving behaviour of their senior partners. The suggestion he'd made hadn't been forgotten either and she'd spent many hours dwelling on it, trying to decide the best move to make.

She made her way into the kitchen, smiling as she saw everyone introducing themselves, helping themselves to drinks and giving Frank loads of attention that he was loving and lapping up. She'd take the covers off the platters on the table shortly and they could all just pick and nibble as they wished. The deli up on the main road had come up trumps when she'd asked them for help and she was sure there would be something tasty for everyone to enjoy.

'Grace.'

She turned to see Jake looking her way.

'Seb and I are going to bring in your gift before we get ourselves too comfortable. Please, can you stay out here until I call on you?'

She looked around at her friends before turning back and replying, 'O-k-a-y. That sounds a tad ominous. What on earth have you got me that is so big it requires two people to sort it out?'

'That, my little buttercup,' he dropped a kiss on her nose, 'is for me and Seb to know and you to find out shortly. We won't be long.'

Seb also grinned at her as he followed his brother out.

'Oh, what do you think it is, Grace?'

'I have no idea, Debs, but I believe there is someone in our midst who might – Mel?'

'Ha, don't look at me. I'm afraid I'm as much in the dark as the rest of you. After we clicked so well at Jake's Sunday lunch, I don't think he trusted me to keep it to myself.'

'Well, you may as well have a glass of wine while we wait. Here…'

Lydia thrust a glass of something white and cold in her hand from which she took a large glug. She wasn't good with surprises and they made her nervous.

They were sitting around the table chatting – Allan and Cedric had brought out a couple of the dining table chairs to accommodate the two extra guests – when Jake called to her from the hallway.

Everyone got up, eager to see what this birthday surprise was.

She walked into the hallway and was surprised to see the coffee table from the lounge sitting by the front door. Stepping into the lounge, with everyone crowding around behind her, she found Jake in front of the sofa over by the window and in his hand was the corner of a sheet which was hiding something in the middle of the room.

'Are you ready?' he asked.

'As I'm ever going to be…'

'Very well. Grace Mitchell, happy birthday!'

He yanked the sheet off and revealed a beautiful chaise longue.

Grace stared at it, utterly speechless. Of all the things she could have imagined him giving her as a birthday present, this would never have made it onto the list. The "oohs and aahs" of her friends were giving a voice to her own turbulent emotions.

She knew instantly that he'd made this for her himself – this was no shop-bought gift – and it was his thoughtfulness that was bringing the tears to her eyes.

'Grace? Do you like it?'

'Jake, I do, I really do. I'm just so surprised.'

'Do you recognise it?'

'Huh?' She looked at him in confusion.

'Look closer…'

She moved nearer and stopped, drinking in the loveliness of the piece. It was upholstered in deep, plush, dark purple velvet. The back was in the traditional chaise longue style where it swept downwards in a gentle curve. The legs were… hang on! The legs…

She bent down and looked closer at the head of the chaise.

No!

It wasn't possible… was it?

She looked up at him and he gave her a small nod.

'This is my old sofa?'

'Yes, it is.'

'But…'

'I saw how you felt about it when I took it away and what it meant to you. When I went upstairs to use your loo that night, your bedroom door was open and I saw the space you have underneath the back window. That's when I had the idea to do this for you.'

'And how you knew what colour to use?'

'Yes.'

This time there was no holding back the tears. To think that this man cared enough to return her old memories, was something she'd never experienced in all her adult life.

'Now, Seb and I will take it upstairs while you allow your friends to have a seat on the rather gorgeous, even if I do say it myself,' he grinned cheekily, 'sofa that has brought us all here today.'

242

THIRTY-SEVEN

Grace sat in her courtyard, a glass of wine in one hand with the other one being firmly held by Jake and the warmth of Frank lying under the table by her feet. It was now early evening. Everyone was a little merry and chatting together like they'd been friends all their days.

'Grace, I heard tell in the office that you got a dose of the Forbes hairdryer the other day? Is that true?'

She looked across the table to Seb, annoyed with him for bringing it up when she was supposed to be chilling and enjoying herself.

'Yes, it's true.'

'Why? What happened?'

She sighed. Clearly her short answer hadn't given a big enough hint that she didn't want to discuss this.

'I hadn't finished the paperwork on the Rollsteen merger and he wanted to go through it.'

'But that wasn't due until Thursday – I heard he had a go at you on Monday?'

'That's right. If I hadn't taken the day off on Sunday, it would have been ready but as I did, it wasn't yet complete.'

'Did you tell him that? That you were well within your preparation time.'

'Tried to but he wasn't in the mood to listen.'

'I'll bet you felt great after that. All those extra hours you'd already put in and they still weren't good enough.'

'You could say that. Let's just say you nearly got your wish of seeing him impaled on that damn trophy!'

'The trophy the company won on the back of our hard work.'

The latter comment was made with a cynicism that was impossible to miss.

'Look, I know this really isn't the time and place but I do need to ask, Grace, have you given any more thought to my suggestion?'

'Oh, what suggestion is this?'

Lydia looked at her with interest and Debbie's head popped out from behind Allan's shoulder as she leant forward to hear more.

Grace brought them up to speed on the conversation she'd had with Seb and the offer he'd extended to her.

'Grace, that's a wonderful idea. If your bosses are behaving so badly, they don't deserve your loyalty or your expertise. If you're going to be giving sweat, blood and tears, then let them be for your own benefit and not someone else's.'

'I hear you, Lydia, but it's such a big step and what if we take this plunge into the unknown and we end up with no clients?'

'Surely some of your current clients would come with you?'

'They might but they're not guaranteed. Lip service is easy but following through is a rarity. I've seen that often enough.'

'I'll be your client.'

All heads swivelled in Allan's direction. He hadn't

spoken much throughout the day although he'd always been smiling whenever Grace had looked over at him.

'Say again?'

'I'll give you my business. Well, some of it.'

'What do you mean by "some of it", Allan?'

'Well, Seb, as I'm sure you would most likely recommend, I don't keep all my eggs in one basket. I have various companies after having been advised early in my business career that diversity keeps you strong. Some come under the A.R.T.I banner but many have been kept quite independent.'

'Such as?'

'Have you heard of "Joysticker Gaming"?'

'Err, yes. Find someone who's into their computer games who hasn't.'

'That's mine. I keep a low profile on it although I still get involved with the development because that's where the fun lies. Anyway, I've felt for a time now that the solicitors who usually deal with the patents and so forth haven't been as "dedicated", shall we say, as I think they should be. I'd be happy to take on your services if this is something you think would suit your business model.'

Grace looked at Seb as he looked back at her. Patents was one of Seb's strong points and the area he worked on most often when there were mergers being forged.

'You would do that?'

Allan gave her a small smile accompanied with a little shrug.

'I would. Despite being classed as a big business myself, I hate to see employees being treated so unfairly. It's a form of bullying and I detest it. If you do choose to take that step, I'll do what I can to support you. I also have an extensive property portfolio which is another separate company – do you happen to do conveyancing?'

Grace felt a fountain of joy bubble up inside her and she

couldn't help but laugh at Allan's hopeful expression.

'That's not something we can offer at the moment but who's to say it won't be added at a later date.'

'*We* offer? Is that you saying you're up for this, Grace?'

She looked at Seb and smiled. 'I'm ready for us to sit down and have a bloody good talk about it.'

'Err, Allan, may I ask a question – you may or may not know the answer but I need to ask anyway. If one of your residents was having security problems, would you expect them to bring it to you or would it be considered nothing to do with you?'

'Lydia! Don't! Shush!'

Debbie's loud hiss had everyone turning to look at her.

'No, Debbie, I won't shush. With two solicitors and a property mogul sitting around this table, now is the perfect time to ask the question.'

'What do you mean by "security problems", Lydia?'

The tone of Allan's voice as he asked the question was a surprise to Grace although that was soon forgotten as Lydia told them about the extortion attempt and the attack on Debbie a few nights before.

'Why didn't you tell me about this, Debbie?'

'I didn't want to worry you.'

Grace felt for her friend. She knew how she felt about Allan and her fear of scaring him off. However, given the way he was looking at her right now, she didn't think Debbie need have any concerns there. She stepped in to take the heat off her.

'Lydia, it is probably worth letting the management company know of the problems. Has it only been your shop that's been targeted?'

'No. I also had a visit from these thugs. Like Miss Debbie here, I gave them short-shrift and sent them on their way. I thought they'd picked on me because of my colour but I've spoken with the other shopkeepers in the mews since Miss Debbie's attack and we've learnt that we've all been visited. None of us, however, have experienced anything further. Well, not yet anyway.'

'What did the police say?'

'That they'd look into it but as Miss Debbie here was unable to provide a description of her attacker, they couldn't say the two events were related.'

'Even with the smell?'

'Circumstantial, Miss Grace. Not enough to go on apparently.'

'Well, speak with your management company – they may be able to sort out some kind of security or at least send someone who can suggest ways of dealing with such things.'

'Can we please change the subject now? I came here to enjoy myself and forget about Wednesday night. Grace, you still haven't opened your birthday presents and when are you going to share out the cake that Lydia and I slaved over to make for you?'

'Slaved over? What she means, Grace, is that madam here walked up to Bait's and asked her to create something wonderful for you!'

'Lydia! You weren't supposed to say that!'

Grace burst out laughing as her friends chuntered between them. The serious mood had been broken and she was happy to move on to more light-hearted chatter. She would worry about this latest development tomorrow.

'Have you had a good day?'

'Oh, yes! One of the best. Although I'm worried about what Lydia told us.'

'Sshhh…'

Jake put his finger gently against Grace's lips. 'That's a worry for another day, tonight is all about you.'

He took the bowl from her hands, placed it on the worktop and pulled her into his arms, kissing her until she felt her toes curl up inside her shoes.

'Why don't we leave the clearing up until the morning,' he whispered in her ear, 'and go upstairs to see just how good that old sofa now looks in your bedroom.'

A frisson of electric anticipation swept through her. Had the moment finally arrived?

'Will it just be the chaise longue you'll be admiring?'

His warm gaze ran down her body.

'Definitely not.'

'What about Frank?'

'He gave it his seal of approval back in the workshop.'

'You know what I mean,' she giggled.

'I don't think you need to worry about Frank.'

Jake inclined his head towards the corner where the spare dog bed lived and she saw that Frank was already curled up in it, fast asleep and tiny little snores accompanied the rise and fall of his chest.

'So much for having a chaperone…'

'My lady, you are now all mine for ravishing!'

With these words, Grace found herself being swung up into his arms and as they made their way up the stairs, she figured she was about to get the best birthday present ever.

THIRTY-EIGHT

'Good morning, Debs, what's going on?'

Debbie looked up to see Allan walking through the door. She hadn't heard the bell tinkle over the noise of the drilling and banging outside that had been going on since seven-thirty that morning.

'Hey, you. Want a cuppa?'

'Sure. Is the mews having a makeover?'

'Of sorts. Further to Grace's advice to speak with the management company, a bloke came round last week, spoke to all the shopkeepers, had a good look at the area and went away to write up a report. We received letters on Monday telling us that gates would be put on the entryways to make the area at the back safer. They'll require fobs for opening to give extra security. They're also putting a gate in at the top of the mews.'

'Really? How on earth is that going to work?'

'Security guards, apparently. The gate will be open during the day with a security guard keeping watch on who comes in and out and then a night guard will open the gate for Luigi's clientele. They're also putting up extra security lights that will have motion sensors and CCTV will be installed at a later date.'

'Wow! They're really going all out.'

'I guess they have to. With so much attention being focused on the safety of women, it doesn't look good if they don't take these things seriously.'

'I suppose so, when you put it like that.'

'Anyway, keep an eye out while I make you that coffee.'

When she returned, Allan was standing at one of the windows, watching the man outside drilling the holes for the new gate.

'Are you any good at DIY?' she asked him while handing over his mug.

'Gosh, no! Absolutely terrible. My home would be more like a demolition site if I were to pick up a hammer. No, I always get a man in for things like that.'

'Allan, where exactly do you live? I'm not clamouring for an invite to your place,' *Liar!* screamed her head, that's exactly what she was after, 'but when you mention "home" I have no idea where that is.'

'Earl's Court. I have a house there. Well, it's between Earl's Court and South Kensington but Earl's Court is the nearest tube. It's handy for getting to the office in Hammersmith.'

'I see.'

It also explained why it was so easy for him to travel down to see her. It was only a handful of stops on the tube.

'You are welcome to come and visit any time you like. I've never asked because I thought you liked going out and about.'

'I do like our trips out but it's also nice to stay in, crash out on the sofa and watch trash on Netflix in your comfy clothes.'

'Okay. We'll do that the next time.'

'Great!'

Her cheeky little heart skipped with joy at this news. Maybe she'd now be able to move the relationship along if they were alone because it sure as heck wasn't doing much out in public and the thought of snogging him on the same sofa she'd once snogged Dale hadn't been sitting well with her at all.

'I was wondering if you'd be able to come out with me this afternoon? There's something I want to show you. Is Lydia around to look after the shop?'

Debbie looked at the time.

'She's gone over to the salon at Tooting to check everything's okay there. She should be back just after one.'

'Good. I'll come back then. In the meantime, I'll pop up to the office for a bit and see what's going on.'

'Allan, aren't you big business moguls supposed to spend every minute behind your desks, cracking the whip?'

'Not when you employ the right staff.'

He gave her his shy little smile, followed by a wink, as he headed out the door. Debs couldn't help but laugh. Allan winking? He really was coming out of his shell.

'Where are we going?'

Debbie waved to Lydia as they left the shop and turned up the hill.

'It's a surprise.'

'Will there be food as I'm starving?'

'No but we could maybe take a little picnic.'

Allan inclined his head towards the bakery.

'I like the way you think, young man. Come on, let me introduce you to Bait.'

'Bait?'

'Real name Bet, as in the name of the bakery, but because the shop entrance is down the side, in the mews, we call her Bait as the smell of her products lures shoppers down into our little bit of paradise.'

Allan laughed as they walked in the door and he was still smiling when she made the introductions. As he looked down at the delicious looking sandwiches already made up in the display case, Bait gave her a wink and a nod of approval and Debbie felt a blush go across her cheeks.

Once they'd decided on their sandwiches and had thrown in some extra cakes which were simply too tempting to ignore, they said their goodbyes and went back out.

'This way.'

He took her hand and they headed off towards Putney Bridge although they took a right turn before reaching the river itself.

'Ready to share the surprise yet?'

'Nope! But we're almost there.'

They made their way through a small pedestrian area which had a café and a pub and the tables outside were all occupied by people enjoying the late summer sun. Rounding a corner, they went onto the riverside path and walked along it for about a minute until they came to a tall block of flats.

She followed him up the path and round to the front door where a doorman, resplendent in his grey suit and cap, opened it for them.

'Good afternoon, Mr Ross. Ma'am.'

'Good afternoon, James. Thank you.'

They moved through the plush lobby, bypassing the two main elevators, and came to a stop at a third set of doors set back in the corner. Allan tapped the pad with a fob and the doors opened.

'After you.'

Debbie stepped in and Allan joined her. He tapped the fob again and the doors closed.

'Er, aren't there usually buttons to push which take you to the correct floor?'

'It depends on the elevator. This one's a little special.'

Before she could ask why, the doors slid quietly open and they walked out into a large hallway. The marble floor gleamed and the huge, floor-to-ceiling mirror at one end made the space feel double the size.

She turned to find Allan watching her.

'What?'

'Nothing. Just looking at you taking this in.'

'That's a bloody big mirror – I was just thinking how I'm glad I'm not the one cleaning it.'

He chuckled as he took her hand again.

'Come on, nearly time for your surprise.'

They turned towards a large set of double doors and she wondered what was going to be on the other side. If he'd organised a lunchtime set from Take That, complete with Robbie Williams, then she would love him for ever.

He let go of her hand, passed her the carrier bag with the yummies inside, and pushed both of the doors open wide. He moved to one side as she walked in behind him.

'Oh! My! Goodness!'

Her head turned from side to side as she took in the vast open space in front of her. A bank of full-length windows provided a view to die for across the Thames. She walked over and looked out across the rooftops of London.

'Good view, huh?'

'I'd say so.'

'Come over here…'

He led her round past the opulent open-plan kitchen – were those worktops actually black marble? – and along into the seating area. She knew this because the largest sofa she had ever seen was placed in a position that looked out through more floor-to-ceiling windows and provided the most perfect sight of the towers belonging to Battersea Power Station.

'Blimey! Check those out. They're amazing.'

'It gets better.'

He undid the lock on the window and slid it into the wall. He then pushed the other one and it too glided into the space specially designed to hide them when the room was opened up to the outside.

Debbie placed the carrier bag on the coffee table and stepped out onto a decked area. That was the moment she saw the infinity pool, just a few steps down, and she felt as though she'd walked into another world.

This was the kind of pad you saw in Hollywood movies. The ones where the movie stars and rock gods lived. Glossy magazines like Hello and Vogue killed to do photoshoots in apartments like this.

'Do you like it?'

'Allan, this place is amazing. I adore this view and I really wish I'd brought my cozzie so I could have stolen a dip in that pool.'

'There's still more to see. You need to have the full tour.'

He took her hand and led her through to the bedrooms which were so big, she could have fitted her flat in them twice over. The bed in the master suite was larger than her lounge!

The bathrooms were done out with pale marble flooring, shining white porcelain tiles and understated chrome fittings. They all boasted luxurious walk-in showers and claw-footed baths. There was even a gym room with a sauna and steam-room leading off from it.

Everything about this place was tasteful and it was

impossible not to fall in love with it. It also screamed outrageously expensive and Debbie couldn't help but feel slightly envious of whoever was lucky enough to live here.

When they'd gone full circle and had returned to the kitchen and dining area – and yes, the worktops *were* black marble – Allan pulled out one of the barstools from under the breakfast bar, indicating for her to sit on it as he pulled another out for himself.

'So, do you like it?'

'Allan, what's not to like? This apartment is stunning. That view... those bedrooms... that pool... it's just... well... amazing. I can't think of enough words to express that.'

'Good. That's good.'

'Why? Are you thinking of buying it? Did you want my opinion on it first?'

If he was buying this place, those cosy nights on the sofa were *so* definitely going to happen!

'Erm, not quite. You see, I used to own it but I don't anymore.'

'What? You've sold it? Why would you do that?'

'I haven't sold it but it's no longer mine. It's yours.'

THIRTY-NINE

Debbie stared at him for a few seconds, her ears refusing to take in what he'd just said.

'I'm sorry... what?'

'You heard me.'

'I may have heard you, Allan, but that doesn't mean my brain is making any sense of what you said.'

'This apartment is now yours.'

He slipped off his stool, walked around the counter into the kitchen, opened a drawer and pulled out a thick envelope which he slid across the cool marble towards her.

'The deeds. It's your name on them.'

'Allan... I... I can't accept this. It's too much. It's not right.'

She pushed the envelope back towards him and stepped down from her own stool.

'I need some air!'

She walked round to the living area and the wide-open doors which beckoned her back onto the decking. She noticed this time that there was a walled, paved area beyond the decking, with a table and chairs and she went and sat down. The blustering breeze from the river subsided in the sheltered spot and the tranquillity of the space began to soothe her racing mind.

She sat alone for a short time, glad that Allan respected her need for some space. He'd dropped a bombshell on her – okay, it was a blooming brilliant bombshell in the grand scheme of things – but she needed to get her head around it.

She was staring out over the water when a movement caught the corner of her eye, causing her to turn her head. Allan was walking towards her, carrying a tray and she could see he'd put their sandwiches onto plates.

'Here, you need to eat.'

'Thank you.'

She took a few bites before placing her sandwich back on the plate.

'Allan, you're such an incredibly kind man but I can't accept this.'

'Why not?'

'Because it's too much. A bunch of flowers is one thing, even tickets to the ballet are okay but a luxury penthouse apartment that must be worth millions of pounds… that's just a step too far.'

'So, it's the cost that's really the issue. You do like the apartment?'

'Of course, it's the cost. People don't go around giving away apartments like this.'

He didn't reply for a few minutes and she went back to eating the other half of her sandwich.

'Okay. Hear me out on this.'

She looked at him and waited for him to speak.

'If I earned fifty pounds a week and bought you a ten-pound bunch of flowers, would you be annoyed with me?'

'Yes, because it's a fifth of your wages and too much money for you to spend.'

'But if I earned say… a thousand pounds a week and bought you a ten-pound bunch of flowers, would you be annoyed then?'

'No, because your earnings are more than enough to cover that.'

'And you would accept the flowers?'

'Yes, I would. And you already know that because we've been there.'

'Indeed! So, what it comes down to is the ratio of earnings to disposable cash?'

'I s-u-p-p-o-s-e. If you want to look at it like that.'

'We need to look at it like that because that's the issue. Debbie, what I'm about to say is a fact, it's not bragging so please don't think it is. The fact is, the money I earn in a day is almost beyond my understanding. It's far more than I believe I'm worth but that seems to be the way business works. In the grand scheme of things, and referring back to my analogy, I'm earning more than a thousand pounds a week and for me, this flat is equal to a ten-pound bunch of flowers. Which means you can accept it because you said you'd accept the flowers.'

He sat back with a satisfied look on his face.

Debbie stared at him. How the hell did you argue with that kind of logic? She now understood how he'd become so successful. He downplayed his business acumen but she'd just seen it in action and she had no comeback.

'Why are you doing this, Allan? Why are you giving me this flat?'

If the money thing wasn't going to do it, then she needed to find another way of refusing his gift.

She gave him a forceful look across the table and waited for his reply. When one wasn't forthcoming, she gave him a verbal prod.

'Why, Allan? You need to tell me.'

The metal legs of the chair scraped harshly on the

porcelain tiles as he pushed it back and went to stand by the wall, looking over the river. The breeze played with his hair and her whole being itched with the desire to walk over and smooth it down. Eventually, he turned round and looked directly at her.

'Debbie, I've given you the flat because I want you to be safe. I don't want to be worrying about you going home and being attacked. This building has a doorman twenty-four hours a day. You would always be safe. It's only five minutes away from the shop so you would be close to it. It makes so much sense.'

'Alright, another objection – I can't afford to live in a flat like this. There's stuff like council tax, shared maintenance costs and so on. I don't earn enough to live here.'

Infuriatingly, he waved his hand in the air.

'Oh, you don't need to worry about that. I own the other five apartments below this one. They get rented out to foreign businessmen. Those costs you mentioned will just get picked up by my company. I can arrange all that.'

'Allan... for the love of...'

She stopped. She just wasn't getting through to him. Or rather, she was and he was being deliberately obtuse.

She looked up at him, still standing by the wall, looking back out over the river, and sighed.

He turned around and this time there was a look on face that she couldn't quite fathom.

'Debbie... I love you. That's why I want you to be safe. I love you and I just can't cope with the thought of anything happening to you. There, that's the truth of the matter. I didn't want to tell you because I know you don't feel the same way for me and I didn't want to scare you away.'

'Scare me away? Why would that scare me away?'

'Because I'm the nerdy geek who doesn't understand

259

people. People frighten me but you don't. You make me feel safe. I feel better, *normal*, when I'm with you. Take these glasses,' he pulled the thick black frames from his pocket, 'and the fact that they're fake. The little boy in the film believes he's invisible when he puts his glasses on and that's just how I feel. But when we're together, I don't need them. I don't want to be invisible to you. I want you to see me. And I hope that one day you will. See me. And maybe, perhaps, love me even though I'm not good enough for you.'

His impassioned words along with his total lack of belief in himself and thinking he wasn't worthy of being loved, were too much and tears slipped from her eyes as she walked over to stand beside him.

'Allan, I've been *seeing* you since we first met and I already love you.'

'You love me? But you've never said anything.'

'Because I didn't know how you would react. You continually tell me how much people scare you so how on earth was I going to be able to tell you that I loved you. I was worried it would be too much for you to deal with and that *you* might walk out of *my* life and I couldn't have coped with that. I kept it to myself to protect what we have as friends.'

He looked down into her eyes and she held his gaze but for once, she couldn't read what he was thinking.

'What's going through your mind right now?'

'That I want to kiss you. And I mean *really* kiss you!'

'Then could you please get on with it, I think you've made me wait quite long enough. And after you've done that, I want to see if the bed in the master bedroom is as comfortable as it looks. After all, if I'm going to be moving in here, I need to check everything is in order.'

The smile on his face stretched from ear to ear but she only got a glimpse of it before closing her eyes and allowing herself to get lost in the warm depths of being *really* kissed by him.

FORTY

Lydia smiled as she read the text from Debbie. She was running a bit behind but would be with her very soon.

She put the phone down on the counter and went to open the shop door, drawing in a deep breath of the warm, balmy air as she stepped out onto the pavement to open up the shutters. It was the early days of September and once again, the country was experiencing a late Indian summer. It was expected to last another five or so days and then they'd see the temperatures begin to drop as autumn forced her way in.

'Miss Lydia, good morning, are you well today?'

'Mr Cedric, I am indeed well, how are you faring on this fine, fair, day?'

They exchanged grins before walking back through their respective doors. The smell of freshly-baked bread slipped in with her and her stomach rumbled. She didn't normally eat anything until after ten in the morning but she now had a fancy for a bacon roll. She'd maybe pop out and get a couple when Debbie arrived and they could scoff them down with a coffee while Debs filled her in on all her news.

Thankfully, she didn't have too long to wait until Debbie and Allan came bursting through the door.

'Oh, Lydia, I'm so sorry I'm late. Thank you for opening up.'

'It's okay, it's only a few minutes after nine. You could have taken longer. Heck, you could have taken the day off, I wouldn't have minded.'

'Oh, no, not on a Friday. We're far too busy these days but do you mind covering for a few minutes more while I go upstairs and change?'

'Of course not. And when you come back down, I'll pop up to Bait's for some bacon butties, how does that sound?'

'Actually, Lydia, I'm heading up to McDonald's to grab us some breakfast and came down with Debbie to ask you if you wanted anything.'

'Oh, a Maccy D's brekkie! Now you're talking!'

Just the mere thought of their hash browns was enough to make her mouth water.

They all wrote down their requests and Lydia made a point of going over to the far corner, ostensibly to re-arrange a shelf, while the two lovebirds said goodbye. Sure, Allan was going to be back in about fifteen minutes or so but she wasn't so jaded about love that she didn't remember what it felt like to tear yourself away in those heady few weeks of truly discovering each other.

She looked up when she heard the door close and saw Allan walking back up towards the main road.

'I'll only be a couple of minutes, Lyds. I just want to jump into something fresh. I've already had a shower.' Debbie blushed when she said this and Lydia couldn't help the grin that sprung to her lips.

'Is that so? I don't think you need to tell me anything more, your cheeks are doing it for you.'

'Hmph! Blooming blushing thing – it's so embarrassing!'

It was difficult not to laugh at Debbie's moaning as she made her way up the stairs to the flat.

Lydia leant against the counter and thought of how happy her flatmate looked. She was such a lovely girl and it was about time she had some good things come her way, because her year so far had been pretty crap. What with Dale ending their engagement, the extortion thing and then being attacked in her own back-yard – quite literally! – she was long overdue a break.

She bent down to bring out the jewellery stands that they put behind the counter at night and placed them on the corner. The items were only paste and nothing expensive but some idiot looking through the window might think differently and try to break in. One of the long necklaces caught on the handle of a drawer and fell off. She was just bending to pick it up when the shop door opened with a bang and Bait was standing there.

'Where's Debbie? Quick, she needs to come now. Something's happened.'

The look of worry on Bait's face had Lydia springing into action. She ran to the bottom of the stairs and hollered up.

'DEBBIE! COME DOWN! QUICKLY!'

Debbie's face appeared over the bannister at the top.

'What's going on? What's all the noise?'

'Just get down here now!'

Debbie ran down and Lydia saw she was in the middle of putting on her old Converse baseball boots. One was already on and fastened, the other was in her hand.

'Lydia, what's wrong?'

'Debbie, you need to come quick, it's Allan... he's hurt.'

Lydia had heard the expression "the colour drained

from her face" but this was the first time she had ever seen it actually happen. Debbie went as white as a sheet upon hearing Bait's words and, pulling on her remaining boot, ran out of the shop and up the hill, not even bothering to look back to see if Lydia was following.

Lydia grabbed the shop keys, ran out behind her and flicked the lock on the door before pulling it closed.

She arrived at the top of the hill to see a man trying to hold Debbie back from the prostrate body lying in the road. A few feet away, a car, one of those mini-sized SUV things, was skewed across the middle of the road with a dent on the bonnet.

'LET ME PAST! HE'S MY BOYFRIEND! LET ME THROUGH!'

Lydia ran over.

'Please sir, it is her boyfriend, let her go.'

As Debbie pushed past and ran to Allan, Bait came up behind her.

'I saw everything, Lydia. He was waiting to cross the road when the next thing I know, I'm seeing him bouncing off the front of that car.'

'Oh, Bait… how could he have missed seeing that? It's not exactly small.'

'Lydia…' the woman looked really worried.

'What? What is it, Bait?'

'I don't think it was an accident. I think he was pushed.'

'You what? How? Why?'

'I don't want to say for sure but a bloke came up behind where he was standing, waiting. I thought they were both just trying to cross the road but then I heard the screeching brakes, saw Allan go down and the bloke was gone.'

'Oh, no!'

She ran to Debbie, her head spinning with this information and in the distance, she could hear the sound of sirens.

'Allan, Allan, oh my love, Allan…'

Debbie was crouched on the ground, tenderly brushing his hair off his face and trying to get a response from the body lying beside her.

'Here, duck, put this over him.'

Someone handed Lydia a blanket as she stooped beside Debbie. She knelt down and was just about to straighten Allan's shirt when something caught her eye. She pushed the shirt to one side and let out a gasp.

'Oh, no! He's been stabbed!'

FORTY-ONE

'Okay, keep me informed.'

Grace said goodbye and dropped her mobile on her desk. She turned to look out the window, her head reeling from Lydia's call. They'd just arrived at the hospital and Allan had been rushed into surgery.

The door of her office slammed open and she turned to see Seb standing there, looking worried.

'It's just come on the news that Allan has been taken to hospital – is this true? Have you heard anything?'

'Close the door, please.'

She waited until Seb did as she asked and beckoned him over to her desk.

'I have more information but it's not being released to the press at this time. He was stabbed while waiting to cross the road.'

'What? But... why?'

She shrugged.

'That's what we don't know and it's what the police are keeping back from the media. As you can imagine, given who he is, the media are now all over this. He's just been taken into the operating theatre. We don't know how bad it is yet.'

'Grace… you need to speak to Jake.'

'Why? I mean, sure, I'll need to let him know what's going on, and I will as soon as I have more news to tell him…'

'No, you need to speak to him now.'

Something in Seb's face stopped her pushing it further. She cocked her head at him, trying to encourage him to say more. It worked with her clients; she was hoping it would work with him.

'Don't look at me like that, Grace Mitchell. I know what you're doing. Look, I've said more than I should have done. Please, just speak with him.'

'Okay! Fine! I'll call him now.'

She picked up her phone and brought up Jake's number.

'Seb, sod off. I'm not talking to him with you standing here listening.'

'Oh, sorry. Wasn't thinking.'

He quickly left her office and she hit the call button.

'Hi, Jake, are you at home? Oh good, I'm on my way to see you, I'll be there soon.'

A sixth sense was telling her that whatever she needed to hear from Jake, it was better to hear it in person.

A moment later she had her coat on, her PC was switched off and she called through to her secretary.

'Emma, can you cancel all my meetings for this afternoon and clear my diary, please? Something's come up and I'm going to be out of the office for the rest of the day.'

'Oh, damn it!'

Grace arrived on the tube station platform just in time to see the Wimbledon train close its doors. She looked at the board and saw it was ten minutes till the next one. In the grand scheme of things, ten minutes wasn't that long but it was enough when her mind was wildly racing in all directions.

What was she going to hear when she spoke to Jake? The way Seb had put it across, it sounded ominous, but why would talking to her boyfriend be a cause for concern. And, more to the point, what did Jake have to do with Allan being stabbed? How was he going to be able to help with that?

The next train rumbled into the station and Grace decided to jump on it. She would change at Earl's Court. With luck, she'd be able to pick up an earlier Wimbledon connection there.

The carriage was almost empty and in trying to avoid looking at her reflection in the opposite window, she looked up and read the advertisements above. There was one for some new computer game and she found her thoughts back with Allan again. Why on earth had he been stabbed? Was it a random attack or had he been targeted? If it was the latter, then by who? Did it have anything to do with his Ministry of Defence work? That would be the obvious conclusion, her inner lawyer said.

The questions went round and round until she was standing outside Jake's place. She'd just placed her finger on the buzzer when the gate opened – almost as though he'd been sitting watching out for her.

'Hey, how are you?' he asked gently, as she approached the side door to find him standing there.

'Not great, truth be told, although probably a lot better than Debbie is right now.'

'It's all over the news but little information is being

given out. All they're saying is that he's been in an accident and is currently being operated on.'

'Well, I can tell you a bit more than that.'

'Let me make some coffee.'

She took off her coat, hung it up and took a seat at the kitchen table while Jake put together a jug of coffee and placed the cream jug on the table along with some mugs. While she was sitting, Frank padded into the room, walked over and lay down with his head on her feet. The weight and the warmth gave her a feeling of calm and soothed some of her rattled nerves.

Jake gently put the coffee jug on the table, sat down and she filled him in on what Lydia had told her over the phone.

'Clearly the police feel the stabbing is pertinent information which they're not yet willing to release.'

'Oh, poor Debbie.'

'Indeed! Lydia also passed on that the two of them had only just taken the next step in their relationship last night. How must Debs be feeling to have finally got where she wanted them to be and now it's all been snatched away again. It's so unfair!'

'Hey! You need to be positive. The poor bloke is still in with a chance right now.'

He leant over the table and gave her hand a reassuring squeeze.

'You're right. I'm sorry.'

'No need to apologise to me, my love, I do understand your concern.'

'Anyway, why did Seb insist that I talk to you? As soon as I mentioned to him about the stabbing and the police, he was most adamant that we talked.'

Jake let out a sigh, pushed his chair back, walked over to the window and gazed out into the garden for a moment before turning around, rubbing his face with his hands. She watched the emotions skitter across his face as he finally looked at her again.

'Grace, I used to work with the police as a criminal profiler. I stopped just over five years ago but I still have contacts within the force. That's why Seb told you to speak to me.'

Grace could feel her mouth opening and closing in shock but despite knowing how stupid she looked, she couldn't force out any sound. She managed to drag her eyes away from Jake and onto the coffee pot which presented her with an alternative focus and she poured some into her mug while her thoughts and words reassembled themselves into something closer to coherence.

'Excuse me? You were a profiler for the police? And you're only telling me this now? Would you have ever shared this rather big piece of news if Seb hadn't pushed you on it?'

'Honestly? Probably not.' Jake shook his head. 'I've worked hard to put it in my past and keep it there. I don't like to think about it if I can help it.'

'But you let me think you'd always worked as a carpenter, or in woodwork.'

'I know. I didn't lie to you, honest. I got into woodwork at school and really enjoyed it. It was a hobby and when times were difficult for me, it has always been the one thing that helped to soothe me and make me relax. When you're working on a piece, you have to be focused and attentive and all the troubles of the day, or the case I was working on, would flow away. I would have been the proverbial basket case without it.'

'Why did you give up profiling?'

'There comes a point, or it did for me, where getting inside the heads of serial killers, rapists and the like just becomes too much. Every case leaves a scar. I found myself dwelling more and more on the victims of these

271

people because we were too slow in catching them. It's not like the television shows where they get their man within twenty-four hours – it takes considerably longer and, sometimes, even a number of crimes being committed before the pattern can be seen.'

'How did you get into it? Did you just wake up one day and come to that decision? You see, this is where I'm confused – and a bit upset too. I shared with you my obsession over being a solicitor and yet you never shared this with me despite, as I'm now finding out, it being a rather large part of your life for many years.'

'I trained in psychology with a side-serving of criminology. I would watch films and cop dramas where some bloke walks into the room, stares at a board or reads a file, gives a quick analysis of the perpetrator and before you knew it, the criminal was in handcuffs and slung in the nick by teatime! Something sparked an interest and it came to be that I found I had a knack for sifting through the data to come up with an accurate reading of the situation. It's not some kind of psychic, tea-leaf reading, crystal ball mumbo-jumbo as some might try to tell you, but careful analysis of data, statistics and – eventually – instinct and experience. You begin the journey using the first part and develop the latter as you go along. Like I said, I seemed to have a gift of being able to cut out the unnecessary details and focusing on what was really relevant which produced a reasonable success rate in apprehending the wrong-doers. I began to get calls from outside of the UK and found myself consulting with the FBI for a time.'

'The American wife?'

'You got it! We met not long after I'd arrived Stateside and tied the knot quicker than we should have but I was in a foreign land and got too swept up in the whole experience. See, even profilers can get it wrong.'

He gave her a small wry grin as he took a drink of his

coffee.

'Is that why it broke up? Your marriage?'

'In a roundabout way. Neither of us had understood the demands that would be made on my time and I was called in on cases far more often than I'd expected. Also, you know how huge the US is, not all those cases were in New York where I'd based myself. I found I was travelling all over the country on a moment's notice. It would have put a long-term marriage under great strain; a new fledgling one stood no chance.'

'Did you enjoy it? The work?'

'I loved the challenge. In a way, you're pitting your clinical mind against a criminal one and it's a case of seeing who will win. The downside, however, is that the "game" too often involves the lives of real people being snuffed out.'

She could understand the challenging aspect of his role. It was the same challenge that got her buzzing when a new file with a new client within was placed on her desk. After taking another drink of her coffee, she asked, 'Why did you turn your back on it?'

'There was a case concerning a serial rapist in the States – you understand I can't go into details – and I was asked to have a look at it. I did my profiling thing, shared my thoughts but the SAC, Special Agent in Charge, was one of the non-believers of profiling and he ignored the information. Four more women were raped and killed before they caught the guy. He was the perfect fit to my profile. Had the SAC taken my input on board, then maybe those four women would still be alive. And if not all four, definitely three. I walked away after that. Those were four new scars on my mind that needn't have been there.'

This time, it was Grace who reached over the table to give his hand the reassuring squeeze.

'And every time you think about it or talk about it, it

reawakens the pain?'

'It does. Do you now understand why I never told you?'

'Yes, I do. No one likes to relive painful memories and the unnecessary death of four women is a lot to deal with. Has it ever been proven that profiling is beneficial?'

'They ran an experiment back in the early 2010s where one police region was trained in using profile techniques. The three neighbouring forces or areas were not and they continued in the standard methods of crime solving. A year later, the region trained in profiling had an increase of more than 260% of crimes solved in comparison to the three others.'

'Wow! Bloody hell! That's some clean-up rate!'

'It sure is. It has also helped to push profiling on and make it more of a regular tool for crime solving.'

'But without you?'

'Yeah, without me. Been there, done that, came away with an FBI t-shirt and a ton of scars. Now, the only scars I have to deal with are when the chisel slips and nearly takes a finger off.'

'And I'm guessing Seb told me to speak with you because you still have police friends who may be able to do something here?'

'Yup! He's nothing if not subtle, my little bro.'

'Subtle? Sorry, that's not a word that would find its way into my vocab when describing Sebastian Andrews.'

Jake laughed at that as she took another drink of her coffee, shuddering at the bitter taste of the now cold liquid.

'Shall I make us another pot?'

Grace looked at the time and stood up.

'Actually, I'm going to go over to the hospital to be with Debbie and Lydia, if that's okay with you?'

Jake came over and took her in his arms.

'Of course, it is. I'll get on to my old mates in the Met and see if I can find out anything. I can't make any promises, it has been a while, but I'll give it a try.'

'Thank you.'

She pulled her coat on and was about to walk out the door when she stopped and turned back.

'Jake… one thing I've realised today is that we don't know what's coming next and what opportunities we miss every day, so I want to say… I want to tell you… I love you. I've felt it for a while but it's something I've never said to anyone before. I don't know why but now I am… saying it. I love you very much and I'm grateful for every day that you are in my life.'

Before she'd finished speaking, she was swept up in a hug as Jake wrapped his arms around her and held her as close as was possible.

'I love you, Grace. Have done from the day we met. I had to let you say it first though, I knew I'd only scare you off if I said it too soon.'

She pulled back a bit to look at him.

'Have you been profiling me, Jake Valentine?'

'Maybe a little tiny bit…'

'Well, you can stop that right now! From here on in, live with the surprises!'

'Oh, I think I can do that. Call me when you get to the hospital.'

'I will.'

She gave him another kiss before heading out the door.

As she walked back to the train station, she mulled over what she'd learnt. And to think he'd been profiling her? Cheeky bugger!

But she was smiling as she thought it for one thing was certain – he'd definitely sussed her out good and proper!

FORTY-TWO

'You've been very lucky, Mr Ross, the blade just nicked your kidney. Another centimetre and it could have been a very different story.'

Debbie held Allan's hand as the doctor informed them of the potential damage he could have sustained from the stabbing.

'Can you remember anything, Mr Ross?'

Allan looked at the detective who'd asked the question and she watched his brow wrinkle up as he tried to recall the events which had led to him now being in a hospital bed.

'I was waiting for a gap in the traffic when I sensed someone really close behind me. I twisted round to tell them to back off but before I could say anything, there was a sharp pain in my back and side and I felt myself falling. I remember being hit by a car but after that, it's all a blank.'

'I think, Mr Ross, it was your action of twisting round which saved your life. Had you not, you'd have been dead on arrival at the hospital from internal bleeding. Being stabbed in the kidneys tends to be fatal, more often than not.'

Debbie gulped at hearing this. To know Allan had been so close to death was something she was having a problem dealing with.

'DI Halliwell, is there any way this could be related to the incidents I reported?'

'I can't say at this time, Miss Stanford. Our investigations are still ongoing. We've been able to pull dash-cam footage from a couple of buses that were in the area at the time of the incident so we're hopeful we can gather more details from them. For now, however, I just need to ask you to be patient.'

Allan turned his head to look at the man standing quietly at the end of the bed.

'When can I go home, Doctor?'

'I'm afraid you're going to be our guest for a few more days yet, Mr Ross. We need to ensure the kidney is functioning properly and that it hasn't been compromised from the surgery. Renal failure is just as big a killer so I'd rather be safe than sorry.'

'Thank you, Doctor, for all that you've done.'

'It's what I'm here for, Miss Stanford, but thank you.'

'Mr Ross,' Allan and Debbie returned their attention to the detective. 'The news has been released that you've survived the attack but we're concerned about press intrusion given your public status. To ensure your continued safety, we'll be placing an officer inside the door to be with you at all times.'

'Inside the door? Don't you mean outside?'

'Not on this occasion, Miss Stanford. The risk of untrustworthy journalists disguising themselves as doctors or nurses is too great so we're playing it safe by having the protection officer in the room. Bob there will look out for you.'

'Oh, okay. Thank you.' She looked over to the officer

who had just placed a seat by the side of the door. 'Thank you, Bob.'

'No problem, miss.'

It all sounded rather odd to Debbie but she was too tired to argue. Had it really only been three days since she'd waved Allan off as he went to buy their breakfast? It felt like an eternity and she hadn't left the hospital once in all that time. Lydia and Grace had taken turns to be with her, with Lydia bringing her a change of clothes each day. Allan's mother had arrived a few hours after he'd been brought to the hospital and they'd kept each other company through the first night as they waited to hear if the surgery to repair the kidney had been successful or if they were going to have to go back in to remove it.

It had certainly been the most unusual meeting of a boyfriend's mum that she'd ever experienced but they'd quickly bonded as they'd passed the long dark hours of the night by sharing stories about Allan. Hearing more about his childhood and things he'd had to endure – which he'd omitted to share with her or had possibly forgotten – only made her love him more.

The doctor and the detective were leaving the room when Jake stuck his head in.

'Hey, are you up for a visitor?'

'Of course I am.'

Debbie noticed how Allan had immediately perked up at seeing a new face but she was also conscious of the shadows under his eyes. He still needed plenty of rest and she was going to make sure he got it.

'Jake, I don't want to be rude, but can we keep it short, please. Allan's still in a critical state at the moment and must take it easy.'

'I hear you, Debs. I really only wanted to say hello and to let you know I'm thinking of you. I've had a word with some old police friends. I'm guessing Grace may have brought you up to speed on all that, and they've asked me to stress to you the need for you to remain in your room at all times.'

'What?'

Debbie's chair made a horrible, teeth-gritting, screech as she stood up.

'Do they think whoever did this may come back to finish the job?'

'No, they don't, but as I believe the detective mentioned, they are concerned about the media presence outside. This is for your protection and also for the other patients in the building.'

'Oh, right, sure. That makes sense. Sorry, Jake, I'm just tired and wrung-out.'

'Debs, I probably worded it badly. It's fine. So, I'm out of here and you, dude,' he pointed at Allan, 'are going to do as the doctor has ordered and rest. I'll catch up with you both later.'

He gave them a quick two fingered salute as he left the room.

'I like Jake. He was kind to me at Grace's party. I didn't feel nerdy or geeky with him.'

'Yes, he is comfortable to be around. I guess his psychoanalytic background helps him to adjust to how he needs to behave with people.'

'Hmm, maybe it does.'

'His visit also proves one thing.'

'What?'

'You now have more than one friend. And as I'm technically now your girlfriend, it means you had a vacancy which has been filled three times over. Possibly more…'

'More?'

'Both Seb and Cedric have sent get well wishes and gifts and have said they can't wait until they're allowed to come and visit.'

'Aww, that's nice.'

'They're just as nice as you are, Allan Ross. Now try and get some sleep.'

She placed a soft kiss on his cheek as he closed his eyes and with a nod to the policeman sitting on the chair by the door, she placed her own head on the bed and tried to catch up on some zeds herself.

It felt like she'd barely closed her eyes when loud voices, banging and shouting woke Debbie up. She immediately looked at Allan and seeing her fear reflected on his face, she instantly sought to reassure him.

'Hey, it's okay. I'm here and so is Bob. You're safe. Perfectly safe.'

She glanced over to see Bob standing to attention in front of the door as she took Allan's hand in hers, holding it tight while gently smoothing his hair across his face, hoping the soft gesture would appease him.

In truth, if there was any trouble, she'd be about as much use as a half-melted icicle but reassuring Allan had to be her priority – his health was still too fragile for him to be stressed in any way.

She was about to walk over to the door for a look outside when the policeman put his hand up to stop her.

'Please, Miss Stanford, I need you to stay over there.'

'But—'

'It's not up for discussion. This is for your safety. Please move back to the other side of the bed.'

Debbie did as she was asked while Bob carefully peered through a small gap in the blinds.

The sounds of a commotion carried on for several more

minutes and then everything went quiet. Bob appeared to relax, gave her a smile and resumed his place back on his chair.

She looked at Allan and saw him grimacing.

'Allan? Are you okay? Do I need to call the doctor?'

'Nooooooo, you need to let go of my hand!'

She looked down and saw both of her hands were now gripping Allan's for dear life.

'Oh, babes, I'm sorry.'

At that moment, the door to the room opened and Jake strode back in, holding his phone in his hand.

'Debbie, is this the man who came into the shop and who you suspect also attacked you in your backyard?'

He thrust the phone in her direction and she gasped when she saw stinky Moustache Man glaring back at her.

'Oh, my, yes. Yes, that's him.'

'And,' he quickly swiped his phone before showing it to her again, 'do you recognise this man?'

'He was with him in the shop. I'd recognise those ratty features anywhere.'

'Then I can advise you that the police now have both of these men in custody.'

'They did come back, didn't they? You lied to us.'

'I confess that, yes, I lied but only to keep you safe and stop you worrying. I know Allan needs to be stress-free. We set up a dummy room, three doors along, with police protection on the outside to make it easily identifiable. The two of them arrived dressed as porters pushing a gurney. We knew we had the right men because one of them carried the smell you had previously described, Debbie.'

Feeling her legs giving way underneath her once again, Debbie quickly parked herself back down on her seat.

'So, it really is over now. Allan and I are safe?'

'Yes, you are.'

'Do we know why they were going after us?'

'Not yet. At this time, we still know very little but the police are hopeful that having these two in custody will bring us all some answers. Now, you both relax and I'll pop in with Grace this evening for a catch-up.'

When he'd left, and Bob the policeman had taken up his new position outside the door, Allan took her hand and kissed it.

'I just knew talking to you that night was going to turn out to be the best thing I've ever done in my life.'

'What, nearly getting you killed?'

'It'll be something to tell the grandkids.'

'Oh, really? Confident of those, are you?'

'Maybe. But I am confident that I love you.'

'And I love you. Now rest. I want you home as soon as possible.'

FORTY-THREE

'Hey, Lydia, Merry Christmas. Cedric, Merry Christmas.'

'Merry Christmas, Grace, and to you, Jake. Gosh it's bitter cold today.'

'Well, Lyds, it is the twenty-fifth of December, I think it's supposed to be. Just be glad it's frosty and not snowy.'

'Yeah, I should be grateful for that, I suppose.'

Grace smiled at the doorman as they walked into the lobby and waited for him to announce their arrival to Debbie up in her penthouse apartment.

'Do you know how many Debbie's feeding today, Grace?'

'Nine, I believe. Her parents and Allan's mum are also joining us.'

'Oh blimey! I hope she copes okay – that's a fair number.'

'From the conversation we had last night, I think the mothers are vying with each other to do their bit in the kitchen – Debbie's hardly getting a look-in.'

'Then, just between us, that means the meal should be more than just edible. I love Debbie to bits but I'm under no illusion that her cooking skills need some more polishing.'

The four of them were laughing as the elevator doors slid open and they stepped out into the marble-floored hallway.

'You know, this still throws me every time I visit.'

'How so, Lyds?'

'Because this is only the hallway and yet it's almost the size of the flat.'

'Would you like to live here instead?'

'No, Cedric, you know I don't.'

'You don't regret declining Debbie's offer for you to continue being her flatmate here?'

'Nope! Not in the slightest. Besides, I knew it was unlikely that Allan would move back out once he was fully recovered. Debbie loved having him around as she looked after him when he left the hospital and she was dreading him leaving although she never told him. Luckily, he had no inclination to leave and I would have just ended up being a gooseberry.'

'You're all here! Come in, come in. Let me take your coats. Merry Christmas.'

Grace handed over her coat and stood back to let Debbie do her gracious hostess bit. She took a look around and admired the beautiful decorations that had been put up. It all looked very festive and helped to make the apartment cosier. Debs had only been saying a few weeks ago that she needed to put her interior decorator skills into action because as much as she loved her new home, it still lacked the cosy feel she preferred. Allan was all for getting a professional in to do the job but Debs had put her foot down on that one. It was her home and as far as she was concerned, she'd be the one to put her special mark on it.

'Come on through and meet the parents.'

Grace smiled and hugged Kate, Allan's mum. They'd

spent several hours together at the hospital but it was the first time she'd met Debbie's mum and dad. They were both nice and friendly and she had no problem seeing where Debbie got her sunny, happy disposition from.

'Where's Allan?'

'He's out on the terrace, putting the final touches to the fire pit for later.'

'Fire pit?'

'Yes, he's got this idea in his head that it will be nice to sit all cosied up outside later tonight, around a fire and toasting marshmallows while drinking hot chocolates spiced with liqueurs. I don't expect you to join us but I'll go out to humour him.'

'I think that sounds quite lovely, Debbie. As long as you have nice cosy throws, I'm all in.'

'Ah, bless you, Grace. We definitely have cosy throws. Oh, here he is – Allan, our guests have arrived.'

Grace turned around and did a double take. She'd grown used to seeing Allan without the thick, black-framed glasses but his new hair-cut was something else. It was no longer all swept forward over his face but cut short and swept back, revealing the beautiful bone structure of his face and his slim fine nose.

'Wow! Allan! Fabulous hair-cut. It makes such a difference.'

'Thank you, Grace. It's kind of you to say so. Debbie's been nagging me to have it cut for a while now so I finally gave in. I've told her this is her Christmas present! Besides, with all the media attention over the last few months, everyone now knows what I look like. I need a new disguise!'

They all chuckled at this and exchanged chit-chat until Kate came over and told them it was time to take their seats at the table.

'I can't get over how peaceful it is up here.'

Grace snuggled deeper into the cashmere throws over her shoulders and across her legs and tilted her head to look up at the inky-black sky overhead.

'We don't get much street noise up here although it does depend on wind direction. Hearing the toot of a ship's horn still delights me though.'

Debbie smiled at everyone as she passed round the plates of giant marshmallows and the toasting sticks.

'How are you feeling now, Allan? Any after-effects from your... well...?'

'Thank you for asking, Cedric. On the whole I feel pretty good. I currently have to go for renal testing on a monthly basis but that should decrease over time if the results are consistently good. I do get moments when I suddenly seize up because the muscles have gone into a cramp but they soon pass and it's happening less frequently as the muscles are healing.'

'Have you heard anything further from the police? There does seem to be quite the air of mystery around this.'

Debbie shook her head.

'Nothing, Grace.'

'Actually, I can fill you in.'

Everyone turned to look at Jake.

'You know? And have said nothing?' Grace glared at him.

'I was only given the go-ahead to share the details last night and decided to wait until we were all together to avoid repeating myself.'

'Well, I think you now have our undivided attention, Jake, if you would like to enlighten us all.' Cedric cast his gentle smile over everyone as he spoke.

'Well, where to begin really. Firstly, the mews had come on to the radar of a gang of Albanian drug smugglers. These gangs, among many other nationalities, are a growing menace in all the cities across the country but more so in London. They'd been looking for an area that would work as a cover for their activities and the mews ticked all the boxes.'

'It did? How?'

'Well firstly, Debs, that alleyway which runs along the back of your courtyard? It goes all the way down to the river. Their plan was to smuggle the drugs up the Thames in small boats, offload them on the shore just below your terrace here and then transport them to the mews via the alleyway, thus keeping the contraband hidden from sight. The reason for the extortion part of the plan was to get all the shopkeepers to move out so they could move their own people in, which would enable them to launder the money from the sale of the drugs.'

'Blimey! They had it all thought out, didn't they? But I still don't understand why they went after Allan – what did they hope to gain from that? Why did they think hurting him would make me move out?'

Jake looked over to Allan who nodded to him to continue.

'Debbie, do you recall Allan saying at Grace's party that he had a property portfolio?'

'Yes.'

'Well, the mews is part of the portfolio.'

'It is?'

Debbie turned to Allan.

'Care to explain?'

Under her hard expression, Allan gave a little shrug.

'The previous management company were taking the piss which I realised the day I visited and you received that

287

letter. As soon as I read it, I knew they were on the take. I originally intended to only buy up the leases but that was going to take far too long. It was quicker and easier to simply buy the company instead. Let's just say I made them an offer they couldn't refuse.'

'Unfortunately, for Allan, the Albanians had already made an approach and an offer which was initially accepted but then subsequently declined when Allan put in his. From that aspect, it was just pure bad timing on Allan's part. As it was, the Albanians had their heart set on owning this piece of land outright – they couldn't risk anyone getting wind of what they were doing and having to answer to a management company would have cramped their style.'

'But how would killing Allan help them in any way? That's what I don't get.'

'Their thinking was, that with the head of the property company gone, all the "stock" as it were would be sold off and they'd be able to get possession of the mews that way. I mean, as plans go, it held water.'

'So how come you now know all this?'

'The two blokes who were doing the groundwork – like the extortion, etcetera – proceeded to sing like the proverbial canaries once we got our hands on them. They'd failed in their mission and this put targets on their backs from the baron of the cartel. In exchange for the information, they will get protection. They also provided details that enabled the police to go on a raid two nights ago where they got everyone in their sights – including the baron at the top.'

'So now everyone is locked up? The mews is completely safe again?'

'They are, Lydia, and it is.'

'And just to add, I will be keeping the new security measures in place. Just in case any other gangs come sniffing around.'

'Thank you, Allan. That's good to hear.'

'Well, everyone, on that joyful note, I think we can absolutely say that this has been a very Merry Christmas.'

Grace held her mug of hot chocolate in the air and smiled as her friends all followed suit.

'Merry Christmas.'

FORTY-FOUR

January again.

Lydia closed the door of the flat behind her and gingerly made her way down the outside metal staircase. It was as icy as anything tonight and she didn't want to fall and break something. It was the first Tuesday in January and she was meeting up with Grace and Debbie for their first Pie & Prosecco night for several months. With all that had gone on, their weekly get-togethers had fallen by the wayside but they'd made a promise at Christmas to get them back on track in the New Year.

She hurried up the mews and sent Debbie a text to let her know she was on her way. By the time she reached the bridge over the river, Debs was there waiting for her.

'I'm really looking forward to this. I've missed our special nights out.'

'Me too,' Debbie replied. 'Alyson won't remember who we are.'

'Have you heard from Grace?'

'She's on her way too.'

'Oh good. I'm starving.'

They were only just in the door of the pub when Grace arrived. It didn't take long for them to remove their coats, get comfortable and put in their usual request for a bottle of Prosecco and three glasses.

When Alyson returned with their order, she said how delighted she was to see them back, placed the menus on the table while informing them of the night's specials and advised she'd be back shortly to take their order.

'Well, ladies, here we are again. What a year it's been.'

Lydia filled the glasses as she spoke.

'You can darn well say that again!' Debbie's words were accompanied with a shudder.

'If you recall, we made our Prosecco Pact last year – shall we go round the table and see how we've done?'

Grace laughed.

'If you feel we must.'

'I think it would be nice.'

'Okay, Lydia, as you've brought it up, you can go first.'

She smiled at Debbie as she drew in a breath.

'I think it would be fair to say that I've accomplished my mission. The extraction from my marriage may not have been made in a manner that any of us could have envisioned but I think, ultimately, it has worked out quite well.'

'What is the story with you and Cedric? Do we have an update?'

'Well, Grace, the latest is that sometimes I sleep at his place, sometimes he sleeps at mine and sometimes we sleep on our own. We're in no rush to go further than that and we both love having our own space and our own time to ourselves. If that'll change in the future... well, only time will tell. So, that's currently one out of three achieved for the pact. Grace?'

'Okay. I said I was going to be a partner before I was

forty and I promised to make more time for myself and make my house into a home. And now that Seb and I are forging ahead with our own business, my partnership will be a reality very soon. And definitely before my fortieth birthday.'

'How is it all progressing?'

'The bastards called McArthur and Forbes are seething at losing both Seb and I. They have since offered the partnerships we once wanted but we both declined. With Allan promising us his business, we're in a good, strong, starting position and we'll be making approaches to other companies we've worked with in the past as soon as we have a date for our doors to officially open. I just need to complete a few more modules on my business course to get my certificate and then we'll both meet the Solicitors Regulation Authority. After that, we're on our way.'

'It must be so exciting.'

'It is, Debbie. I hadn't realised how stagnant I'd become at work until I began walking this new path. It's another reason I declined the partnership offer. This is far more fun.'

'And your house was looking lovely when we were over after Christmas. It certainly looked homely to me. Or maybe that was just the sight of Frank lying sprawled out on your sofa.'

'Oh, Lyds, I love that dog and his slave to bits. If it hadn't been for the pact, I'd never have gone out to look for furniture and the part of my life that has been the most rewarding over the last year would never have happened. The thought of not having met Jake doesn't bear thinking about. I don't know where we're headed or how it's all going to turn out but I'm certainly far more flexible in how I approach my life now. So, I reckon that's two out of three for the Prosecco Pact.'

'Yup, I would say it is. I'm afraid, Debbie, it's your

turn.'

Lydia hoped Debbie didn't feel too bad about failing her part of the pact. It wasn't her fault her engagement had turned out to be a farce. Hopefully, though, she felt she was in a better place now and that it had all worked out for the best.

'Okay, ladies, I guess this moment had to come.'

She let out a large sigh and Lydia just wanted to give her a big hug.

'My part of the mission was to have a date set for my wedding…' she stopped for a moment to look down at the table before raising her head and squealing, 'and I can tell you now that it's taking place on the fifteenth of August!'

'WHAT?'

Lydia and Grace looked at each other in amazement as Debbie stuck her left hand over the table for them to both admire her new ruby and diamond engagement ring.

'Oh, Debbie, it's gorgeous.'

'Allan said he chose the ruby because it reminded him of the red dress I was wearing the night we met.'

'It's gorgeous, Debbie. Congratulations. I'm very happy for you although when did he propose because you weren't wearing this in the shop earlier.'

Debbie grinned.

'He asked me on New Year's Eve but it didn't seem fair to tell you first so I kept the ring off during the day until we were together tonight. I wanted to tell you both at once.'

'Aw, thank you, Debbie. I'm really touched you did that.'

Grace turned to Debbie and gave her a hug.

'Well, Grace, you may not be so touched when I say I'm hoping you'll both be my bridesmaids and Lydia, I'm tasking you with making the dresses, including mine.'

'You what?'

Lydia just about choked at this.

'You heard me. I wouldn't trust anyone else. And, with that, I think we can safely say that I too have accomplished my mission and it's three out of three for the Prosecco Pact.'

'I'll drink to that!'

Grace lifted her glass and Lydia and Debs chinked theirs against it.

'Well, ladies, we still have one final bit of business to conclude before we give Alyson our orders.'

Debbie and Grace looked at each other in confusion before turning back to Lydia.

'We do?'

'Yes. We need to decide if we're doing another one for this year.'

'No way!'

'Hell no!'

She laughed. 'I'm guessing that's a "no" then?'

'You guessed damn right. This last year has done for me. I just want to get married and have a nice quiet life. I'll pass, thank you very much.'

'In that case, I think we need to raise our glasses and simply say, 'To Prosecco!'

Debbie and Grace lifted their glasses and the three of them said as one...

'To Prosecco!'

ABOUT THE AUTHOR

Kiltie Jackson spent her childhood years growing up in Scotland. Most of these early years were spent in and around Glasgow although for a short period of time, she wreaked havoc at a boarding school in the Highlands.

By the age of seventeen, she had her own flat which she shared with a couple of cats for a few years while working as a waitress in a cocktail bar (she's sure there's a song in there somewhere!) and serving customers in a fashionable clothing outlet before moving down to London to chalk up a plethora of experience which is now finding its way into her writing.

Once she'd wrung the last bit of fun out of the smoky capital, she moved up to the Midlands and now lives in Staffordshire with one grumpy husband and another six feisty felines.

Her little home is known as Moggy Towers even though, despite having plenty of moggies, there are no towers! The cats kindly allow her and Mr Mogs to share their home as long as the mortgage continues to be paid.

Since the age of three, Kiltie has been an avid reader although it was many years later before she decided to put pen to paper – or fingers to keyboard – to begin giving life to the stories in her head. Her debut novel was released in September 2017 and her fourth book was a US Amazon bestseller in Time Travel Romance.

Kiltie loves to write fiery and feisty female characters and puts the blame for this firmly on the doorsteps of

Anne Shirley from Anne of Green Gables and George Kirrin from The Famous Five.

When asked what her best memories are, Kiltie will tell you - Queuing up overnight outside the Glasgow Apollo to buy her Live-Aid ticket. Being at Live-Aid. Winning an MTV competition to meet Bon Jovi in Sweden. (Although, if Mr Mogs is in earshot, the latter is changed to her wedding day.)

Her main motto in life used to be "Old enough to know better, young enough not to care!" but that has since been replaced with "Too many stories, not a fast enough typist!"

You can follow Kiltie on the following platforms:

www.kiltiejackson.com

www.facebook.com/kiltiejackson

www.instagram.com/kiltiejackson

www.twitter.com/kiltiejackson

Printed in Great Britain
by Amazon

36948652R00169